D1236814

WHEN I WAS
OTHERWISE

When I Was Otherwise

Stephen Benatar

St. Martin's/Marek
New York

ACKNOWLEDGEMENTS

To Leonard Mosley, whose fascinating book *Backs to the Wall*
(Weidenfeld & Nicolson, 1971) about Londoners' experiences
in wartime helped me immeasurably in the chapter concerning
Daisy's own wartime experiences.

To my wife, for her constant encouragement, reading and
re-reading, for her invaluable suggestions and for her (sort of)
long-suffering acceptance: writers don't *always* make the very
easiest of husbands!

To Victoria Barrow – once more – for her infinite patience and
concern, for her careful scrutiny of every word and every
exclamation mark: the copy editor *par excellence*. Thank you,
Victoria, enormously.

To Maureen Rissik especially but also to everybody else who
has been connected with the production of this book . . . my
really heartfelt gratitude.

First Published in Great Britain in 1983 by The Bodley Head Limited

First U.S. Edition

10 9 8 7 6 5 4 3 2 1

To the memory of both my parents,
Gran, Jack and Molla, Joan
– and Nancy

Man knows where first he ships himself, but he
Can never tell where shall his landing be.
Robert Herrick

Part One

I

On Wednesday 23rd March 1983 there appeared in the *Guardian* the following report:

An inquest is to be held on the two elderly women whose bodies were found on Monday in the dilapidated North London house they shared with a man who was the brother of one of them and the brother-in-law of the other. Post-mortem examinations yesterday revealed that they had both died from natural causes—but that the older woman had been dead for up to a year.

As the story of the hermit-like existence of the Stormont family emerged yesterday, a spokesman for Barnet Council and for the local health authority defended doctors and social workers who had to deal with them. 'It's a bizarre case. You can't make people go to hospital or have meals-on-wheels if they won't have it. But we did try,' the spokesman said.

The two women and the 76-year-old widower refused all offers of help. But for months the grimy windows of the house in Alderton Crescent, Hendon, hid a gruesome secret. Mrs Daisy Stormont, in her middle eighties, lay dead, while Mrs Marsha Poynton, 67, and Mr Daniel Stormont continued their strange, reclusive existence. A police spokesman said that at one time Marsha had slept in the same room as her dead sister-in-law, unable or unwilling to leave her chair.

Police were alerted twice in the last twelve months by neighbours who were concerned about the family's health, but were turned away by Mrs Poynton, who spoke to them only through the letter box.

Last week police were alerted a third time, forced the lock on the front door, and found Marsha ill in bed. The family doctor called for an ambulance, but she refused to leave the house. A home help called at the weekend and on Monday found Marsha apparently dead.

Later, the skeletal remains of Daisy were discovered.

Mr Stormont, now recovering in council care, did not wish to speak to anyone yesterday—not even to a relative from Australia.

2

'Well, here I am, you see. Turned up again. Just like the bad penny. I've brought a cake.'

'Hello, Daisy. Oh, isn't your cheek cold! How wonderful to see you.'

'And you, dear. My things are in the car.'

'Dan can get them later. He's just slipped out to the shops.'

'I haven't been in this house for years.'

Marsha closed the front door and, having tried unsuccessfully to relieve her sister-in-law of her coat and woollen gloves, led her into the lounge. She had turned on the fire half an hour earlier and Daisy made straight for it, standing with her back to the imitation live coals, rubbing her hands.

'Ah! This is a bit more like it. I may begin almost to feel human again—you never know!'

'I'll just pop and put the kettle on, shall I?'

'That's the spirit.' Daisy gave her slightly throaty laugh. 'Talking of which—I almost brought a bottle of scotch with me. But the pubs were closed.'

'I'm very glad of it; drink is such a price these days.' In the doorway Marsha hesitated. 'Oh. Would you like just a tiny drop of whisky now? Instead of the tea?'

'What a lovely thought, dear: a real piece of inspiration. Oh, do you think we should? No, tea will be *very* nice.'

'I'm going to pour us both a whisky!' said Marsha, wickedly.

'Very well, dear; I can see there won't be any stopping you!'

'No, there won't.'

'The bit's between your teeth!'

'I shan't be a minute, Daisy. It's in the kitchen.'

'Might as well put the kettle on then, at the same time.'

A moment later she informed the empty room:

'But what a funny place to keep your whisky! Never heard of anything so extraordinary in my entire life!'

On Marsha's return, Daisy had taken off her coat and hung it carelessly over the back of a chair. She had also thrown off her woolly pomponned hat and run her fingers through her tight black curls. She was a short woman, trim, but even in her late seventies (Dan and Marsha had the previous night decided on *at least* seventy-eight) a sturdy one. Her white blouse looked a little grubby; her green jacket and pleated skirt could also have done with a clean. But her solid black lace-ups shone as though they'd just been polished. Daisy had pulled up one of the armchairs very close to the fire and a part of the element was reflected in the leather of her left shoe.

'Now you be careful that you don't get chilblains!'

'My dear girl, why should I? Such things exist solely in the mind. They only search out the frightened folk.'

'Well, they certainly search out me!'

Marsha set down the tray and handed Daisy her glass, which had been filled in the kitchen. Then she took the coat out and put it in the hall.

'You must have a very steady hand, dear,' said Daisy. 'You didn't spill a drop.'

'Yes, I think I have got a steady hand. Of course, I didn't fill the glasses to the brim.'

'That's true, dear, I noticed. Anyhow—here's mud in your eye! Happy times!'

They drank.

'I see they changed the wallpaper. Just as well. Not that this one's much of an improvement.'

'Why, what's the matter with it?' Marsha's laugh was a little nervous.

Daisy merely shrugged.

'I always considered Erica had quite nice taste,' said Marsha; never having thoroughly learned to leave well alone.

'Oh, *taste*. Yes, I daresay. But did you ever see anything so utterly wishy-washy in all your life?'

'Now, Daisy . . .'

'Naturally I'm referring to the wallpaper.' Daisy looked about her with disdain. 'Dull. No spirit of adventure.'

She added, as though it were the final and most crushing epithet that could possibly be brought to bear on that or any other subject: 'Suburban.'

'I really don't think it's so bad.'

'Yes, I know, dear. I daresay you're right.' Daisy gazed into her empty glass for an instant. She gave a sigh and was about to put it down on the floor beside her chair, when Marsha stood up and took it from her and placed it on the tray. 'Mean-spirited,' said Daisy.

Marsha smiled. 'I really don't see how a wallpaper can be called mean-spirited.'

'Don't you?'

'I must say, Daisy, that you're looking awfully well.'

'What's that?' Daisy fiddled a moment with the bulky hearing-aid which she carried in her breast pocket. It gave a high-pitched whistle. 'Oh, drat this thing! I'll swear it has a mind of its own.'

'Like you, Daisy.' Marsha mouthed the words and pointed.

Daisy chuckled. 'Yes, dear, just like me! You've hit the nail right on the head. *Just* like me. Thank goodness! Ah, that's got it!' she said, triumphant, as if she'd just swatted a persistent fly. 'Now, what was it that you were saying?'

'I said that you were looking awfully well.'

'Yes. Well. One has to keep going, doesn't one? One has to keep one's pecker up. Somehow.' She brooded over that for several seconds, and then rallied, to illustrate her own maxim. 'Not that my appearance would ever pity me, even on my deathbed. I always had a good colour.'

Indeed, Daisy had such a good colour that she looked a

little like a rag doll with small round patches of red sewn on to either cheek. It wasn't quite what Marsha had foreseen when once, long ago, she had given her a few hints on how to apply her make-up.

Daisy had a portrait of herself, in oils, done by Augustus John. If Marsha had ever been painted, water colours might have been more appropriate. Marsha was wearing a beige woollen dress, only a shade or two lighter than her softly waved brown hair. She was now sixty, yet one could still see—despite the lines of disappointment—that she had once been very pretty.

She glanced at the clock on the mantelpiece.

'Dan's a long time,' she said. 'All he had to get was a tin of peas and a jar of marmalade. Oh—and a box of tissues. I left them off my shopping list this morning.'

'How is Dan?'

'Marvellous. Considering.'

'I think it very strange,' Daisy said, 'that no one let me know, until after the funeral. Very strange indeed. And I shall make no bones about telling him so, either.'

Marsha looked embarrassed. 'He didn't think you'd want to come, Daisy. After all, you and Erica . . .'

'Oh, what nonsense! The merest little tiff, that's all. We were always quite the best of friends. And he could at least have given me the option.'

She pursed her lips and shook her head several times, emphatically.

'Besides, it must have looked so strange. Not that one cares anything about that, of course. But . . . I suppose everyone came back for drinks and things, after the service?'

Marsha nodded.

There was a silence.

'And what did you have? At this little do of yours?'

'I'm not quite sure one should describe it as a "do".'

'Well, describe it as anything you like.'

'It was really all quite simple. We had tea and sandwiches.' Marsha started to tick things off on her fingers. 'Three sorts: scrambled egg, grated cheese, and sardine. I mixed a little salad cream with the cheese. Also we had chocolate cup cakes

13

and assorted biscuits and I'd made a sponge. It was quite a light one.'

'Just tea?'

'Earl Grey. Everybody liked it. I had to make three pots.'

'Three? That does sound a success.' But Daisy now seemed reconciled to having missed it. 'Did you say you'd put the kettle on?'

'Oh, yes, I did. Thank you for reminding me.' Marsha got to her feet and picked up the small tray. 'Chocolate cup cakes, by the way, might seem a slightly funny thing to some but they were always a particular favourite of Erica's.'

'Oh—did she come, too?'

'No, of course not. She—'

Marsha suddenly realized that she'd been caught out and they both laughed with great enjoyment. 'Oh, I'm sure we shouldn't, but you're so absurd. I'd almost forgotten what a tonic you are, Daisy! I shan't be long with that cup of tea,' she promised. But at the door, again, she hesitated. Daisy was hopeful.

'Oh, Daisy. Before Dan comes. You won't speak of the wallpaper again, or anything like that?'

'Don't worry, dear. I'm not a fool.'

'No, no, of course I didn't mean—'

'But what about *after* he comes?'

Their laughter was renewed. 'You big stiff. But your talk of making no bones worried me a little. And you do realize, don't you, how fond he was of Erica? We don't want to upset him. It was so good of him to offer us his home.'
Daisy stared.

'He may have offered *you* his home,' she said, 'but I'm only here for the weekend.'

'Oh, didn't he tell you in his letter? Then I suppose he thought it better to do so in person. I shouldn't be spoiling his surprise.'

'Ha! But now that you've gone as far as this you might as well carry on. I won't say anything if you don't.'

At first Marsha seemed uncertain.

'Well, all right. But, anyway, I've more or less told you already. You see, Dan knows that you aren't very happy

14

where you are. Just as he knew that *I* couldn't really afford to stay on in that poky little flat of mine. And so he thought it might be a good idea . . . since he was now all on his own in this great house of his . . .'

Daisy certainly didn't think of it as a great house: a three-bedroomed semi-detached in Hendon, rejoicing under the lovely name of Shangri-La.

'The three of us together . . . ,' she murmured, meditatively. 'Well, I don't know, dear. I'm not absolutely sure about that . . . Do you realize I haven't seen Dan for a full five years?' she said, partly to avoid the necessity of having to commit herself straightaway (though the idea did have one or two appealing advantages) but more especially to stop Marsha from thinking that she was simply going to jump at it, as though she could imagine nothing better. You should never, of course, let anyone believe you were too available.

'Is that so?' asked Marsha. 'My goodness, doesn't time fly?'

'Erica was in Germany, visiting her family, or some such thing. And before that I hadn't set eyes on him for . . . well, I don't know how long . . . except that I can tell you he was still just a bag of skin and bones *then*, whenever it was, so you can imagine my surprise when I suddenly saw this great fat chap who was opening the front door to me . . .'

'Oh, I wouldn't exactly say *fat*.'

'Well, I certainly did and Dan himself didn't appear to mind. But bloated, then, if you'd prefer. Definitely unhealthy.'

'In any case, fat or not, he's the most saintly person that I've ever met. He's always trying to do what's right.'

'Oh, *saintly*,' said Daisy. 'Yes, maybe. Well, I can imagine, of course, that most of us try to do what we can.'

'Anyway, about our all living together . . . Dan says he's sure that it's what Henry would have wanted.'

'And how do you feel about it yourself, dear? When you're not under the influence of the drink, I mean?'

But at that moment they suddenly heard a key in the front door. Or rather, Marsha did.

In the minute or two before her brother-in-law came into the room, Daisy—having to remind herself not to expect the slim young man she still mainly visualized—briefly remembered something.

3

One Saturday morning in the spring of 1936 she had been on Rosslyn Hill, in Hampstead, when she had seen someone whom she recognized across the street. She hailed him cheerily. 'Dan! Dan!' How nice. She would get him to buy her a cup of coffee in that smart new café which she'd just passed.

But he didn't hear her. All he'd been doing was disposing of something—an empty cigarette packet, she thought—in one of those rubbish bins attached to a lamppost; but he appeared oddly preoccupied with what he'd done and as he started walking slowly onwards he kept glancing back over his shoulder—quite furtively it seemed.

Daisy was intrigued. For the moment she didn't call a second time. She simply stood and watched.

As she did so, she saw Dan suddenly turn and hurry back to the rubbish bin. He still looked furtive—and this time, little wonder. He actually peered into it, put his hand in and then pulled something out: yes, it *was* a cigarette packet: presumably the same one that he'd just dropped in. What extremely strange behaviour—even from a Stormont.

Now he was crossing the street, but still he didn't see her. He made off quickly down the hill. She followed. The same thing happened. The cigarette packet went into a rubbish bin on *this* side of the road; and then he slowed his pace again and looked back several times as though to make sure of something.

But this was thrilling, thought Daisy. Thrilling. What a story she'd have to tell them at the club! Memories of Bulldog Drummond and Sexton Blake and sinister German spy rings

16

rushed fleetingly to mind. The coded message in the cigarette! The contact whom you daren't acknowledge! (*His* life, *your* life could both depend on it!) The watcher in the shadows! The winging knife between the shoulder blades! For an enraptured moment Daisy scanned the street. A Norland nanny pushed her pram. (Ah, but was there in fact a baby under all the coverings? And didn't she have a rather mannish gait?) A slouching old woman wearing two over-coats—and mittens showing fingers as grey as slate—shuffled by with bulging carrier bags: was *she* all that she seemed? A young man passed, who gave the impression that he might be going from door to door searching for work; but was that striped tie one he had the right to wear—what did he really carry in his small black case—didn't he have a slightly foreign look? Daisy turned and watched reflections in a window, ostensibly gazing at books. Her childhood was not so far behind her, thank God (nor would it ever be), that she hadn't retained a true delight in the bizarre—and the magical ability to turn it to account. Imagination and a sense of fun! Curiosity and wonder! A *sine qua non*. Each one of them.

It was the old woman with the carrier bags who stopped at the rubbish bin!—who retrieved the cigarette packet, opened it, stared at it; Daisy saw her satisfaction, even in profile. She saw, too, that Dan, almost at a standstill, had witnessed it from further down the hill.

But what now? Was it over? He had quickened his pace once more. Daisy had to run in order to catch up with him.

'Dan!' she called again. 'Dan!'

This time he heard her. He turned, looking surprised but welcoming, and hurried back towards her.

'Hello, Daisy! What are *you* doing here?'

'And I could put the same question! I've been watching you, you know.'

When she said that, he actually blushed—a grown man of nearly thirty who could still blush! 'What do you mean, old girl?'

She described what she had seen.

'Are you being blackmailed?' she asked. 'Have you murdered your wife?' But no such luck, of course.

'Oh, well, not quite that,' he answered, smiling foolishly.

'What, then?'

'Nothing much. Really. Nothing at all, in fact.'

'Oh, yes, I could certainly see that,' she informed him drily.

'Well, the thing is, you can't just go up to a person and hand them a couple of pounds as if they just had no pride at all—I mean, can you? And at times like this, those of us who are lucky enough to have a job . . .' With his eyes, as much as with the gesture of his hands, he pleaded for her understanding.

'Did you say—a couple of *pounds*?'

He tried to turn it into a joke. 'I thought she was never going to find it, suddenly crossing the road like that. I thought she'd given up looking in the bins at precisely the wrong moment.'

'For heaven's sake, dear! How often do you go berserk?'

'Oh, hardly ever, hardly ever. It's just, as I say, when there are so many thousands out of work and desperately feeling the pinch . . .'

She suddenly thought of Andrew and the attitude that he had towards his job—his loathing for it and his feeling of martyrdom. But all she said was, 'I shouldn't think that *she* was ever *in* work—or would ever have wanted to be. She's probably been a hobo all her life. And good luck to her, too!'

'She can't have started out like that.'

'Oh, well, one hopes she was a bit cleaner, at any rate!'

'And she didn't look exactly carefree.'

'But if you're still in the mood for doling out charity you can treat me to a cup of coffee.'

'Of course! With pleasure.'

'There's a place up the road that does scones with Devon-shire cream and strawberry jam. Gather ye rosebuds while ye may!'

'What were you doing here, anyway?' he asked again, when they were seated and their order had been taken.

'Oh, just enjoying my constitutional. I've been wandering on the Heath.'

'No wonder you look so fit.'

'I like to have roses in my cheeks.' Yet, these days, he didn't think they were entirely supplied either by exercise or by fresh air. Daisy had glamorized herself. He thought it suited her. Then he remembered having heard something about this from Erica, who had heard of it from Marsha. 'But what about you? Were you on a constitutional, too?'

'No. I was on my way to buy a special sort of cake for Erica. Chocolate. We bought one once before and she enjoyed it so much I thought I'd come up here today and surprise her.'

'Nobody ever buys me special cakes to surprise me!' she said forlornly.

At that moment the coffee and scones and cream arrived.

'Do you like chocolate cake?'

'It's always been my favourite!'

'Then accompany me to the cakeshop and I'll buy you one, as well! We can't have poor old Daisy wandering around London feeling pathetic.'

'No, we can't,' she agreed jovially. 'You're absolutely right!' She asked, a little belatedly, 'How *is* Erica, by the way?'

'She's very well.'

'And your mother?'

'Not quite herself, as a matter of fact. She's had 'flu. It's pulled her down a bit.'

'Oh. Fading a little, is she, dear?'

'Well, hardly. She's only in her fifties.'

'Ah. I didn't realize.'

Daisy finished her scone. She used her forefinger to wipe around the plate. 'I hope it's clean! I don't much care if it isn't!'

'Have another.'

'I don't think that I should.'

'Sure?'

'Are *you* going to?'

'No. I'll be having lunch in an hour.'

'What! Don't tell me you'll be bothering with lunch, after *this*?' She accepted the second scone.

Later she rummaged for her cigarettes; but couldn't find them. 'It doesn't matter. I'm better off without.'

'I'll go and get you some,' he offered.

'You're such a dear. But you must let me pay you. No—wait.' She'd found her own packet, after all, right at the bottom of her handbag. 'How lucky. You might have had to go for miles. Here—have one—they're Turkish, I'm afraid.'

'But you've only got two.'

'Oh, never mind. I have a gallant young admirer who buys them for me.'

She leaned back and blew a trio of smoke rings.

'But I wonder if I *had* let you go and buy me a packet whether I'd have found two pound notes tucked away inside it! Perhaps I missed my opportunity.'

'I do wish you'd forget that.'

'Travelling in hairnets and costume jewellery is clearly more lucrative than I thought. I must confess, I always considered it a peculiar thing for your parents to have put you into, but it appears now that I ought to beg their pardon. You must take this pretty pink box with you when we go. I think it would show up very nicely in a rubbish bin.'

He was silent. He waited for her to finish her second cup of coffee; glanced pointedly at his watch.

'I hope you realize, of course, dear, that she'll only spend it all on drink?'

'How do you know?'

'How do I know? I've been through my own do-gooding phase—naturally. We all have. Not that I don't still try to do my bit,' she added, hurriedly.

She blew some more smoke rings. A toddler at the next table, chained to his high chair, stood up and pointed. Ecstasy and awe were intermingled.

'You seem to have another admirer.' He had felt resentful but this spectacle of frowning delight and of chubby, grasping fingers made him laugh instead.

'Yes. Shall we go?' She stubbed out the remainder of her cigarette. 'I suppose you both mean to have children,' she observed, when they had left the café.

'Well, we both want them. But so far, unfortunately—'

Sudden sympathy blended with ferocity; he was surprised at the extent of both. 'Yes! It's always the way! Those who really want them and who would make good parents . . .' She shrugged. 'I hear that Marsha's about to produce at any moment,' she remarked.

He nodded. 'It's overdue already.'

'Yes. Disgusting. I mean to say—couldn't they wait at *all*?' But she gave him no opportunity of answering. 'You saw that child in there just now?'

'Naturally,' he said, a little coldly.

'Such innocence! Such trust! Such spontaneity! Where will all of that be in a year or two? That mother looked plebeian.' She had worked herself into a small frenzy. 'People have no right—!' Dan was glad to have come in sight of their destination.

But there was just one chocolate cake remaining.

'What shall we do? I suppose we could get them to cut it in half?' He looked around, with an equal lack of enthusiasm, at the other less interesting cakes on display.

'Nonsense. You take that back to Erica—the pair of you enjoy it—forget about me. As though it makes a ha'p'orth of difference. Fattening, anyway.'

He felt touched. 'I think I've got the solution.'

'Yes?'

'You'll simply have to share it with us. You must come to tea this afternoon.'

'You're one in a million, dear, but Erica might not like it. I mean—she may have other things to do.'

'No, I'm sure not. I'll ring her straightaway.'

'Besides, I don't quite know what I'd do with myself till teatime. I think it wouldn't be worth my while going home, you see.'

'Then, Daisy, you must come to lunch!' he cried.

He was, essentially, a very simple man.

4

They had had a small party to celebrate: Marsha, Dan and Daisy. The latter had insisted on going out to an off-licence for a bottle of Johnny Walker. She'd also bought some peanuts and some crisps. They had now finished their dinner, but were still sitting at the table over coffee. 'And later we can eat the rest of the cake.' They had begun it—again at Daisy's insistence—to accompany the tinned fruit and cream which Marsha had provided for dessert.

'But, Daisy, you extravagant mortal, that cake would do beautifully for tomorrow; there's a good three pieces left.'

'I don't want it tomorrow. I want it tonight. Tomorrow let the cupboard be bare; tonight, while there's cake, let's eat, drink and be merry and banish all thought of frugality . . . Not to mention stinginess,' she added to herself.

'Daisy, I may be careful, but I am not stingy.'

'Good God! Who ever said you were, dear? Instant death to such a preacher of sedition!' She raised an imaginary sword and glanced about her, glaringly, for an assailant. 'Daisy the swashbuckler! A son of Robin Hood.'

'And rather merry into the bargain,' laughed her sister-in-law; but still with a trace of reproval.

'What! On just a spoonful or two of pear juice and a bit of cream? No, but it was very nice, dear, very nice indeed. You were always a first-rate little cook. Me, I never had the patience to slave before a stove. There was always something more exciting that I wanted to be getting on with.'

Which wasn't wholly accurate: during one period of her life she had not only cooked well but had even quite enjoyed it.

Marsha said, 'It might have been very different, of course, if you'd been married for longer to Henry.'

'Ah, yes,' murmured Dan, who always grew more than usually sentimental on spirits—and more than usually red-complexioned. 'Poor Henry. Poor Henry. What *year* was it, Daisy, that you married him?' The first part and the second were not consciously connected.

'It was 1934,' supplied Marsha at once.

'Was it as long ago as that?'

'Yes. I'd have been eighteen, and you—let's see—'

'I was a year younger than he was.'

Daisy said to Dan: 'Oh, I remember the way you and Henry giggled at the altar—for all the world like a pair of silly schoolgirls!' She chuckled. 'It's about the only thing that I do remember of that day.'

'Well, he should never have had me as best man! We always set each other off.'

'Yes, I remember that and I remember the way that I did *not* get on with Florence—of course, that wasn't just the wedding day. Why did she have this horrible fixation about everybody's age? As though it ever *mattered*! Well, let's just say that for the few months Henry lived she and I maintained an uneasy truce—and after that we simply kept out of one another's way. Terrible woman! I don't mean to be rude—I forget she was your mother.'

Marsha didn't look too pleased.

'It was a quiet wedding,' said Dan, quickly. 'There couldn't have been any other best man. That's why you had to have me.'

He smiled.

It didn't work.

'It all seems so long ago now,' said Daisy, 'so wholly unrelated to anything that happens now.' She sat back—let her glance travel round the ceiling, as though seeking for something in it to admire. 'And I daresay she was really very nice . . . If you ever got to know her properly, I mean. Naturally.' She shook her head, pondering life's impossibilities.

'The trouble was,' said Marsha—and didn't see Dan now mutely appeal to her across the table—'the trouble was, I think, that she believed you had him too much under your thumb. He was very young, remember, and impressionable.'

'Ha!' muttered Daisy. 'The pot calling the kettle black!'

But her mutter was rendered inaudible by Dan, who spoke simultaneously.

'In 1934? He must have been twenty-eight by then.'

'But very young for twenty-eight,' persisted Marsha. 'Though I'm sure that what really exasperated Mother—one can talk about it now, can't one, Daisy?—was never being able to find out.' Her look was almost impish. 'We none of us could ever find out!'

'But who *wants* to talk about it now?' cried Daisy. '*I* certainly don't! Find out what?' she asked, suspiciously.

'Why, how many years you'd deducted on giving your age to the vicar! We made bets; we laid snares; of course, I can't think why none of us ever went along to—'

Suddenly, the hearing-aid gave one of its more piercing screeches; then settled for a lower, steadier note. When quiet had been restored, Daisy apologized for having missed the whole of Marsha's answer.

'No matter. I don't suppose it was important. But . . . What were we saying now? I think I met your mother last in 1945. That was the year of your divorce, wasn't it? I was coming out of a film, I remember. It was called *The Wicked Lady*. And there, slap bang on the pavement, was Florence.'

This was hardly the road to conciliation.

'Surely there don't need to be any secrets between us *now*, Daisy? Not when we've all of us grown ancient?'

'Oh, At Shangri-La one never grows ancient,' observed Dan, with apparent joviality. 'Didn't you know?' But he looked at Marsha quite beseechingly; and this time she couldn't fail to see. She remembered then her obligations —and was suddenly a different woman.

'You mean, we'll get to be six hundred and still look just like girls?'

Her remorse was distilled from the same malt and barley as its counterpart, but there was now an urgency which made her almost gabble.

'Oh, I'm all for that, aren't you, Daisy? Do you remember the film? I saw it three times. I used to think Ronald Colman terribly dashing. But what will happen, Dan, when we set foot outside the house? Will we suddenly age, *horribly*? Look all of thirty-nine? Oh—how grotesque!'

It was very strange, thought Daisy, sitting there tight-lipped, that she should have happened to hit upon that particular adjective. 'Grotesque' described it all down to a tee. The present performance of course, let alone any that was still to come.

But Dan was very much relieved. 'We'll just have to keep ourselves all safe and snug indoors.'

'Well, that suits me. The older I get the less far I want to venture from my home, anyway. I don't even like the thought of holidays any more. I don't know why. I think I feel afraid.'

Daisy felt afraid, too—she always had—but as she had once said to Henry she would never have owned up to it. No, she hadn't said it, had she? But she would have done, if it hadn't involved owning up to it.

Dan was anxious to draw her back into their conversation. 'What do you think about all that, Daisy?'

'I'd take a dose,' she said. 'That's what I'd do: I'd take a dose. If I thought that I should never want to venture far from home!' She mimed the glass of poison to her lips; tipped back her head to swallow the stuff down. 'I'll tell you this: it's only the thought of the club which has prevented me from doing it, over and over again.'

'So you still go to the club, do you? I didn't know that it existed any more.'

'Why shouldn't it exist?'

'No reason. You still go there, anyway?'

'Just try to keep me from it!' said Daisy. 'Not only is it somewhere to go to in the evenings—and one can't just sit about at home, like a vegetable, night after night—some can; I can't; no. It also seems to me the last bastion of civilization around these parts—not that it *is* around these parts, thank God—at least Regent Street still has a bit of dignity about it, a small remnant of the old days, not much. London isn't what it used to be. No.' She looked at them indignantly, as though the charge could be laid squarely at their own door.

'But what do you do at the club, Daisy?' asked Marsha. 'Do you just discuss things all the time? That sounds horribly intellectual.'

25

'Who said anything about discussing things? Yes, of course we *do* discuss things; the people there have *minds*. Some of them. The ones who aren't just silly asses like anybody else. And what a relief that is: to find people who can talk, who don't just worry about the laundry, and making the beds, and what little Johnny did at school today. But one doesn't *have* to talk. Most of the time I simply play the giddy goat. I don't suppose you'd recognize me.'

'Are you so different, then?'

'I'm *alive*—that's how I'm different. I dance. I sing. I flirt. I do everything. Outrageously. "Good old Daisy!" they shout. "Always the life and soul of the party! You can always rely on Daisy." "Yes," I cry. "You can!"'

Dan burped, discreetly. 'What sort of songs do you usually sing at the club?'

'All sorts!'

'I used to have a party piece once,' said Marsha.

'The one they're always requesting, of course—no originality, that's what I tell them!—is "Daisy". It's my theme song.

" 'Daisy, Daisy, give me your answer, do.
I'm half crazy, just for the love of you.
It won't be a stylish marriage . . ." '

Her voice was rather gravelly but had a lilt to it. In any case, her panache alone would have disarmed criticism. As she sang, she stood up and pirouetted around the furniture, waving her arms about a good deal. The joints of her hands were swollen with arthritis, and—despite that look of sturdiness—her legs were really far from steady; quite soon, in fact, she would need to have a stick; but as she told them now—and told them, too, on many a subsequent occasion —'There's life in the old dog yet! Life in the old dog yet!'

Undoubtedly, however, this was the only way in which she ever used that adjective aloud, in reference to herself.

5

They settled down into their new way of life. Spring had come. The nearby park was filled with blossom. Daisy acquired a favourite bench. Every day, while the fine weather held, it was a pleasure to sit and watch the young men and women in their fresh white shorts and shirts and sweaters bouncing about gaily on the tennis courts. Gradually she got to know them. There were two in particular to whom she always cried out 'Good Luck!' as they passed along the path in front of her; and though for the first few days they only smiled at her, a little shyly, on the fourth or fifth day they actually stopped and talked. The first one was Homayoun and he was very dark and handsome and he came from Iran—although she preferred to use its real name and speak of it as Persia. The other was called Félix, a tall, blond Swiss boy with a charming smile and proper, muscular thighs. They were studying at a language school across the road and liked to come for exercise during their lunchtime break. 'How did you know to wear white, dear?' she asked Homayoun, after patting the bench a little for them to sit beside her. 'Oh, I daresay it's a custom where you come from too, isn't it?—yes, very nice.' And the two boys smiled and nodded happily, so they were well away.

They were both extremely nice young men; they obviously came from *very* good families—that was something you could always tell, despite their colour or their lack of any decent language in which to communicate. They themselves didn't smoke—'and quite right, dears, you're very sensible, I wish I was!'—but they brought her cigarettes, when they discovered that she did. That was on only the second day they stopped to have a chat! And on the third one they introduced three friends—all from the same class—and suggested she should join the five of them for coffee. They took her to a snack bar and they all had baked beans and fried bread, followed by apple turnovers with their coffee, and they wouldn't let her pay for a thing, not a thing, no matter how she tried. *And* they bought her more cigarettes, when she attempted to get up and buy some for herself. It was quite unheard of. So she did her best to be as entertaining as she could—which you could tell that they appreciated enormously—and at the same time to help them with their English. She told them about how she was now retired but how till very recently she used to be a physiotherapist (she got that across, amidst much hilarity, by massaging Félix's shoulders)—and oh, how she missed it. 'You know what my patients used to say? When I massaged them? They said it was like the touch of angels' wings brushing over them, just like angels' wings. They all said it. And it was! But—look! —I used to work too hard: see how my poor muscles are wasted away.' And she slipped one arm out of her coat and jacket, to show them. 'Oh, I used to put too much of myself into my work—far too much—I pummelled and punched and pulled—and great big hulking fellows some of them were—like you, dear,' (to Félix) 'only bigger—they weighed six times as much as I did—I was always a little shrimp. But tough. Wiry. Yet in the end I just wore myself out with it; well, you can hardly be surprised at it. Can you? And now I feel useless. Quite useless!' She pursed her lips up, bitterly. 'Useless. Thrown out on to the scrap-heap. I'd better come and be a teacher, though. Do you think they'd have me?' She ended on a chuckle. 'An old reprobate like me? I mean "old" in the sense of . . . having nothing to do with age.'

'You—teacher,' they said. They smiled and nodded very vigorously. 'Good teacher. Very good teacher.' It was amazing, the amount they seemed to understand.

'Oh, my word, the stories I could tell you!' She lifted both her hands and brought them down expressively upon the table. 'About some of my patients, for instance. Mostly celebrities of one sort or another—stage or society or something of that kind. There's one little anecdote I simply must tell you. I'm sure you don't have anything like this at home!' Then she told them her story about 'Fruity' Tamworth—and how he met his come-uppance, at the hands of Lord Oswestry; and they grinned and roared at the outrageousness of it just the same as she did. 'And it's *true!*' she concluded gaily. 'Every last word of it. All perfectly true. And that tells you something about the state of the English aristocracy between the wars! Doesn't it?'

It was the happiest lunchtime imaginable—how she galvanized that sleepy little place!—and the only tiny damper on the whole occasion was the thought that it was Friday and she wouldn't see Homayoun or Félix or any of their jolly, laughing friends till Monday at the very earliest. (She remembered how it had already been bad enough the previous Friday—and *that* was before the two young men had spoken!) Even Helga, the only female in the party, seemed a pleasant sort of girl, though a little puddingy perhaps, both in manner and appearance, and in no way really worthy of the others; she had a broad, good-humoured smile, however. Daisy conceived the sudden, very happy notion of inviting them to lunch on Sunday. 'I must repay your hospitality,' she said. 'And you will see how a normal English family conducts itself on the sabbath, after its return from church; which will certainly do you good.' She beamed. She wrote her name and address down for them on a smoothed-out paper napkin. Marsha would be pleased, she thought; she always enjoyed the cooking. And she herself would contribute a cake, or a block of ice-cream; maybe a flagon or two of cider. Devon cider.

Drake he's in his hammock till the great Armadas come.
(Capten, art tha sleepin' there below?)
Slung atween the round shot, listenin' for the drum,
An' dreamin' arl the time o' Plymouth Hoe . . .

Yes, it might be a very nice idea, as well, to teach them a bit of real English poetry. She liked Sir Henry Newbolt. And Kipling. (Boots—boots—boots—boots—movin' up an' down again!) As she sat on alone in the snack bar, after the others had all gone, but over the final cup of coffee which they had left her, she reflected that really—despite everything —life was still pretty good.

6

And there were other things, too, besides all these beautiful new friends. There were her books, for instance. There were her visits to the bank and to the hairdresser's—not to transact business necessarily or to have her hair done—but just to say hello and be given a cup of tea, with biscuits (at the bank) or a cigarette (at the hairdresser's) and a look at the *Financial Times* or the problem page of *Woman's Own* (what muck! —but something to take your mind off things a little). And there were sunny days like this—with always the chance of getting into conversation. (Preferably with someone young, lively and interested; it **was funny** how the lively ones were so often drawn towards herself, as though they could sense immediately a kindred spirit. 'Why *me*?' she would say. 'What do they ever seen in *my* ugly mug, I'd like to know!')

There was also, of course, her little car; her Austin Seven; her *sine qua non*; her winged and fiery chariot.

Yes, thank heaven . . . At least she could still pooter about in that—like Mr Toad—the world her oyster. (Hendon was all very well, she supposed—even quite nice in a suburban sort of way—but it was very much off the map.) Without this faithful ferryman of hers (Charon's counterpart, maybe, who brought the souls of the *living* across the river Styx—or down the Finchley road—*away* from Hades; yes, that too began with an H)—without him she would go crazy. Life would be unbearable. She'd take a dose.

With a car, there were always people you could see. You were still somebody whilst you were mobile; an entity, a life force to be reckoned with. Without it, you were little better than a zombie. Incredible that Madge Fairweather should ever have suggested that she, Daisy, was now getting too —well, *there* was an example of the living dead for you, if you liked: Madge Fairweather, with her ghastly posture and her soft pudgy whiteness, her dowager's hump and her silly teetery legs in their disgustingly vainglorious stockings (vein glorious!): with her interminable droolings over her long-dead husband who was supposed to have been a saint—what a ridiculously overworked word that was!—and probably had been, too, if he had managed to put up with *her* for more than two weeks together, let alone bring her up breakfast in bed and say, 'There, there!' which had seemed to be his principal occupation in life and his principal line of dialogue. Saint or else prize ninny?—Daisy thought that *she* could answer which. But, no, she certainly had precious little need of any Madge Fairweather. ('My Fairweather friend,' she always called her. Madge herself didn't ever seem to see the joke. That showed you.) Even without her, Daisy still had Edgar and Vera in Blandford Street, bless them, Bill in West Kensington (despite that shrew of a wife of his), young Malcolm in Notting Hill. (Never tell Marsha about *that*.) And that nice and intelligent—though not very pretty—little thing, Phoebe, with whom he lived. Daisy didn't exactly approve of that, but at least it was done without hypocrisy, and dear Phoebe was always offering her another glass of sherry—and, after all, why not? The young were more sensible now than they had ever been. She'd willingly throw in her lot with their generation any day of the week, rather than with their so-called elders and betters. Ha! And then, of course, there was the club. Without her trusty little Austin, how often could she ever have got down *there*?

(But how *extraordinary* of Madge Fairweather! What an *extraordinary* thing to say! Yet the woman was clearly jealous. And no wonder—since she just sat and guzzled chocolates all day, about four to every one she ever offered you, while half-wittedly gawping at the television set, quite literally open-mouthed! She had a highly plebeian cast of soul. She was the sort of person who always wanted to label people, label them and limit them, file them away in some neat little pigeonhole, so she then thought she knew exactly what they were, exactly how they would behave or exactly how much they were worth. People *and* things: she labelled the one by their pedigree, their job, their age; the other by their price. In short—she had the Florence complex. And when you'd said that, of course, you had said everything. Poor soul.)

The club. She remembered Marsha's reaction: 'But what do you *do* there?' She would have to tell Marsha all about Madge Fairweather, clearly; perhaps she would do it when she got home this afternoon; or would she go to the library first—put off that deadening moment of return for just an hour or two longer—try to stay out, if she could, until suppertime? Then she would hold Madge up to her as a Warning and an Example; but do so, naturally, with tact. She wasn't quite certain how—not yet—but she was bound to think of something when the proper time arrived. It seemed she always did.

7

'Oh, Daisy, how could you? How could you? You really are the limit. You're quite impossible.'

'Impossible? Why? What have I done?' She busily adjusted the tiny lever on her hearing-aid. 'Wait a minute, wait a minute,' she said crossly. 'You don't want to waste fine rhetoric on the desert air.'

'Honestly!' Marsha appealed to Dan. She'd been in the midst of clearing away the supper things; the two others were still seated at the table. 'Can't *you* say something to her?'

'I must admit, Daisy, I think it isn't very considerate towards poor Marsha. To suddenly spring it on her like this.'

'Dear heaven,' said Daisy, 'it's only Friday night. They won't be here till Sunday. How much notice does she *need*? Six months and a printed invitation?'

'You know I do the weekend's shopping on a Friday.'

'What was that?'

'I always do the weekend's shopping on a Friday!'

'I'm only surprised you don't do it on a Monday and have done with it! Then you'd have all day Sunday to *plan* for it!'

'Well, I tell you, I just couldn't bear to live my life in the muddle that you live yours!'

32

After a moment, however, Marsha spread her hands and spoke in a lower voice.

'Besides—you don't even know what they like to eat. Does this man from Persia eat normal food, for instance? I don't suppose it even occurred to you to ask.'

She didn't wait for an answer.

'And how do you ever imagine we're going to sit five extra people round this table? It will only take six at the outside.'

'Well, I suppose that's a relatively minor problem,' said Dan.

'But it just shows you that she doesn't *think*. And what about all the extra expense? Is the housekeeping simply supposed to stretch? I rack my brains to make economies and then she just comes along— And, no, Dan, I don't see why *you* should be expected to fork out, I really don't.'

'Nobody is expected to do anything! I intend to do all the shopping myself,' said Daisy grandly, '*and* to pay for it out of my own pocket. It won't matter if I have to go without a few little things for a week or two—like cough lozenges or aspirin or the batteries for this infernal aid. I really can't think what all the fuss is about. A simple act of Christian charity to homesick strangers in a wintery land—*that's* what it started out as. I thought you'd be pleased. I didn't know that Marsha would carry on as though I'd landed her with the feeding of the five thousand.'

'Rubbish. You didn't think of us at all. And you know perfectly well that you won't be the one to do the shopping —or to pay for it, either.'

'Furthermore, I shall buy everything already cooked,' said Daisy, loftily.

'A typical Sunday dinner *this* is going to be!'

'I can't help that. I shall certainly do my best.'

'Yes, and I suppose you'll set the table, too, and get the house all ready—'

'There was never a house more ready than this one is.'

'—and see to all the washing up afterwards.'

'Naturally.'

'We'll each help with those things,' said Dan.

'Well, I keep on *offering*,' said Daisy.

There was a silence. Marsha resumed her clearing of the table. 'Here. Let me do that for you.' Marsha said nothing. 'Here's the custard jug.' Silence. 'Would you like me to try and carry that tray? I think that I could probably manage it.'

Dan returned from the front door with the shaken table-cloth; and Daisy was able to relax again.

Marsha continued to sulk for the rest of the evening.

'In any case you ought to be glad of having the opportunity to make new friends. Both of you. I am,' Daisy said, while Dan was trying to listen to a radio play. 'Making friends, indeed, is one of the greatest pleasures that I know of.' She added after a moment, with her characteristic low chuckle: 'Keeping them is sometimes less of a pleasure. I occasionally wonder if it's worth it.'

When she got no noticeable response, she said a few seconds later, 'Is this thing any good? What's it all about? I wish you had a television. *Everybody* has a television these days. I mean, everybody who is anybody. They all think it's extraordinary at the club. "What do you *do*," they say, "the evenings when the club's not open?" "Nothing!" I say. "*Nothing*! Just stare at the carpet and go crazy." Thank God I've got inner resources, though I don't know *what* I'd do if I hadn't! What's happening now?' she asked.

Dan tried to give her a quick resumé. 'No, no, it doesn't matter,' she said. 'I can't hear a word—you and the wireless in competition. You enjoy yourself. Forget about me.'

She was silent for a short while. She adjusted her hearing-aid.

It whistled.

She tapped her foot a little, in time to a tune that sounded better inside her own head than it did when she tried to hum it.

'Have you sent off your Christmas cards yet?' she said to Marsha.

Silence—except for the radio.

'The best friend I ever had, you know, was Marie. (Though I don't know why people can't pronounce that name properly these days. It's as if they'd never heard of Marie Corelli—or Stopes—or Tempest—or biscuits. I suppose the

34

same people would pronounce Nice biscuits nice!).' She made a richly contemptuous tcht. 'Where was I, then?'

Nobody answered.

'Oh, yes. Marie. Now, there was a sensible woman; the most sensible and the most sensitive woman I ever met. (Sometimes I think the *only* sensible and sensitive woman I ever met! That was a joke.) I mean, sensitive to the needs of others—naturally. There's not a day passes when I don't think of her. And no one has any idea how much I still miss her! No. Not at all!'

She tapped her foot some more.

The leading male character in the play was declaring his love for the leading female character. Daisy listened for a couple of minutes. He was getting quite passionate.

'Silly ass!' she said. 'Can't think why he doesn't find something better to do with his time. Poor fellow is all I can say. Deserves everything he'll get. Bill could tell him a thing or two! Oh, my word, but couldn't he just! I don't know how you've got the patience to put up with all that tripe.'

Dan—with his customary good-humoured forbearance —got up and turned the radio off.

'Oh, I see you haven't.' The cessation of sound seemed to make her immediately more cheerful. 'Wise chap! There's hope for you yet, dear.'

Marsha said curtly: 'Dan was trying to listen to that play.' It was the first time that she had spoken for ages.

'Yes, I know, dear. I didn't quite hear what you said, but I daresay that you're perfectly right!' Anything to be conciliatory, she thought; she chuckled. 'And welcome back to the land of the living!'

So obviously Marsha, too, had a bit more discrimination than she sometimes gave her credit for; and, in the end, the only thing her recovery had needed was for all that filth and cacophony to be switched off. 'Love stories, dear! I ask you! Oh, ye gods and little fishes!'

'Daisy, I said—'

'It isn't important,' interrupted Dan.

'But it *is* important!' replied Marsha. 'Of course it is.'

'That's right, dear. You tell him!' Daisy clapped her hands

encouragingly. Marsha clearly had her dander up over something, but at least she'd stopped moping. This would surely be a good moment to speak about Madge Fairweather.

'So I shouldn't think there's ever been much of a love story for *her*,' she ended up triumphantly, 'other than on the most nauseating "I-hope-your-egg's-all-right-there-there!" sort of level. Perhaps you could call it *tepid* . . . almost . . . if you were someone, that is, with something of a penchant for overstatement.'

Marsha didn't say anything about this then—indeed, she hardly appeared to be listening—but the following afternoon it was clear she wished to make amends. She and Dan had been to a jumble sale and had brought Daisy back a framed piece of woolwork that could have been Victorian—'a real collector's item,' cried Daisy ecstatically, 'I shall treasure it for ever!'—except that the colours seemed almost too fresh for that. But the text was certainly Victorian!—'and not at all in keeping, dear, with all those pretty flowers and butterflies and trees that look like lollipops! "Judge not, that ye be not judged"! Oh, thank you, dear. It's the nicest present that I've had in centuries!' And several times during the course of the evening she gave Marsha a sudden impulsive kiss.

Indeed, it was a happy evening. Especially as dear, sweet Dan had insisted on paying for everything, even for the cider (though strictly, of course, on the q.t.!) and all her cups of coffee and cigarettes were safe.

She felt so pleased with the pair of them.

It was doubly unfortunate, then, that the following day Marsha should again become upset . . . being every bit as angry when the students *didn't* come to lunch as she had been when she'd first been told they would.

8

'Thank you, dear. That's very good of you,' said Daisy, taking the hot-water bottle which Marsha was holding out to her. 'These autumn nights are getting rather nippy. Don't *you* find that?' Daisy was already in bed, but she had her hearing-aid clipped into the pocket of her pyjama jacket (it was a man's one—striped) in expectation of Marsha's visit. 'Don't run along at once, dear—unless you're very busy. Of course you're always very busy; sometimes I don't know how you do it. I take my hat off to you, I really do. Or I would, if I had it on, I mean! But why don't you just sit down a moment and rest your poor old legs? I'm feeling a little . . . a little lonely, dear . . . tonight. That chair is a nice and comfortable one; just sling the handbag on the floor—oh, anywhere, it doesn't matter. "A *handbag*, Mr Worthing?" Yes, I must say, you and Dan have made it all quite comfortable for me. On the whole. But then, of course, it *is* six months since I moved in—would you believe it?—it hardly seems a week or two to me. And, incredibly, we still appear to be surviving, don't we?'

'We certainly do!'

'But . . .'

'Yes, Daisy?'

'I often wonder who she was, dear, don't you?'

'Who?'

'The woman who did that tapestry thing. Many's the time I've lain here—just propped up against these pillows—staring up at it. And thinking.'

'Perhaps she's still alive?'

But Daisy shook her head, decisively. 'No. I feel it in my bones she's not.' And she didn't add that, alive, she would have been just another woman; not someone you could speculate upon with any degree of satisfaction. 'Anyway, I certainly hope that *I* shall never fall into the habit of judging people.'

'Well, I suppose no one can avoid it, really.'

'No, you're quite right, dear. Quite right. You usually are, of course.'

'Oh, oh, oh. All this soft soap. What might you be after, Lady Jane?'

'Yes—and don't forget the flannel, dear. Soft soap *and* flannel! My word, you've just reminded me, though—I used to grow mustard-and-cress on a flannel once, when I was knee-high to a grasshopper. And delicious it was, too. Cress sandwiches; the best I've ever tasted. They were. It's true! But . . . Now what were we saying? Oh, yes, dear, I was thinking a little about your own case. I don't see how you can help judging people when you have to go through all the rigmarole of a divorce. Do you?'

Marsha gave a shrug. 'Well, that was a long time ago, Daisy.'

'And now one can see that the fault was evenly divided—is that what you're saying? You just weren't compatible?' Daisy nodded. 'Although you, dear, were probably a lot more compatible than he was, if the truth were known; that was always my own view of the matter, at any rate.'

'Do you know something? It was exactly forty-one years ago, last June, that we got married.'

'Good gracious! Almost an anniversary. We ought to celebrate. Except that he was a bad 'un, of course. Not that you could help liking him though.'

'If you didn't have to live with him.'

'Quite! Oh, spoken like a true philosopher! Upon my soul, do you ever know a man until you've lived with him?—and then, after that, dear, do you ever want to?'

Marsha raised both eyebrows. 'Yet I always thought, Daisy, that in your opinion men could do no wrong.'

'Oh, men, maybe. Men. But who ever said anything about husbands?'

They laughed.

Daisy nodded again, sympathetically. 'Yes, you had a raw deal, if you ask me. A very raw deal, indeed. We both did! But poor Marsha. That's what I always say; poor old Marsha. If only the cards hadn't been stacked so high against you. And you started off with such a *very* good hand, as well, dear. What sheer rotten luck that you couldn't have played it just a little better! But you can tell me all about it if you like.'

9

Yet what was there to tell? It was all such a dull little story.

On the night that Andrew Poynton had proposed she had sung 'If you were the only boy in the world' to him. They'd been alone, in the garden, but there could have been others within earshot. He had been woefully embarrassed.

That was Marsha's party piece. (Although she had only twice sung it at an actual party.) She possessed a pretty voice.

But undoubtedly the prettiest thing about her was her face.

Once, when she'd been dressing for a dance and a cousin had been staying in the house, this child had lain there on the carpet with her chin cupped in both hands—and just solemnly gazed: Marsha at eighteen was the most beautiful thing that she'd ever seen up till then, she was to say later, many years later, when most of Marsha's looks were gone and her life was nothing but a bleak routine, joyless and wearisome.

Of course, her school reports had never been good. Her last one (well, not counting the finishing school at Lausanne) had actually bemoaned the fact that Marsha was all 'bubble' and had strongly recommended that she should do her best to develop some worthwhile interests. But even then one of her teachers had said that her personality was as charming as her face and that it was quite impossible not to be enchanted by her!

The real problem, though—as she herself saw it in after-years—was her appalling lack of experience. If only she had known then about the things which might have been possible! If only she had known about theatrical schools!—or that it was indeed not unheard-of to defy your parents over matters more important than a smuggled-out lipstick.

She married the first man who asked her; not because she thought she wouldn't have plenty of other opportunities, but because he was handsome and there was a lovely moon and

she was impatient to be the mistress of her own establish-
ment, to entertain her own friends without supervision, and
to tell the cook what to prepare.

Also she was very much moved by the sentiments expressed in that old, slow favourite of hers—even if Andrew
(almost ungallantly) did rather cut across them to offer for
her hand.

She hadn't realized then how easily he grew embarrassed.
Amazingly it wasn't so much their wedding—nor its pre-
liminary introductions to family and to friends—that made
her cognizant. It was their first breakfast-time in Austria,
when she absent-mindedly asked within their waiter's hearing whether he took sugar in his coffee. For the rest of that
morning he hardly spoke to her.

He was embarrassed again, in a dozen trivial ways, before
and after the arrival of their first child. Once, she had been
very sick behind a telephone kiosk—he had stalked on
huffily, resolutely dissociated. Later, when her pregnancy
was more apparent, he showed reluctance to go out with her
at all; and later yet, if she were pushing the pram, he would
usually walk in front, or behind, or on the other side of the
road. He would never have considered—under ordinary
circumstances—pushing it himself.

He was twenty-two when he married her; but whereas he
seemed only seventeen in some ways, he seemed like twenty-
seven (or forty-seven) in others; and very soon Marsha had
begun to call him a stick-in-the-mud, disappointed that he
wouldn't take her out more often and increasingly impatient
with his assertion (constantly reiterated) that savings and
insurance were the things that mattered. After a few years, he
said, he would be earning more; they would be settled; time
then to think of theatres and dances and holidays abroad. He
worked on the Stock Exchange. It was a job he loathed, but
especially because he loathed it, he claimed, he had to stick at
it. She didn't understand why.

He was a stick-in-the-mud; he was a puritan. He was also a
boor—although once, when she actually put it in a note
rebelliously explaining her absence from the breakfast table,
she spelt it Boer (three times, complete with capital letters,

exclamation marks and underlinings). This was the morning after she had given a small dinner party which, demonstrably, he had not found very interesting. He had first begun to yawn, broadly and loudly, and then he had picked up a newspaper—opening it wide and ostentatiously rustling its sheets. Finally, he had brought into the room an alarm clock, which had gone off stridently at midnight, making everybody jump.

It had been impossible to pass it off as a joke—though of course she had tried to do so.

Her friends might have pretended to believe her; her husband's eyes—if not his actual words—had plainly denied its being one.

She had preferred it when he'd been self-conscious, even to the point of lunacy.

Yet in some measure she—inadvertently—had her revenge, soon afterwards. Andrew invited his boss home to dinner. His boss was merely humourless but his boss's wife would have made Lady Bracknell seem an easy mixer. Marsha had suggested that it might help things to have another couple present. Evelyn Franklin was a schoolfriend —and the daughter of a lord. Wouldn't she and her husband perhaps be worthy to sit at the same table as Colonel and Mrs Chin?

Unfortunately, at the last moment, Evelyn phoned to say that John seemed to have caught something; he was feeling rather ill.

'Oh, but you can't let me down—you just can't! Think how *awful* it would be! Oh, Evie—please! I've been depending on you.'

They came. During the meal John Franklin had to leave the table: three times. The third time, like the drowning man, he didn't come back. The cloakroom was next door to the dining-room; it was a modern house—the walls were paper thin. Through most of the fish course (and a lot of the duck) they heard him retching. Even the strawberries and cream were difficult to get down. When he wasn't retching he was groaning: a great deal of the conversation had to be repeated. But although at length Evelyn—with one or two mysterious gestures—did slip apologetically away, neither the Chins nor Andrew acknowledged anything unusual. It would have been hard to say who displayed the greatest valour in the face of nearly overwhelming odds. They talked about the weather. They talked about the Depression. They talked about the annexation of Austria, three months earlier. They even talked about Chaplin. Their smiles were grisly. Marsha—who anyway wouldn't have had much to contribute to some of these subjects but who was normally put down as a very sympathetic listener—said scarcely a word. She came to feel thoroughly miserable; ashamed, as much as anything, at the thought of her own heartlessness.

In the end she grew quite hysterical. She started laughing. This was when Colonel and Mrs Chin, who had had to rush away immediately after dinner, thanked her for 'such a very charming evening. Quite delightful. Really.'

'Yes, wasn't it fun?' she replied. 'I'm so glad you enjoyed it.'

It was totally the wrong thing to have said—at least in Andrew's eyes. (He didn't suggest what might have been the right thing.) He was furious in his disappointment, and later on morose. It was all her fault. It was she who'd wanted the Franklins in the first place. It was she who'd insisted on their coming, when Evelyn had telephoned. She had hardly done or said a single thing all evening to add to the general entertainment.

At the height of his fury he even hinted that she might have contrived the whole affair. Out of spite. She hadn't wanted him to make a good impression. 'That's why you laughed in their faces when they left.'

Their divorce was still some seven years in the future, and there was a whole world war to be fought out in the meantime. Yet that was the evening when she first started clinging seriously to the possibility of it—as a hope, and a solace, and a refuge.

IO

'Well, I'm not surprised, dear. Not at *all* surprised. Henry, too, was a very poor stick of a man. Oh, yes, a very poor stick indeed.' She was always forgetting the tiresome fact of their having been related—Henry and Marsha and Dan. 'Thank you for telling me all that. You didn't have to. But I'm very glad you did. You look a little peaky, dear, you really ought to go to bed. But . . . Just imagine his bringing in an alarm clock to speed the parting guest! What a lot you must have had to put up with! I never knew he had it in him! Yet I always liked that quiet, dry sense of humour of his; that sharp, ironic wit. It goes with such panache—I recognized it then. And he was certainly very handsome. You can forgive a man a lot, I always find, if he's young and handsome and can make you laugh.'

'Well, I'm not so sure,' responded Marsha.

'What was that, dear? No, of course you're not. Why should you be? Handsome is as handsome does—*that's* what I say. But . . .' (she fiddled impatiently with her hearing-aid) 'you yourself always had the looks of the family, didn't you, dear? I mean the Stormonts. Dan and Henry didn't get very much of 'em—especially Dan! He looked just like a thin, gangly monkey when he was younger, with sleeked-down gingery hair, and he looks just like a slower, puffier version now, with hardly any hair at all to speak of, gingery or otherwise! Not that that matters, of course. He has a nice, lazy, easy-going sort of face—to match his personality. Not much get-up-and-go, however—oh, well, you can't have everything—none of you ever showed much of that! Of course, it usually works out in this life that it's the brothers who get all the beauty and the sisters who are left to look like monkeys. So you, dear, did very well for yourself. I mean —in that respect. But . . . Why *did* your mother never

43

encourage you to develop more resources? I've often wondered.'

'I suppose that in those days people just didn't consider it so necessary for women to be educated.'

'Well, I don't know, dear. *I* managed to scratch together an education of some kind. Of course, that wasn't quite in those days, I grant you. Your mother herself was reasonably well-educated. In a way. According to her lights. I must say, it seems very strange. And it wasn't only you! To have let Dan go into hairnets and Henry into Selfridge's . . . ! Didn't your father ever have a say in it?'

Marsha merely shrugged. 'I really can't remember.'

No. Marsha's father had been a distinctly poor sort of a fish. Daisy *did* remember.

And besides that, she already knew the rest of the answer quite well—anyway, with regard to Marsha. Florence had just wanted to keep her daughter dependent on her, in her old age. That was mainly why she had organized the divorce: to have an unpaid companion to dance grateful and admiring attendance on her in her final years. And how wonderfully Florence had succeeded!

'I wonder what she's doing now.'

'Who?'

'Your mother.'

Marsha stared at her. 'But, Daisy, my mother is dead.'

Daisy stared back at her a moment; suddenly appeared to give herself a little shake.

'Yes, I know *that*, dear.'

She passed one hand across her forehead, and spoke almost with vehemence.

'I meant, of course—I wonder what she's doing now, in the afterlife. Don't you believe in heaven? Don't you believe that we go *on*?'

'Yes . . . I think I do.'

'Well, then?' She put her hand back to her forehead, kept it there a little, shaded her eyes with it. 'Don't go for just a minute—there's a dear.'

'Aren't you feeling well, Daisy?'

'Of course I'm feeling well. I think that someone must just

have walked across my grave, that's all. What a ridiculous expression! I certainly hope they had the good manners to wipe their feet well, before they did so!'

Marsha began to relax. 'You're not sitting in a draught or something?'

'Yes, I am. I'm sitting in a something. I'm sitting in a bed.'

They both chuckled. 'Oh, you arsiponum!' After a moment, she administered one further test.

'What do you suppose heaven will be like, Daisy?'

'A colossal bore, most probably.'

'Oh—you don't!'

'It depends on whom you have to meet there. I hope there's not a lot of idiotic women, all doing good works. Suppose I had to be polite to my own mother—let alone yours?' (There seemed nothing much wrong *there*, thought Marsha.) 'That was just my little joke, of course.'

'I know it was, Daisy.'

'My word, I do believe you're getting quite broad-minded in your old age! There's hope for you yet!'

'I'm very relieved to hear it!'

'No, but I don't really mean it, dear—you know me—not a word. Shall I tell you what I intend to do the minute I arrive?'

'In heaven?'

'Yes. Paint the town red—you might have guessed. "Great Scot," they'll say, "who's this the wind's blown in? Hold on to your hats, boys! This place will never be the same again —oh, *hallelujah*!" Besides which, I intend to catch up on a few of the shows I was sorry to have missed in London. I mean, I'd like to see Burbage and Garrick and Kean. And —of course—keep up with all that's going on when I'm no longer here to see it.'

But Marsha shook her head; smiling; bewildered.

'Oh, Daisy, how can that be? What's past is past. Nothing can bring it back.'

'Oh, ye of little faith!'

'Well, it's no good pretending I can understand! But do you really believe it could be possible?'

'I do! I do! If that's the sort of thing you're after.'

'Then I'll just have to think about it. I know I've never been as clever as you, Daisy.'

' "Be good, sweet maid, and let who will be clever." '

It was a moment of rare harmony between them.

'And do you know how else I see it?' asked Daisy. 'I see it as a sort of might-have-been place, where you can relive your life as it really ought to have been lived. All the right people responding in the right way. Your true potential unimpeded. I wouldn't *mind*, dear, finding myself in a place like that. Would you?'

'No; it sounds quite beautiful.'

'And probably all poppycock—if the truth were known!'

'I shan't believe that.'

'You please yourself, dear. You'll be as mad as I am before you're through!'

Marsha stood up. 'Well, Daisy, in that case I could certainly do worse. But now I think that I'd better be on my way. You need to get your beauty sleep. I need to make Dan his good-night cup of Horlicks.'

'Yes, of course. I mustn't keep you. We really ought to call you Martha—not Marsha.' Daisy gave a wide yawn.

'Oh, don't do that—you're making me do it, too!'

'Now just look at you—you poor old thing! You should have been in your bed *hours* ago. Tell Dan to make his own Horlicks!'

'Here, let me take your aid for you and put it on the table. Do your pillows need plumping again? Is that a little better?'

Daisy didn't hear, but nevertheless she supplied the right answer. 'That's very nice; thank you, dear.' She gave another yawn. 'Thank you for my hot-water bottle. Just the way I like it. Thank you for sitting and listening to me. Been jawing the hind legs off a donkey—*as* usual! But tonight, dear, *you* provided a fair amount of the jawing yourself! Still—mum's the word—I shan't tell on you! Don't forget to say goodnight to Dan for me.'

Marsha bent and kissed her on the cheek. (It was still as rouged as in the daytime.) Daisy mumbled her usual nocturnal benediction.

'Sweet repose. Half the bed and all the clothes . . . God bless. Happy dreams.'

'Thank you, Daisy. Sleep well.' When Marsha passed her room again, some fifteen minutes later, Daisy was deeply and rhythmically snoring.

Part Two

II

When Marsha had been married a few weeks Daisy telephoned her.

'Hello! I want to come and visit you. I want to meet your groom—properly, I mean. Didn't have a chance to speak two words to him at the wedding.'

Marsha, feeling skittish, having been brought up always to observe the little politenesses of life, considered asking, 'Who is that, please?' But she couldn't quite bring herself to do it.

'Why, Daisy! Hello! Good morning! How are you?'

She felt pleased with herself—that she had thought (for once) of the right retort so quickly. It was a much kinder and much more subtle manner of teaching her sister-in-law a little lesson.

'Oh, not so bad. Not so dusty. You know—*considering*.'

It was a dampening and very necessary reminder. Marsha felt quite humbled.

The thing was, so very much had happened in her own life in the last six months that she'd forgotten how short a time it really was; and although she'd never been wholly certain (no one had) how much Daisy had truly *cared* for Henry, she now saw that she'd been selfish and unthinking.

For, after all, the wonder was, surely, not that Daisy had forgotten some of the silly little niceties, but that she was still managing to function even *adequately*, let alone robustly, let alone with so much courage. She was a veritable lesson in bravery. (And Marsha had supposed that *she* was going to be the teacher!) How could Daisy bear to come and visit newly-weds?—and such very playful newly-weds, too, Marsha told herself, always billing and cooing—such bliss—just the way she'd imagined it was going to be—with Andrew amusingly trying to pretend that he was far too serious for all that type of thing, acting like an old curmudgeon but only wanting to lead her on. Why, just last night!—the way he'd given a groan when she had rolled over on to his side of the bed for a cuddle! The way he had actually got out and padded round to *her* side of it and then put one of the pillows between them and threatened her with separate rooms if she didn't behave herself! So? Was to be on *ration*, was it? His favours weren't just to be had as though they were provided two a penny! He was the master of the house, and she must earn them! What a lark! Well, in the end, of course, she had certainly managed to earn them—along with his grumbles and his grudging sigh of resignation. (In fact, she rather thought she had earned better than she had got—but no matter—there were some things which, even in fun, it was rather better not to mention.) But all these delightful and tantalizing—and presumably typical—goings-on! Daisy herself had been a bride not much more than a year ago, and though of course she wouldn't be invited up to the bedroom, she must surely remember how it was. Had she simply decided, then, to take the bull by the horns? Yes, that was it. It would entirely fit her character.

Marsha remembered Daisy at the funeral: so dramatic in black, such a grim-faced, plucky little woman.

She remembered her at her own wedding; still in mourning, so that every eye went straight towards her, the one stark figure in a sea of white and pastel, still a little grim-faced. 'So they didn't try and get you to postpone this business. I should think not, either! I hope that you'd have put your foot down if they had! You probably wouldn't.'

She had given them a pair of double sheets and a beautiful double blanket as a wedding gift—a marvellously useful and generous present. Then Erica had seen the blanket and inspected it very closely; and they had found a monogram on the pair of sheets. Marsha had mentioned all this to her mother, never dreaming that such revelations would be passed on. News of it had got to Daisy. 'D.H. on the sheets!' Daisy had exclaimed. 'D.H.? Well—naturally! Where do you think I bought the wretched things?'

She had insisted that D. H. Evans was still *D. H.* Evans, wasn't it, or had even department stores succumbed to the modern mania for change and for excitement?'

'Change, change, change!' she had reportedly cried out. 'Nobody can do without it! Well, quite right too! I'd take a dose if everything remained the same! I should, really!'

It had still been a very useful and a very generous present, Marsha had declared; and she only hoped to heaven that Daisy wouldn't make any mention of it in front of her—ever.

'Yes, of course you may come and visit us!' she now cried gaily down the telephone. 'You know you never need to ask.'

'Well, I wasn't sure if *you* were ever going to,' replied Daisy, with her gruff laugh.

'Oh, you're one of the very people we've been meaning to get in touch with. In fact,' said Marsha, 'you're right at the top of our list!'

'Oh, well done, me!' said Daisy. 'Then I hadn't been forgotten, after all.'

Marsha had to admit (to herself) that she had perhaps been a little neglectful. Between the funeral and the wedding she had only visited Daisy once—there had been so very, very much to see to—and although she had telephoned on a number of different occasions (well, two or three at any rate) Daisy had either been out or about to go out.

'The merry widow,' Erica had christened her.

'Oh, Erica,' said Marsha with a chirrup, 'I don't think that's very kind of you!'

'Better than the original version!' remarked Dan—but with a slightly strained sort of grin; he, of all of them, had always been closest to Henry.

'Oh, what do you mean: the original version?' Marsha stared at them both prettily, prepared to be appalled.

'The merry *black* widow!' said Erica. The two of them giggled together very naughtily. It seemed immensely funny.

'Oh, don't! You mustn't,' Marsha gasped at last. 'You know I simply can't bear spiders. Creepy-crawlies! Ugh! I dream about them. If I were ever to start associating Daisy with anything like that . . .'

Dan said: 'Oh, come off it, Marsha! There was never any woman less like a creepy-crawly than Daisy.'

It was a smiling yet none the less uncharacteristically stern rebuke; and it had the desired effect on both wife and sister.

Marsha soon began to hum melodies from *The Merry Widow*, not with any satiric intent, but simply because these were the first tunes that came to mind and she thought, in a slightly chastened mood, that her singing might please Dan. It did please him. He loved to listen to his sister's voice (Erica, unfortunately, was tone-deaf) and when they'd been younger, indeed, had often requested her to sing the popular songs of the moment to him.

'Do you remember that time on holiday when it rained all afternoon,' she said, 'and the two of us had that competition to see who could recognize the most tunes which the other hummed?'

'And you won hands down!' laughed Dan. 'It cost me a whole shilling.'

'Yes. Happy days. Ah, happy days!' she said. (No, she didn't mean that, of course. Well, she didn't mean precisely that. It was sometimes difficult to know, even inside her own head, just what she did mean! Oh, how she wished sometimes that she had been born clever!)

She finished singing 'Velia' and then she said, 'Well, talking of *The Merry Widow*—did you both go to see *The Gay Divorcée*? Oh, that was great fun, too.'

They hadn't, however.

'Oh, but you must, you must, if ever you get the chance. And I'll tell you a little secret. I'm wildly in love with Fred Astaire.'

'Then we'll tell Andrew, if you're not careful.'

'Oh, he already knows—that grumpy old puss.' She pouted. 'He doesn't share my passion.'

'If he's a grumpy old puss,' said Erica, 'six days *before* the wedding, what will he be like, six years *after* it?' They all laughed, for some reason. 'And if he is, anyway, I'm sure it's only nerves.'

'Yes, yes, you're right. Oh, my, is that the time? Well, I must simply fly. I only meant to stay a minute. And perhaps I oughtn't to be speaking so much about merry widows or gay divorcées—perhaps it's tempting providence. But if ever I am a gay divorcée I do so hope that Fred Astaire will still be there!' She arranged her veil before the mirror.

'I never,' said Erica, 'I never knew anyone who talked so quickly and so breathlessly as you—not when you're talking about shows or films or dances or Fred Astaire, at any rate.'

'I must grow up,' said Marsha, very slowly, and pausing in her flight towards Dan at the door. 'I am very soon about to be a wife and a mother.'

And then this sudden dignity was shattered when she clapped her hand up to her mouth and giggled and said, 'Oh, I didn't mean—'

Erica said, 'Well, don't grow up too quickly; you're very charming as you are,' and Marsha darted back to plant a grateful kiss upon her sister-in-law's cheek.

It was such a pity, she thought, that she couldn't quite feel the same about her *other* sister-in-law. Then they could all have linked arms and sung 'Three little maids from school are we' in a very jolly and high-stepping and united trio. (Except that Erica was tone-deaf and Daisy couldn't stand her—and Erica, of course, couldn't stand Daisy either—which somehow diminished the possibilities of such a bright eventuality. It was a shame. Never having had sisters of her own, Marsha hadn't foreseen that sisters-in-law could be anything but sheer delight, a sort of extension of one's schooldays that would go on for ever; and she often felt it might be her own fault that she didn't get on better with Daisy.)

'When shall I come, then?' Daisy's voice rasped unmusically down the telephone in just the same way that it rasped unmusically when *not* down the telephone. Marsha was still a little surprised, even now, that distance didn't do anything to soften Daisy's personality. 'I don't suppose that you'll be wanting me for Sunday lunch?'

She added quickly: 'And don't say, "Mmm! Braised, I think!"—because even then I'm sure I'd be too tough! *Far* too tough!'

Marsha responded feebly. 'Oh—er—yes. Sunday? This one?'

'Or arrange it for one evening if that would suit you better—I don't care. Are you free on Saturday? Yes, *this* Saturday. I hate to make plans about six months in advance. You might have changed your minds about wanting to have me then!' The forceful laughter which followed this remark, to point out, of course, that it had merely been a joke, made Marsha withdraw her ear very quickly from the receiver. 'I'm assuming that you don't mind feeding me, you see.'

'Daisy, we shall be delighted and honoured and privileged to feed you!'

'My, my, that's a very pretty speech! I don't believe one word of it.'

'But I mean it.'

'Well, even so, you mustn't put yourself out, dear, not on my account; or your cook, either. Even pot luck will be a splendid treat—for me. At home, I just live on a sandwich. Now and then, that is, when I remember to think about it.'

'Oh, you poor thing! You've got to look after yourself, Daisy.'

'Oh, I can't be bothered. And I don't want you to bother either. I'm just not worth it. No. Pot luck will be extremely nice. Now—when am I to blight your lives for you? *Are* you free on Sunday?'

'Yes, but . . .' Marsha had been thinking. If Daisy was invited to Sunday lunch she would probably remain till bedtime; and now she used her ingenuity. 'Why don't we say, though, Saturday evening? An evening makes it more of an occasion. It's like going to the cinema in the afternoon and coming out when it's still daylight; you feel it's a bit of an anticlimax, don't you? I know that *I* do.'

'And I'm an occasion, am I?'

'Most definitely you are!' Marsha felt that somebody should be patting her on the back for the way that she was handling this. (Perhaps Miss Myers, who'd always been her very favourite teacher. Such a darling!) Ten out of ten for tact, old thing!

Daisy chuckled happily.

'Of course you're an occasion. It's such a long time since I've seen you; and Andrew is simply dying for this meeting —he's heard so much about you. Didn't I *say* that you were right at the top of our list?'

'I'll tell you what, then,' said Daisy. 'Hold on to your hat, dear! I'll come to dinner on Saturday night—*and* stay for lunch on Sunday. Now wouldn't that be a real holiday! And I'm sure, of course, you have the room.'

She sounded so pleased at being able to present this perfect compromise—so certain that she'd be giving quite as much pleasure as she'd be receiving—that Marsha couldn't even think of it as cheek. Daisy, she knew, would never dream that she was being an imposition.

Besides, it *would* be a little break for her. And faced with all of that, what on earth could Marsha say?

So she said it with as great an appearance of joy and willingness as she could manage. Miss Myers would really have been proud of her! (*Her personality is just as charming as her face!*) So would Old Knick-Knacks. Even the dreaded Mrs Troop would probably have given an approving nod. Marsha felt elated by her own performance; and momentarily determined to follow the ideal of Noble Behaviour throughout the remainder of her life.

(*It is quite impossible not to be enchanted by her!*)

Daisy thanked her, very suitably—there! further reproof for Marsha's want of insight and charity at the beginning —told her that she was one in a million; that she was not to go to all the trouble and expense of putting flowers in her bedroom, no matter how much she might love them; and asked whether she should bring her own hot-water bottle. Then she rang off; having assured her that she would be there on Saturday—unsinkable, sunny side up, pestering the living daylights out of the pair of them—at four o'clock, in time for tea.

12

Despite her black dress at his wedding, Andrew couldn't remember her. (He could remember very little of his own wedding. Nor could Marsha. She had once said, 'Oh, wouldn't it be lovely if we could go through it all a second time, feeling totally relaxed?' 'Heaven forbid,' he had answered. Wholly deadpan, as usual. 'What a card!' she informed all her friends, anxiously.) Even not remembering her, even not remembering much of what he'd heard of her (his attention was inclined to wander if the conversation wasn't to do with business or racing or politics) he was appalled by the news which Marsha tried to break to him extremely gently when he came home from work that evening. At first, yes, she did try for gentleness; yet he was so disgusted by the mere fact of her dining with them on Saturday that she thought it better to hurry the news of her breakfasting with them on Sunday; in addition, of course, to her lunching with them a little later in the day. Extremely gentle, then, it wasn't, but it was quick and clean—and even merciful: she mentioned neither the certainty of afternoon tea on Saturday nor the strong probability of afternoon tea on Sunday; not that, by this time, either of these points could have made a great deal of difference.

'You'll simply have to phone her back. Now. Tell her that you made a mistake.'

'Oh, Andy, I couldn't. What would I say?'

'Tell her you'd forgotten that we were going out. Or going away. Tell her you'd forgotten that we were moving.'

But the awful thing was: it didn't *sound* like a joke.

Nevertheless, she laughed. He must be recovering. This time he wasn't going to sulk.

'Well, I'll tell you one thing,' he said. 'If *she* comes—I go.'

'Temporarily or permanently?'

'No, I'm perfectly serious. We don't need to have her for the whole damned weekend.'

She didn't say anything.

'At least you must put her off for Sunday.'

'I can't. I won't. She seemed so pleased. Oh, I've just remembered, Andy. I've got you a present. I'll run and fetch it!'

It was a little peace-offering which she'd prepared in advance. Indeed, she'd rushed out to get it almost as soon as she'd replaced the receiver that morning. She had taken it into the kitchen to wash but had then forgotten all about it. She returned to the drawing-room now, carrying it upon a teaplate.

'A peach?' he asked, as though it were something that he'd never seen before.

'Not just a common-and-garden peach,' she said—proudly—knowing how very fond he was even of those. '*This* is an English peach. I went off to the West End for it, specially. *And* there's another in the pantry—but it looked more delicate, just bringing in the one. But both of them are for you,' she added hopefully, when he merely gazed at the extended plate and said nothing. 'I'm told they have the most incredible flavour.'

'My God, how much did that cost?'

'I got them cheap,' she lied. 'It was a bargain.' She still held out the teaplate. 'Taste it,' she said. 'Or will it spoil your dinner? No—because then I'll get your sherry and that should bring back your appetite. Oh—but would you like a fruit knife? How silly of me; I forgot.'

'How much was it?'

'I'm not going to tell you—and it's extremely rude to ask. Here; take just one bite. Use your fingers. Then maybe I'll take a bite, as well—that is, if you should feel like offering it—but you must certainly have the first.'

'No, no,' he said. 'I'm not going to eat both the peaches. What do you think I am? But at that price we're going to eat them properly—for desert—and at the table using a knife and fork. This way, in any case, without even a napkin, I'd be bound to drip juice down my suit.'

'Whatever you say,' she answered.

'Well, anyhow, thank you for them. I'm not saying it wasn't extravagant, of course, yet it was also very kind. But didn't you have anything else to do with your time?'

'No. *Pas une chose.* I'll go and pour our sherry.'

He smiled, a little tightly.

'But I am still not going to have that woman inflicted on us for the whole weekend!'

'That woman is Henry's wife. Widow. She's your sister-in-law. Please. I think we do owe it to her.'

Impulsively, she went down on her knees beside his chair and started to run her fingers along his thigh. 'Please, pretty please,' she repeated, wheedlingly. 'And if you're a very good boy I'll tell you what I'll do . . .'

'For heaven's sake! Not here! Mary might come in.'

'Not *that*, you silly! Or that as well, if you like! But I was going to say that I'd sing to you: "If you were the only boy in the world and I were the only girl": our song.'

'I don't want you to sing to me. And do get up!' he said. He glanced nervously towards the door.

She ran her fingers along his leg again.

'Before I do,' she said wickedly, that mischievous twinkle in her eye that all her chums at Hillingdon had grown to take delight in, 'before I do . . . may Daisy come and stay with us, Andy? May she? I've got such itchy fingers! What do you say, darling? Next weekend? Yes? Yes? May she?'

13

It was not the most auspicious of beginnings; especially when Andrew had said in bed that night (although he hadn't, thank goodness, been repeating that master-and-slave strategy of the night before, fun on occasions of course but tiresome if employed too often), 'Well, anyway . . . Just so long as she doesn't *talk*! If she's like *some* of your friends—the two of you together—talk, talk, talk—'

'I'll give her a notepad and pencil as soon as she steps inside the doorway,' Marsha had promised.

'*Does* she talk?'

'Well, don't forget that she's only recently suffered a bereavement.'

'But is she one of those silly, twittering females you see such a lot of?'

In the darkness Marsha pouted—as she guided his hand towards her breast. 'You always used to say that you *preferred* silly females.'

'Never.'

'Yes, you did. You said you were glad I wasn't brainy. You said you didn't care for brainy types.'

'Oh, that. That isn't the same thing at all. I only meant I was glad I wasn't marrying a bluestocking.'

'Because, you mean, you wouldn't be able to impress her with all your cleverness the way I'm impressed?'

'Are you impressed?'

'I'm not saying. I might be. Perhaps.'

'Then tell me what impresses you. Does *this* impress you?' She giggled.

But Daisy did talk. Bereavement or no bereavement, Daisy talked . . . and talked. Yet she wasn't silly. And she wasn't a bluestocking. Marsha began to hope that, despite a half-past-three arrival, total disaster might somehow be avoided. The splendid thing about Daisy was that she could always give just as good as she got, and after a time Marsha sat back admiringly and with a great deal of relief. She even thought she might be learning something.

'I'm so sorry,' Andrew had said, after they had shaken hands. 'We've actually finished our lunch. But if you'd only let us know we could have held some back.'

'Why, what did you have?'

'Cold meat and boiled potatoes and peas; followed by apple tart and custard.'

'Well, that's all right, then. They're not my favourites. It wouldn't have been worth it.' She chuckled, and sat down in the chair which he'd just vacated. 'Besides, I shall eat a larger tea in order to make up.'

And she looked at him to see what he would have to say in answer to *that*. For the moment all he could think of, however, was to mutter something about its no doubt being very nice but he had brought home a lot of work from the office and therefore if she would be so very good as to excuse him for a while . . .

'No, no, I shall not be so very good—not at all,' said Daisy. 'Sit down. I've hardly spoken to you yet. I've had no chance to test your mettle. Do you know—I heard a funny story about you? I heard that you were shy! Somebody actually told me you were shy!'

'Who told you that?'

'And do you know another thing? I suppose the two of us are in a way related—no matter how much we may deplore the fact to our families or try to conceal it altogether from the world outside. So that's a second reason why you shouldn't leave the room the minute that I enter it; and therefore—if you do—I shall assume it's simply because you haven't got the guts to stay. Who cares about politeness?—it's guts that interest me.'

He sat down, then, with a show of some reluctance; and further asserted his independence by refusing to be drawn too quickly into conversation.

'I must say, you're looking very well,' observed Marsha, for the second time.

'Oh, my looks have never pitied me!' declared Daisy. 'And why should they indeed? It's usually other people who have pitied me my looks!'

Marsha laughed.

'That was my little joke, you know,' said Daisy, confidentially, to Andrew. 'It isn't that I actually mind your not laughing. It's just that I don't want you to go round saying to your friends—"That poor woman! Everyone commiserates with her upon her face; and I can truly understand why!" I take it that you've got some friends?'

'A few.'

'My word, I bet you gabble when you get together!' She turned back to Marsha. 'Talking about my face, though—if you can bear it—will you tell me something quite honestly? Do you think I might look better if I wore make-up?'

'Have you never worn make-up, Daisy?'

'No. Never. I used to think that it was the muckiest stuff imaginable. Still do—in a way. But recently I've been wondering. I'm in danger of being converted!'

'Well, why don't you experiment a little? Wouldn't that be the thing to do?'

'Oh—I don't know—can I really be bothered? Though I daresay you're right, of course.'

'If you like—after tea—I'll take you upstairs to my dressing-table, and we could try out one or two effects.'

'Now, that seems like a bit of genuine inspiration! With a cup of tea to fortify us both! Though we might soon be wishing it had been something a little stronger! I hope not.'

'Oh, I think it sounds like fun!' said Marsha—meaning it. She enjoyed messing about with cosmetics (she always felt she might have been a beautician or a hairdresser) and this was the sort of jolly occupation she had often imagined sisters going in for—though she had never yet done it with Erica. She stood up. 'I'll just go and see if Mary needs a hand with the tea, then, shall I?'

'Yes, hurry it up a bit,' advised Daisy enthusiastically. 'What another very good idea! Marriage obviously agrees with you. Can't say I see why, though,' she said to Andrew, conversationally, as soon as Marsha had left the room.

'Would I be right in assuming that that's another joke?' he enquired, rather coldly.

'Well, if the cap fits wear it—that's what I always say! Does marriage agree with *you*?'

'Are you usually this outspoken, Daisy?'

'I don't like to deal merely in small talk, if that's what you mean. I don't find it interesting and it teaches you nothing. I always like to *know* about people, you see. I'm not sure whether or not I've replied to your question.'

'Snap,' he answered drily.

'Tell me something, though—outspoken or not.' Daisy leaned forward conspiratorially. 'How do you get on with your mother-in-law?'

'I don't,' said Andrew succinctly; but then at once added, with automatic caution, 'Of course, I can't really say whose fault that is.'

Daisy had never much believed in caution, and in her case, certainly, it was *never* automatic. 'Isn't she an utter pain?' she enquired, with a chuckle. 'Isn't she vile? I don't get on with her either,' she added, informatively, 'and I can say perfectly well whose fault that is. Indeed, I often have. I hope I may continue long to do so. My word, I believe that you're actually smiling. Or is it some trick of the light?'

'Do you know, Daisy, I've never heard anybody else say one unpleasant word about Florence?'

'She dabbles in hypnosis.'

'And I've got to admit it's almost a relief.'

'Yes, of course you have.'

'Why? Do you dabble in hypnosis, too?'

'You've got a nice smile. You should use it far more often. Oh, now, don't clam up on me again! Just when I've discovered how almost handsome you can be!'

Marsha came back into the room. She was followed shortly by the tea.

'Has he been entertaining you, Daisy?'

'Brilliantly. We've been getting on like a house on fire. Haven't we?'

'If you say so.'

Marsha was impressed. 'I should tell you, Daisy, that that sounds like fulsome praise, coming from Andy. He would be perfectly capable, you know, of saying "No! Not at all!" to a question of that sort. What people fail to realize about this husband of mine'—Marsha went behind his chair as she was speaking and put her arms around his neck—'is that at heart he's very droll.' She bent and laid her own cheek against his. 'He's a card, an absolute card.'

Daisy saw Andrew's expression while Marsha was doing this. She didn't quite understand it, because she thought that any man would delight in having a very pretty woman, even if not a very bright one, show adoration of this kind (as any woman, presumably, would delight in having a very handsome man do the same thing), but she imagined that he might be one of those unusual creatures who looked below the surface—remembered that beauty was only skin-deep and that real treasure was often buried far beneath the ground; and so she nodded at him, sympathetically.

Marsha, seeing this nod, interpreted it as the smiling indulgence which she knew all the world felt towards young lovers but which she was faintly surprised to find that Daisy felt, too!

It made her feel almost ashamed again, as she had felt four days earlier, on the telephone.

Daisy was incredibly brave. And kind. And misjudged. She felt uneasily conscious of the way that she herself had been inclined to misjudge her.

She suddenly wanted to share things.

'Shall we tell her, Andy?'

'Tell her what?'

'Tell her what, indeed. Only that this rather clever young man and I . . . would you believe it, Daisy? . . . we're already expecting a baby. What do you think of that?'

14

Another thing about Daisy's visit that staved off disaster was the discovery, during tea, that she played chess.

'*What?* I was brought up on it! Check and checkmate were probably my first and second words!'

Andrew's enquiry had been uttered with a bleak formality; he *still* wasn't expecting a lot of mitigation.

Her answer, therefore, drew a strong reaction.

'Then you must, I think, be the most civilized person to have come into this house in all the months we've had it.'

'Oh, spoken like a true gentleman! *And* a very wise one!'

'I tried to teach Marsha once. It was hopeless.'

'I just couldn't get the hang of it at all!' agreed Marsha, with happy modesty.

'Yes, I know, dear,' said Daisy. 'It was exactly the same with my own parents. My father was an inveterate chess player; my mother couldn't even learn the simplest moves.'

But something about her manner kept them from replying.

'Or *wouldn't*, more like it,' she continued, after a pause, 'because, of course, it was all done out of spite. She didn't want to give him the satisfaction of being superior to her in even the smallest way.'

She glared at them.

'And yet couldn't she see? He was superior to her in almost every way that he could have been: in intellect, in breeding, in just plain goodness of heart. Oh, she was so *petty*! She said he bored her; that little things pleased little minds; that he didn't have any get-up-and-go.'

She shrugged.

'Well, it was certainly true, that last bit; he didn't; otherwise he simply would have; got up and gone, I mean—just wouldn't have stood for the way she ran that household, with her cheap denigrations and her joyless assumptions. But it was her own fault: what had she ever done to try and nurture the manhood that he had in him? She'd smothered it, that's what she'd done—just smothered it—all the while knowing perfectly well what she did, of course.'

Daisy laughed—a sad and very bitter sound.

'Believe it or not, she was even resentful of the way he liked his work; of the escape it gave him from *her*, and of the concern he used to lavish on his pupils, while she herself was left high and dry to slave away the best years of her life, she said, at home. I heard her claim once that there was something unnatural about the way he felt towards those little boys. I believe he hated the holidays. He lived for the children whom he taught and tried to push on as he himself had never been pushed on; and for his books and for his games of chess. And perhaps—I don't know—in his quiet and totally undemonstrative way—even for yours truly. Poor fellow. But I could never give him much.'

When she'd finished speaking, there was a long, slightly stunned sort of silence, like there sometimes was, thought Marsha, at the conclusion of a very dramatic picture that had ended suddenly. Marsha had never known her to reveal so much. She wanted to set down her teacup and reach out with fellow feeling and touch Daisy's hand, yet she knew that such a move would be disruptive—and, anyway, would probably annoy Andy. (Daisy, too, quite possibly.) But she was still the first of them to speak.

'You must have given him a lot. You said that you played chess with him.'

'Oh, for what it was worth. Yes. I was certainly the only one who ever did—at home. My brother never did. He was too much the apple of his mother's eye, and trod too carefully in her footsteps. But that's why my mother always hated me. She was jealous of the enjoyment that we had together over the chessboard. Oh, my word, the numbers of games that got interrupted and "accidentally" upset! (You could never leave a game unfinished hoping to come back to it!) The number of pieces that constantly got lost and had to be replaced or improvised!'

'But you said your father tried to teach her!' Marsha was so indignant that, unwittingly, she spilled her tea. Her hand shook and the teacup rattled.

Daisy dunked her *langue-de-chat* as though she were holding her mother by the ankles and ducking more than just a biscuit. 'Well, if you cut off your nose to spite your face, I imagine you wouldn't be so very pleased to find that your face could get on perfectly well without it.'

'Poor Daisy. No wonder you disliked her so.'

'Disliked her? Disliked her?' Her mother's head fell off. 'I wouldn't have demeaned myself so much as to do that. I detested her! Still do, of course. Now more than ever.'

'Even though she's dead?'

'What difference does that make?'

Marsha did her best not to sound shocked. Nor even to feel it.

'Well, at least you still had your father, Daisy. At least you still had someone you could love.'

Daisy considered this.

'Yes, I suppose that I did love him. In a way. I certainly felt sorry for him. I wanted to make up for things.' Her expression signified the hopelessness of such a wish; the stupidity of anybody who could entertain it.

'Of *course* you loved him,' said Marsha, ardently.

'I despised him, too. He irritated me. For being such a miserably poor fish. He was happiest, you know, after she had died. I went back to live with him then, to look after him, but I felt angry that he hadn't got away from her years earlier. Eighty-three is hardly the proper age to be making a new start!'

But she added, after a bit: 'Though better than nothing, I suppose! Yes—why not? What does the *age* of a person ever matter—to anyone, that is, whose first name isn't Florence?'

'Oh, yes—exactly!' agreed Marsha, overlooking the last part of this sentence and still swept along by her romantic

67

ardour. 'How old was your mother when she died?'

Daisy gave her a look.

'She was seventy-one.'

'And how many years did your father have . . . ?' Marsha couldn't quite bring herself to say 'of peace?' Yet this had nothing to do with the fact that Daisy had been looking after him.

'Not even two. But count your blessings. I can only say: thank God my mother was the first to go. I'd never have gone back to take care of *her*; no, not in a million years! Nor would that good-for-nothing brother of mine—her precious blue-eyed boy—himself now hag-ridden and buried somewhere in the wilds of Ireland with a teeming brood of daughters, nothing but daughters. Well, it serves him right! Good riddance!' She laughed, sharply.

Marsha said nothing.

'Yes, he's turned out to be a poor fish, too. Well, that's what comes of kowtowing to a domineering woman. He should have done what I did; they should *both* have done what I did: stood up to her, every blood-stained inch of the way. And, my word, did we have a few pitched battles! I learnt at an early age, you know, how to protect myself on the battlefield!' But this time, when she laughed, there appeared to be something rather different about it: a quality, almost, of affection. 'And it's true what they say, of course: attack *is* the best policy of defence. Every time.'

Eventually she seemed to recollect herself.

'Good heavens! Have I been up on my soapbox again? Better pull me off it, someone—if anybody thinks that he's man enough to do it! Cram another cake in my mouth and hope I'll sit here silent, like a stuffed pig!'

'Nobody wants to shut you up, Daisy.'

'Then they must be crackers—all of them—that's the only explanation! But . . . Well, I don't know'—she accepted her third cup of tea—'sometimes I look about me and I think an awful lot of men are just poor fish and an awful lot of women not very much better than . . . oh, what's the one I mean?' She broke off abruptly, impatient with herself. 'The one that bites off her mate's head as soon as he's finished performing his vital function?'

68

'A praying mantis,' said Andrew. It was the first thing that he'd said for a long while, but Marsha knew that he'd been listening and hadn't just lapsed into one of his moody silences—didn't his naming of this horrid creature prove it? She would have been hard put to it, however, to say quite how she knew. His face didn't normally give very much away.

'Yes. Nailed in one, dear! But I thought you'd know, of course. Well, in my view it's a pretty depressing situation. Wouldn't you agree?'

Marsha giggled. 'Well, it really does seem a bit of a cheeky thing to do. And certainly ungrateful.'

'What does?' asked Andrew.

'Well, you know—after they've just—after he's just— Oh, do you think that I'm a praying . . . do you think that I might be one of those things, Daisy? If so, you'd better watch out, Andy. I believe I've found a way to keep you up to scratch!' (Oh, if only, she thought, if only she could have felt as relaxed as this when some of her schoolfriends had been to visit her and Andy! Good old Daisy! She was better than a tonic—or a glass or two of gin! But at the same time she couldn't help feeling an awful pang of regret; and she did so hope that they'd agree to come and see her again, those friends, if she should ever be able to work up the nerve to ask them.)

'Well, I'll tell you one thing,' offered Daisy.

'Yes? What?'

'That good-looking husband of yours—dour, crabby, earnest individual though he well may be—(you know, he could do with a spot more liveliness, we'll have to see what we can think of!)—anyway, looking at *him*, at least I can make one prophecy with some assurance. *He*'ll never be a poor fish. He may be the bane of your existence; but he'll never be a poor fish!'

Marsha laughed. 'Oh, precious bane!' she said happily.

'Did you ever read that?'

'No. And I never read *The Card*, either.' Then she looked down at her lap with carefully suppressed pride. 'But I heard of both of them.'

69

When she raised her eyes again, she was surprised to see that Andrew was smiling; very nearly, grinning. Had she said something naïve? But she didn't mind it if she had—oh, not at all. She would have to call him precious bane again. Perhaps it could get to be a nickname; and in time might even encourage him to find a nickname for her as well. (Not merely 'Marsh' or 'Ma', that she'd grown up with; though even those, she thought, would have been better than nothing.) Actually she had several times suggested one or two things —oh, *very* casually—trying not to let him see what she was up to. But it wasn't easy.

She would have to borrow Andrew's dictionary afterwards —stealthily, without his knowing—and find out just what 'bane' meant.

She smiled back at him; although, sadly, she didn't think he saw.

'I'll tell you what, Daisy. I'll have a game of chess with you, if you like.' His tone grew even more expansive. 'The best of three! And then we'll see which one of us is really the poor fish—and which the praying mantis!'

15

But first there was the business with the make-up—Marsha insisted on that. Daisy indulgently complied ('She wants to use me as a guinea-pig; is determined that I shan't escape!') but Andrew shrugged with some annoyance at the frivolity of it all.

'For heaven's sake, what's wrong with her as she is? At least she doesn't spend half her life in front of a mirror, endlessly prinking and preening!'

Daisy considered this, with her head a little to one side. 'Will somebody tell me, please, if I've just received a compliment? It doesn't happen often and I'd really like to know.'

'No,' said Andrew. 'I don't picture you as the type of person whose life can only be sustained by compliments.'

'Like some that we could mention!' said Marsha, almost

before she'd realized that she had any intention of saying any such thing.

'Meaning?'

And now that she had started, it seemed monstrously easy to go on.

'Meaning that people in glass houses certainly shouldn't throw stones; because *I*'ve seen people prinking and preening themselves in front of a mirror, too; though naturally I shouldn't dream of naming any names.'

He was about to protest.

'Or doesn't posing in front of the wardrobe door just before you have your bath—or just after you've had it—or both —doesn't that happen to count for some reason? I'm very sorry if I thought it did.'

'For heaven's sake, Marsha!' He looked at her as though he couldn't at all understand what had given rise to this; for that matter, she wasn't sure that she could understand it, either. 'Have you gone clean out of your mind? Have you forgotten that we have a visitor?'

'Oh, don't mind me,' said Daisy—who, for once in her life, really wished that people wouldn't. 'I'm still trying to work out whether, on aggregate, I come out of this with a fiercely swollen head or just my usual hangdog expression. Anyway, Marsha, I do admire a man who wants to keep himself in trim. Don't you?'

But this seemed to please neither of them.

'Anyway, I thought,' said Marsha, a little more placating-ly, 'that you had some work which you wanted to get on with.'

'I suppose, now, that it's not enough that I slog at the office all through the week? I'm not even allowed to put my feet up for a short while on a Saturday afternoon?'

'Why don't you just drink another cup of tea and then set out the chessmen?' said Daisy, who had suddenly remembered that blessed are the peacemakers—and conveniently forgotten that she herself had drunk the last drop of tea. 'I don't imagine we'll be long.' She smiled, beatifically.

'Well, just make sure that you're not,' he said.

She decided (though it was something that she'd known

from the beginning, anyway) that she *was* being complimented; only rather more subtly than merely through the lips; because he was obviously impatient—yes, actually impatient—to play chess with her. So she made up her mind at that moment that she would protract their excursion upstairs for as long as she decently could. She turned to Marsha with a merry injunction and a pointing finger.

'Lead on, Macduff!'

Marsha—not quite so merrily—led on.

'Like a lamb to the slaughter!' said Daisy, turning her eyes back momentarily to Andrew. If she was supposed to be referring to herself the simile lacked conviction. 'When you see me next, I hope I shall look a bit like Greta Garbo. Do you think I might look a bit like Greta Garbo?' She slung out her arms and slunk with a supposedly long-legged stride and moody sinuous grace out through the open door.

Upstairs Marsha led her into the bedroom that she shared with Andrew. Daisy glanced around her with much interest. It wasn't often that you had a look at people's bedrooms. The room was only ordinary, but *that* was the wardrobe door, presumably, before which he posed naked—threw out his chest, no doubt, and flexed his muscles. Daisy found the thought unsavoury but exciting. Henry had never stood in front of a mirror and flexed his muscles—at least, never to her knowledge—during the brief course of their marriage. Moreover, he wouldn't have cut a very dashing figure if he had: like his brother Dan—just a bag of skin and bone, and of very *white* skin at that. Besides, she had neither encouraged nudity in him nor indulged in it herself, before him. She even thought, despite her long years as a nurse and physiotherapist, that there was something faintly disgusting in it. More than *faintly* disgusting, too. And yet, all the same . . .

And *that* was the bed in which, if he failed to come up to scratch, Marsha had threatened to bite off his head, when he'd performed his vital function.

Well, he'd already done that, hadn't he? Marsha—who was not yet even twenty—was already pregnant. Daisy quickly turned her face away from the bed and experienced an extension of that feeling of disdain, almost of revulsion. In some ways it *would* be a very much cleaner world if Nature had provided women with the jaws and the digestive system which she had given to a praying mantis.

Though *cleaner*, perhaps, wasn't entirely the right word. No! Definitely it wasn't! Daisy considered all that dripping gore and all the problems of disposal. It would be simpler, she thought, more cheerily, if they were to eat their way straight down to the toenails. Far more practical, in every way. And it would save on the meat bills.

'I've just decided that I may become a cannibal!'

She sat down on the stool that Marsha indicated.

'I'm not sure that I feel like this any longer,' said Marsha.

'Well, that's all right,' Daisy reassured her. 'We can merely sit and talk. And perhaps that's the reason it prays, of course: "Oh, take away these hiccups!" '

'What?'

Daisy descended to Marsha's level. 'What on earth are all these jars for? And how in the name of sweet St Antony do you ever manage to keep track? Naturally, I mean of Padua —not of Egypt.'

She enjoyed her own conceit: presumably the father of monasticism would not have been much interested in ladies' aids to beauty; the restorer of lost property, on the other hand, might have been more concerned for the passing of soft skin; the vanishing bloom of youth; lost roses in the cheek.

'My mother always talked about the saints. I can't think where she supposed that her path and theirs would ever cross!'

Marsha began to explain the purpose of each pot and tube. At first she sounded apathetic, yet as she handled each item her enthusiasm grew. 'Now let me just look at you,' she said to Daisy. 'Let me take a good long stare.'

Daisy was relieved the evenings had drawn in; and that such an examination was being conducted in the softest lamplight. But to take Marsha's mind just a little off what she was examining, she remarked: 'Ah, that's better, dear. I'd have said just now that you were lackadaisical—but of all the things you may be lacking, it certainly isn't one of *those!*'

She chuckled richly; and Marsha smiled politely—having no idea at all what Daisy was talking about.

'Why do you always run yourself down so?' she asked.

'I thought I only ran down other people.'

'Well, you're always speaking about yourself as if you were ugly—'

'When in fact I'm a raving beauty? No. I usually say I've got a *funny* face.'

'You've got a very good bone structure, though—that's what you *have* got. And it expresses character, too; a lot of it.'

'But not beauty?'

Daisy's tongue was very much in cheek, yet Marsha didn't realize.

'Yes, it *does*! In a way.' She suddenly looked not one day older than her nineteen years—and incredibly eager. Daisy was a little touched. They stared at each other for a moment in the mirror, pensive and unsmiling. They could never have stared directly at one another like that.

'But it is true: you don't really make the most of yourself.'

'Who does?'

'Have I really got a free hand?' And yet she still hesitated—picking up first one thing and then another. 'I feel a little nervous.'

'How do you suppose that I feel?'

They were talking as though Marsha had a tattooist's machine. (*Escape into a whole new world of colour! Your life will never be the same again!*)

'Your hair should be a little longer. You've got nice hair, you know. But it would look much softer if you'd let it grow.'

'Like yours, you mean?'

'Yes—possibly. I think this style suits any age.' Unaware she'd made a gaffe, Marsha started happily upon her work. As she smoothed in the foundation cream she lost all hesitancy and worked with instinctive, gifted fingers. But some echo of that last remark lingered in her own mind as surely as it did in Daisy's. She thought: Daisy's mother died five years ago and I know now that she was seventy-one when she did so. Assume that she was forty, then, at the time of Daisy's birth. (Surely a charitable assumption?)

Thirty-six? Was Daisy thirty-six? She had quite nice skin, of course, and if she had never bothered with it very much . . .

Give her the benefit of the doubt, though. Say thirty-five. It was a tidy figure, too; and Marsha hankered after tidiness. (In that, at least, she and Andrew were particularly well suited.)

Thirty-five.

She smiled.

'What suddenly made you think about make-up, Daisy? I mean—since the idea of it obviously wasn't with you from the time of childhood, like it was with me?'

Marsha recalled her own mother having recommended it, a week or two before Daisy's wedding. Her mother had got remarkably short shrift, however: just another in the long list of little conflicts between the pair of them; not exactly pitched battles, though, thank goodness. Henry himself, of course, hadn't seemed to care a great deal one way or the other—would merely have agreed, good-naturedly, with whichever argument he had happened to hear last. (Marsha had loved him and in some ways had been very much like him—she didn't realize this—but she would never have wanted to marry him! She had often wondered why Daisy had; and just as often why Henry had wanted to marry *her*. She had never felt the same perplexity over Erica and Dan.) But it had just occurred to her that Daisy might have met somebody else, who *had* shown a preference for make-up. She felt curious—and full of happy expectation. Not for nothing had her schoolfriends called her a matchmaker. She liked a romance almost as much in real life as she did upon the silver screen.

But she was about to be disappointed; even though Daisy, under the soothing influence of gentle fingers, was prepared to overlook—this once—the *faux pas* that Marsha didn't even know she had committed.

'Oh, the receptionist that I get in the Harrow Road—when I go to practise there on Mondays and Thursdays, you know—she said something much the same as you. It made me think a little. She was nervous about saying it; didn't like

75

to be personal; but somehow felt impelled—even directed—to mention it to me. At least, that's the way she put it, and one couldn't take offence.'

'Oh.'

'A pleasant sort of woman. A good sort of woman. Religious too—and without that awful cant that generally goes with it. Not a bit mealy-mouthed, you know. Her name is Marie. Has a flat in the Fortune Green Road,' she added, as if that somehow might explain it.

'Not too far from here, then,' said Marsha; recovering quickly from her silly disappointment.

'Yes, I know, dear. And what a perfectly shameful waste it is, too! She's sixty-five or so (I tell you that before you ask) and unmarried and where on earth is the sense of it?—that's what I want to know.'

Marsha felt bewildered.

'This world is teeming,' said Daisy, 'with rotten wives and rotten mothers. And then you meet someone like that who would have been a marvellous wife and marvellous mother—you only have to look at her to be convinced of it—and yet no fool has ever asked her. Where's the sense of it?'

'But surely, Daisy, there's more to life than just being married,' said Marsha—who didn't believe that there was for a moment. Bewilderment had now given way to a feeling of surprise. She didn't think that she had ever heard Daisy speak so gently of another woman.

'Well, it's very easy for someone who *is* married,' answered Daisy, 'to trot out a platitude such as that; but there's no denying the fact that children are important to most women, even if a husband isn't—even if they'd give their eye-teeth, sometimes, to be shot of him!' Daisy gave a brief compensatory chuckle.

She started thinking about Henry.

'Anyway, Daisy, don't talk now. It's time for the lipstick.'

16

She remembered when she'd first seen him. He'd had a rather pale and interesting air, an almost ethereal quality, but what had drawn her to him as much as his appearance was the fact that he'd been sitting alone, reading. Daisy very much approved of that. There were not many people you came on at the club who sat lost in a good book, oblivious to the world. She made a beeline for him.

'Well done!' she said. 'The perfect way to spend a wet Saturday afternoon!'

'What?' He looked up with a start, thin-nosed and sandy-haired; his voice a little piping.

'What's more, you add a touch of class. Tone. An air of intellectuality. And this place could certainly do with that!' She laughed. 'My word, yes! The things that can't be told!'

He struggled to get up. For some reason his umbrella stood between his knees. His mackintosh was folded on the small table that pinned him against the wall.

'I wish I'd brought my own book now; you're quite an inspiration! But everybody here just *talks*. Jabber, jabber, jabber! It never *occurs* to them they may be interrupting! No, don't get up.' (He had just managed to do so.) 'I'll sit down. There! Descended to your level.' She noticed that he didn't smile, as he descended back to it himself, but young men with ethereal qualities could hardly be expected to have an earthbound sense of humour. 'Rupert Brooke, I presume?' It would clearly be her duty, though, to try and introduce one.

'Oh, no.' He looked at his book and held it up to her, so that she could see its name. '*If Winter Comes.*'

'Which it has with a vengeance!—you'd better strike out that first syllable! Ah, no, but there's a word to conjure with; to weave into your daydreams. Your every hope is fashioned out of that. It's the only word, I sometimes think, which really keeps me going. On second thoughts you'd better leave it severely alone, dear!'

He looked at her in a friendly but rather puzzled way.

'Don't worry. I haven't gone quite addlepated. Contrary to popular opinion! But I really meant *you*—not what you were reading. You reminded me of Rupert Brooke.'

At that, he did smile. 'Well, I only wish I were Rupert Brooke.'

'But why? Then we wouldn't be holding this intelligent conversation. Of course, you might not set that down as one of the major disadvantages,' she added, with a chuckle.

'It's funny you should say that.'

'What?' She was nearly as startled as he himself had sounded earlier.

'About my looking like a poet. It's my biggest ambition, you see, to be able to write poetry.' His tone was shy and proud and defiant, all at once.

'Well done!' said Daisy. 'I quite take my hat off to you. But I could tell, you know, the very moment I set eyes on you. I could see that you were different. *Rupert Brooke*. It was emblazoned on your forehead!'

'Could you really tell?' Modesty and gratification warred. 'Perhaps you've got a sixth sense!'

'I'll tell you what I have got, though. A raging thirst! It's all this looking at my crystal ball that does it!' She glanced towards the counter at the far end of the room and made the motions of being about to stand up.

'Oh, I'm sorry,' he said. 'How rude of me! What would you like?' They were immensely pleased with one another. 'Coffee?'

'I can't let a stranger buy me coffee!' she protested. 'We don't even know each other's names!' But fortunately they stumbled on the remedy for that. 'Later, of course, they're licensed to serve alcohol,' she said.

When he returned to the table she had hung up his hat and raincoat and put his brolly in a stand. 'We do have *some* facilities, you know. They were all quite damp; you'll give yourself rheumatism. Poets especially should look after themselves,' she told him sternly. 'Are your trousers dry? I'm sure that thing was dripping in your turnups.' She didn't suggest what should be done, however, if such a fear was justified. 'Oh, thank you, dear, for this. That's very sweet of you. You really shouldn't have bothered. And such filthy muck, as well! But never mind; it hits the spot; you're obviously an angel, as well as a poet! Why have I never seen you here before?'

'Well, I suppose the reason might be,' he said quietly, 'that this is the first time I've been.'

She was delighted by his answer.

'So that's why you were reading your book with such absorption! It's just that you were shy! I thought as much right from the start. How lucky that I came along!'

She waited for him to agree. He smiled, and nodded.

'You need someone who knows the ropes.'

'Yes.'

'When this place fills up I'll introduce you to everybody worth being introduced to.'

'Thank you, but . . .'

'We'll lay down the red carpet.'

'I'm not sure that . . .'

'We'll say you're Mr Henry Stormont the famous poet. Don't worry. Nobody will know the difference. Not here. If anyone asks what you've written, just say, "The boy stood on the burning deck", or "She walks in beauty like the night . . ." What's the matter, dear? You're not still shy, are you? Not now that you've got Daisy Todd-Ferrier beside you?'

'Perhaps just a little.'

'And very understandable, too! My goodness, don't think that I don't know what it's like to be shy. I do! I do! Always. Every day of my life. The abyss; the great yawning gulf. I'm terrified. But the trick is—not to show it. You have to play the giddy goat. You have to say: I don't care; I couldn't give a damn. You have to cling tight to your guardian angel, and never doubt that he is there. Who introduced you to the club?'

'I know Mr John slightly. Augustus John. He's one of the members here.'

79

'Oh, you don't have to tell *me* that,' said Daisy, sounding more impatient than impressed—though in fact the opposite was true. 'You know, of course, he means to paint my portrait?' There was a faint implication that this was his motive for having become a member in the first place. 'Is he coming here tonight?' There was a further suggestion that, if so, she might just spare him an odd half-hour for the initial sitting.

'Well, actually I thought he'd be here before this.'

'Excellent,' said Daisy. 'Then the two of us shall await his coming together. No need to hide behind a book. We'll put the world to rights—we'll eat, drink and be merry, shall we? I can recommend the turkey sandwiches.'

She gave her merry and infectious chuckle. 'I can recommend them—but I can't afford them!'

She said, more seriously, 'Well, I ask you, dear: these days, who can?'

Then, as they ate, she told him a lot about herself; and wanted to hear a lot about him, too.

'Now, how many volumes have you published?'

He laughed; yes, it appeared it hadn't been just a flash in the pan—he really did have a sense of humour. Well, if *she* couldn't bring it out in a man, she felt sure that there was nobody who could. (She really pitied anyone who couldn't laugh at the absurdity of it all. You had to. All the time. It was the only thing that kept you sane. No; it was the only thing that kept you *alive*.) She was glad he was enjoying himself.

'You'd better ask me that in another twenty years!'

'1953. I'll note it in my diary.'

'So far I've written just a handful of poems. They're not very good.'

'Who says so? Just tell them they'll have Daisy Todd-Ferrier to reckon with!'

'My family says so.'

'Oh, your *family*! Yes, well . . . I'd be disappointed if they didn't.'

'But you don't even know my family.'

'Yes, I do! Your family is just the same as mine—and everybody else's! Does a prophet *ever* find honour in his own country? No, of course he doesn't! What does your mother say?'

'She says it makes a very charming hobby.'

'You see? Quite typical! They're all the same. And that charming little hobby, of course, must never be allowed to interfere with something important—something really important—like a career at Selfridge's. Oh, goodness, no!'

He was amazed at the indignation which she clearly felt on his behalf; he found it touching but also a little frightening. No, not frightening. Awe-inspiring.

'But . . . Why on earth did she want to put you into Selfridge's? *Selfridge's!*' She said it as she might have said the French Foreign Legion, or the Women's Prison Service. 'No, don't tell me! Security! That grinning tinpot god, Security! Subjection! I wonder that you didn't just stand up and say: Phooey!'

'Phooey?'

'Well, that's what I'd have done!'

'Phooey? To my mother? Besides,' he went on, 'it was my father's decision just as much as hers. And my own, too, of course,' he added quickly.

'You give me the impression that no one ever says phooey to your mother.'

He looked amused. 'Well, actually, I don't know that they ever do . . . since you ask. Perhaps it's just not necessary.' He coughed (rather violently). 'Perhaps she's simply not the type.'

A few weeks later Daisy was able to judge for herself just what type she really was; although she had known it all along, anyway. She was invited to tea at Cavendish Mansions. Henry's parents were there and his brother and sister, and his brother's wife. Daisy felt like a missionary being inspected by the cannibals—except that most of the cannibals would have been too amiable, or soft, or squeamish, actually to take the first bite, and would probably have turned their eyes away while the dish remained recognizable. She didn't count Henry's sister, Marsha, who was a sweet, pretty, spineless nincompoop, but the other two women put her very much in mind of Kipling—who was a man who knew about these sorts of thing if anybody did: 'For the female of the species is more deadly than the male!' (How she would love to meet Kipling and shake him by the hand and say, 'Well done!' Perhaps, she sometimes thought, she ought to write him a letter!) Mrs Stormont in particular was a she-bear, whose husband was one of her cubs as surely as were any of her children. Well, there was nothing unexpected about that! Daisy was only surprised that she hadn't bitten his head off, years ago, in a fashion other than purely metaphorical! But no, it was a wholly representative portrait of a family. And that was why she was here: to help young Henry to escape. (Even on its own, the fact that he wanted to, showed that he was worthy of better things.) 'Daisy,' he'd said, 'sometimes I really feel the need to get away; to cut the apron strings. I think you're stronger than I am. You've got to help me do it.' Daisy, who liked nothing better than a cause and an underdog (as long as the underdog knew he was an underdog and didn't mean to go on lying down), had assured him, warmly, that he'd found himself the proper champion; and had chucklingly brushed aside his protestations of gratitude and admiration and affection. 'Oh, just listen to you! The fledgling poet! The first hot breath of freedom—and what do you become? Lord Byron himself! Or Don Juan! Some silly ass like that. Extravagant and bold. Why shouldn't you, indeed?'

Tea itself was civilized but difficult. To do her justice, Florence Stormont was the only one of the lot with anything at all to say for herself, and if it hadn't been for her, the rest of the family would just have sat around like cushions— cushions somewhat lumpier than those which were actually provided and which had a smell and a padded softness to them that were somehow typical of the furnishings in general, and were undoubtedly one aspect of what made the meeting civilized. The room was tasselled, tapestried, heavy, claustrophobic, but it *was* civilized.

And so was Mrs Stormont's bedroom.

'Miss Todd-Ferrier,' said her hostess, some time after the extremely proper maid had cleared away the extremely proper tea things, 'how can we get to know each other well with the rest of this vexatious mob breathing down our necks like simpletons?' She blew them all kisses as she asked this. 'Shall we adjourn into my bedroom, you and I, to an atmosphere of peace, a rarefied air of tranquillity?'

Daisy felt her heartbeat quicken. They sat themselves in low, elegant chairs that faced one another; the chairs looked fragile but were strong. Daisy had her back to the single bed, luxuriously quilted, highly pillowed, that possibly explained in part why Mr Stormont still walked around with his head on.

'Henry tells me that there's been some talk of marriage?'

Mrs Stormont leaned forward with a gracious, slightly quizzical expression on her face, which suggested that they were girls together and could smile with understanding tolerance at the absurdity of rumour and the gutter press.

'Of course, you know that this can never be.'

'What can't, dear?' Working as a physiotherapist in the Harrow Road for two days a week, where obviously she treated the poorer section of the community—and for next to nothing, too!—(though the richer section, who came to Thayer Street, made up for it!), she had acquired the habit of calling people 'dear'. Sometimes, however, she caught herself still doing it under very different circumstances. Usually it expressed affection. Today, though, it wasn't unintentional. And today it didn't express affection.

But Mrs Stormont appeared to see no irony or insult. 'This marriage,' she said. 'I'm afraid there can't be any question of its ever taking place.' She sounded almost sorry she was forced to make this ruling. 'Of course, you mustn't see that as something personal against yourself.'

'Phooey!' said Daisy.

Even if she got in nothing else, she had been promising herself that. She was glad of the opportunity.

The effect, however, was not entirely what she'd expected. Mrs Stormont gave a dry smile. 'Phooey, yourself,' she returned, equably. 'Though I hope that some of our conversation may possibly rise to a higher level. You're a little older than Henry, aren't you?'

Now *that* she had expected.

'I don't know that I am. And even if I were—what has age got to do with it?'

'Not a great deal, I agree. Certainly five or six—or seven —years is by no means the end of the world.'

'Three,' said Daisy. 'Two-and-a-half.' The admission was forced out of her.

'Personally, I've always found it most sensible to stay at twenty-one.'

'Why? What does anybody know about life at twenty-one? A *hundred* and twenty-one—now, there, perhaps, I could see some point. At that age you might just be beginning to get interesting. It's a moot point though,' she added, looking at her.

'And one we shall some time have to debate quite fully,' said Florence; 'but—for the moment—your being older than Henry means, of course, that you're more experienced than he is. You strike me as a woman of the world. And that does make me wonder, a little, what it is precisely that you see in somebody . . . so comparatively immature . . .'

'Well, surely his own mother shouldn't have to ask a question such as that! I see a person who wants to make something out of his life—who doesn't want just to follow the common herd; a person who—'

'Who will never be rich, you understand,' said Florence, gently. 'Looking around you here, it's quite possible that you may have gathered the impression . . .'

But it had honestly not occurred to Daisy to think a great deal about that side of things. Henry would have to leave Selfridge's, of course, and concentrate upon his writing —that much was clear—so if she'd thought about it at all she had vaguely assumed that *she* would support *him*, until he grew successful or until such time, anyway, as she began upon a family—which, after all, was surely one of the main reasons for anybody's getting married: how lovely to produce another life, to have the care of it, the joy of it, the comfort, even the terror of it! And now she stared at her accuser with so much genuine indignation that Florence's hitherto speculative gaze was lowered.

'Well, never mind that,' the latter said, quite quickly. 'The last thing that either of us wants, I fully realize, is a quarrel on our hands.'

Daisy wasn't altogether so convinced.

'Just tell me what it is,' she asked, 'that you don't like about me.'

'Oh, my dear Miss Todd-Ferrier. What nonsense! What arrant nonsense!'

In any case Daisy felt she knew the answer: it was simply that she was another woman—or, rather, that she was another woman who had a mind and a will of her own. She was not an extra cushion.

'But I shall tell you,' added Florence, when she had finished with her gracefully uncomprehending arm and hand gestures, 'why it is that you can't get married.'

(And the splendidly funny thing, thought Daisy, was that up until about ten minutes ago she herself hadn't been quite certain that she even wanted to!)

'Yes, dear. Tell me why you *think* it is that we shan't be able to get married. One's always ready for a laugh.'

But now the possibility of laughter seemed remote—shared laughter, in any case. The smile on Henry's mother's face, always present to some degree until this very moment, was irrevocably gone.

'I trust that *this*, however, Miss Todd-Ferrier, won't strike you as too amusing. My son is a consumptive. He has tuberculosis. He is a dying man.'

Afterwards, Daisy hoped that her surprise—the cold wave of shock that moved swiftly through her—hadn't shown itself upon her face. And whereas until now she had not felt love for Henry Stormont—simply a wish to enfold him beneath her wing while he came crawling out of his shell with ever-growing strength and confidence—at this moment she experienced a surge of compassion so great that it was almost like love.

And it was heightened by something else.

Even uglier than the blow his mother's words had given her was the manner in which those words had been delivered. '*My* game, I think!' was the chief impression that Daisy received; her opponent clearly thought she had produced a winning card.

Well, that's what she *thought*! But she hadn't quite reckoned with Daisy Todd-Ferrier.

'Oh, I know *that*, Mrs Stormont. Did you really suppose for one moment that I didn't?'

Because you couldn't leave anyone—and especially not a boy as sensitive as he—to die in hands so patently unfeeling.

No, it couldn't have shown itself, her sense of shock; since, if it had, what would have accounted for the astonishment in the other woman's eyes?

'But Henry himself doesn't even know about it! At least —he thinks he's cured. He's spent months of his life in a Swiss sanatorium. Years, altogether.'

Daisy shrugged. 'Anyone with as much medical experience as I, could hardly fail to read the signs, at just a first or second glance.'

'I see.' The Mrs Stormont who now sat avoiding her gaze looked like an ill woman in comparison to the one who had so recently led her into the room, gracious and undoubting, her steel encased in velvet.

Except that her steel was not true steel; or, at any rate, not as the steel of some.

'Besides—who says he *can't* be cured? New ways of treatment are being tried out all the time. To speak of dying is defeatist—wrong! Have you thought, for instance, about taking him to Lourdes?'

'I have no doubt you mean well,' said Florence, with extreme weariness. 'But please don't be naïve.'

'Naïve!' exclaimed Daisy. 'Well, perhaps I am. And I thank the Lord for it, too, in that case—because I'd rather be naïve than arrogant. I think that one should fight. I think that one should tell the truth. To hide from your son the fact that he is dying—if he is—is patronizing, and unforgivable. How dare you underestimate him, or underestimate anybody? How dare you rob him of his chance to show his greatness, his opportunity to be a hero, his opportunity to be a saint? It isn't life that matters; it's the way in which one faces up to it! Well,

I shall tell him, Mrs Stormont, the very moment that we're married; and however long or brief a time we have together I shall expect it to be filled with courage and nobility and beauty.' She stood up and drew herself to her full height. 'We shall make it beautiful,' she forecast. 'We shall make it beautiful together.'

Always one to judge her exits with some care, she then turned and walked slowly from the room; merely pausing at the door to say: 'And please don't worry, Mrs Stormont. I shall do everything I can for him. And may I take this opportunity of wishing you a very happy Christmas?'

17

'Well, how's that? You can turn back to the mirror now and take a look at yourself.'

'No, I can't. I'm paralysed in every limb.'

'But you really don't need to worry. I've been quite sparing about it, you know. Broken you in gently.'

Daisy turned slowly—with her hands held up before her face. She peeked between the fingers.

'Oh, dear God!'

She closed her eyes again.

'No, Daisy, honestly! You mustn't be so *timid*.'

Though accidentally, Marsha had hit upon the right approach. Daisy had never thought of herself as timid. (Nor, in truth, had anybody else.) She despised timidity. Anything was better than that. She would be a clown.

She laid her hands down decisively and fully opened her eyes.

'Grimaldi,' she said.

Marsha, who for some reason thought that this was one of the Ugly Sisters in *King Lear*, which she had studied at school but not to any depth, again arrived at the right answer; though only God knew how. 'No. Cinderella.'

'Really?'

'Grand transformation scene. Come on. Let's go down and surprise Andy.' In all her excitement and absorption she had forgotten that she wasn't pleased with Andrew. 'I shall take a feather with me too, so that I can knock him down with it!'

And she drew one out of a hat; it was all such fun. Then she carefully replaced the hat-box.

'You know, it doesn't feel at all like *me*,' said Daisy.

'It soon will. You'll have to get a whole new wardrobe to go with your whole new personality. I'll come and help you choose it.'

'What? With a mirror on the front?'

They went downstairs. At the entrance to the drawing-room Marsha put a pretend trumpet to her lips and blew a most important fanfare, which seemed to involve a lot of finger movement. 'Tarrah, tarrah!'

Andrew, sprawled a long way down in his chair, didn't even look round. 'Have you any idea of just how long you've been?'

'Not really—but you'll think it time well spent, my love. And please don't spoil it for her. Nor for me.' More loudly she said: 'Will all gentlemen kindly stand up so that they can be conveniently knocked down with a feather? Tarrah, tarrah!'

'It is ten-past-bloody-six.'

'I am the herald of the Queen of Sheba! Please enter here, Your Majesty!'

'Said the spider to the fly!' chortled Daisy, nervously.

Marsha prayed that all was going to be all right—and squeezing herself to one side was suddenly surprised at just how *small* Daisy was. At other times she didn't really give such an impression of shortness, yet at close quarters she made Marsha feel nothing but arms and legs. Yes, with Daisy brushing past her in the doorway now, why, even her head looked only small and vulnerable, as though it wouldn't take much just to snap it off, cleanly, at its root. But on the other hand, while Daisy had been sitting at the dressing-table upstairs and she herself had been standing, she hadn't had this same sensation of power, this feeling that she could just

88

swoop down from the top of her long neck and *gobble* her all up. Perhaps, she thought, she'd been too busy preparing her for the grand entrance!

Daisy went in and said: 'Think of Michelangelo and the Sistine Chapel. Think of da Vinci and the Mona Lisa. Think of Marsha Stormont and . . . but no, don't think of me! Or have I suddenly become a swan? All plucked and ready for the oven?'

'Marsha *Poynton*.'

'Oh, yes.'

'I liked you better as you were.'

Daisy put the back of one hand to her forehead and the other to her breast; but then, before finally petrifying into tragedy, appeared to have a moment of doubt and turned to Marsha seeking confirmation.

'Even from Andrew—that wasn't quite a round of applause?'

It was Andrew himself who answered, 'Do you realize that all this nonsense has taken you both a full hour?'

Ignoring him, Daisy said rather sadly to Marsha—all hope departed—'No, I thought not.' She resumed her stance of heartbreak and of deprivation. 'I vant to be alone!'

Marsha giggled.

'Oh, Andy, truly, doesn't Daisy look attractive?'

'And you needn't just think I'm playing the giddy goat, either. If you don't say yes, I shall stay like this all evening. Perhaps for ever. What an embarrassment! What an eyesore! How would you ever explain it? Something brought from the museum in Cairo? No one would admire your taste. Besides —I couldn't play those games of chess. Three, did you say?' She noticed he'd laid out the chessboard.

'I shouldn't think there's even time for *one*. Not now.'

Marsha had never been able to laugh before when Andrew got the sulks—far from it, indeed—but Daisy seemed to regard the matter as a joke. With Daisy there, even Marsha couldn't take it very seriously. She couldn't help but see the absurd—even the slightly comic—angle.

Daisy abandoned her pose. She questioned Marsha. 'Haven't you dared tell him, then, that he's stuck with me for a good half of tomorrow?' ('What's good about it?' muttered Andrew.) 'Or is it just that he spends Sunday morning in church—and hasn't got a travelling chess set?'

'No travelling chess set,' answered Marsha.

'Yet he does go to church?'

'Sometimes.'

'But *that*'s the reason why they were invented!' Daisy sounded scandalized. 'What's the matter with this man of yours? Doesn't he know *anything*? No wonder he can't smile.'

Then—most incredibly—he did. It was reluctant: a mere quivering of the lips that couldn't be contained—and soon was stubbornly suppressed; but it was, at any rate, a start. Daisy exclaimed:

'Once more unto the breach, dear friends, once more . . .
Cry "God for Harry! England and Saint George!" '

and brandished her sword gleefully on high, looking as though she might actually put down her head and charge.

When she was in certain moods, even Scrooge might have found it difficult to hold out long against Daisy . . .

And amazingly, at the finish, it turned out to be a very good weekend; even a lighthearted one; one of the very best, Marsha thought, that they had spent in their new house. Life was certainly full of surprises. When Daisy left, late on Sunday evening, Andrew said, 'We must do this again sometime. And when we do—I shall definitely beat you hollow!' This weekend, he'd patently had to struggle: out of their seven games, Andrew had lost as many as three.

'I'll make you eat those words!' she said. 'Ha, my friend —ha! Just you wait.'

'Nonsense, you know that I was out of practice.'

'And I suppose that I've been playing twenty times a week? Why must you keep on making that same feeble excuse?'

'I'm going to bone up,' he said.

'I'm going to bone up better!'

And she peeled off one of her black gloves and threw it, provocatively, to the ground.

'There!'

He picked it up. 'To the death! But I suppose, as a general rule, you're fairly busy at weekends?'

'Mmm. Fairly.'

As Marsha and Andrew waved her goodbye and she drove away, hooting cheerily, in her little black Austin—the ancestor, eventually, of a couple of others—they stood together by the garden gate. It was a pleasant autumn evening, with a lovely moon—not at all chilly. Andrew had his arm round Marsha's shoulders; his sleek fair hair gleamed in the lamplight and his eyes had a gleam, as well.

'You've done some nice things to this garden,' he said, as he looked around the small area with apparent, though uncharacteristic, interest. 'You're a girl who's obviously got green fingers.'

'Oh, darling, I am so glad that you think so; though it's a long way past its best—it was much nicer a few weeks ago.'

'Tired?'

'Yes, a bit.' She yawned, as if at the suggestion. 'But peaceful. Happy.'

'How's the little one?'

'Very well, thank you—I hope. But little.' She placed one hand a moment on her stomach. 'And I do hope that I'm not going to grow *enormous*.'

'Me, too,' he said—and with great feeling, although she didn't really notice any seriousness. (She hadn't yet been sick behind the phone-box.) They laughed.

He said, after another few seconds, 'Actually, green fingers isn't all you've got. She's quite a good-looking woman, isn't she? I hadn't realized. You managed to bring it out.'

Marsha felt tremendously content. She had never received so much praise from him before, over so short a period.

'Lipstick fingers, too?'

'Yes.'

'Of course, she does need to do something about her hair. I told her. I can't think why she's never bothered.'

He yawned, as well. 'I imagine she's the type of woman who doesn't worry overmuch about her looks.' Then, mindful of something similar he'd said the day before and of the reaction that it had provoked, he added hurriedly: 'Of course, she has plenty of personality. I suppose she's always got by on that. And she's very intelligent. But quite fun,' he went on, also hurriedly, for fear that this might seem like criticism.

'I am glad,' repeated Marsha; though she wasn't quite sure what she was glad of. Just life, generally.

'I suppose she always knew that she could never be half as pretty as somebody like you,' said Andrew. 'That must have discouraged her—well, it would, wouldn't it? It would discourage any woman.' He spoke suddenly as if he were an authority on the subject. She felt that she was almost brimming over. She led him gently up to bed.

Part Three

18

She was weeping. She had waited until now before finally letting go. She had wept, perhaps, just a dozen times in the whole of her adult life: notably, at some of the mutilations she had long ago witnessed in France, and once in the empty flat on the day of Marie's funeral, after the last of the mourners had departed and she was alone in the stunning silence. This morning, however, in the court, she had stood there small and staunch and scornfully dry-eyed. Unbeatable. She had even, at one point, shaken her fist at the magistrates. (She had immediately claimed that she was knocking away a fly—a ludicrous explanation which the magistrates, thank heaven, had accepted.) And she had brushed aside their offer of a chair with almost the same air of contempt. But now she was crying: sitting in the back seat of her own car, which Malcolm was driving for her—he felt grateful to be occupied. Phoebe, beside him, was twisted round uncomfortably and had one hand on Daisy's skirt, ineffectually patting her knee.

'Couldn't we stop at a pub, Mal?'

He shook his head.

'A coffee bar?'

'No. It's better to get back.' He too was whispering, though Daisy wouldn't have heard them anyway. 'Have we any of that brandy left?'

'I think so. Oh—but isn't this unspeakable? What are we going to do with her?'

'She'll be all right. Get her talking of the past. We'll take her to a film.'

Aloud he said:

'We'll soon be home, Daisy. What we all need is a strong cup of tea! Lots of brandy in it!'

She did make an effort. 'Yes. Just what the doctor ordered. But it's all been such a shock, you see. I've never experienced anything like it in my life. No. Never!'

She blew her nose hard.

This time it seemed that she might finally rally.

'I suppose that I must look a frightful sight!'

'Not a bit of it. And even if you did . . .' said Malcolm. 'You *are* among friends.'

'Yes—and none better. I know that, dear. But just the same . . . who ever thought I'd go and make such a goose of myself?'

She added bitterly: 'At least I waited, though, until I got out of that place!'

'You did indeed. You were incredibly brave in there.'

Unfortunately she didn't hear.

'But my lovely car.' She ran an arthritic hand caressingly over the leather seat; even through thick grey wool the twisted joints were still apparent. 'My dear old Pegasus. My one dependable companion.'

The tears started to well again.

'At least there's a bright side, Daisy.' Too late, Malcolm realized the futility of this. But, perversely, she had heard him and he had to carry on. 'You'll get a bit of money for it. I know someone in the trade and he'll see that you're not done.' He thought that, on the sly, he could probably add an extra thirty pounds or so himself; benefiting, maybe, from his uncle's good example—for Dan had given him an open cheque with which to pay the fine. But Daisy only sniffed.

'Money! Is *that* the bright side you talk of?'

Feeling piqued, he answered: 'No, the really bright side, of course, is that the woman wasn't killed. We can all thank our lucky stars for that. And how!'

'She was hardly even hurt,' said Daisy.

'A broken leg?'

'Well, she needn't have broken it. That was her fault. She evidently didn't know the proper way to fall.'

Malcolm kept silent.

'Besides, she was too fat. You never saw such mounds of flesh. And if it hadn't been for all that weight . . .'

(In fact, it had been mentioned in the court how good Daisy had been with her; taking charge with sympathy and efficiency until the ambulance arrived—although she herself had obviously received a shock.)

'Or if it hadn't been for your gross inattention . . .' said Malcolm. 'And on a pedestrian crossing!'

'What was that?' The aid gave its familiar piercing whistle. 'What did you say?'

Phoebe had turned and pressed his arm. 'Almost there now, Daisy. Have you ever seen such heavy traffic? That's what he said.'

'Oh.' She slumped back against the seat and glanced without interest at some of the offending traffic. 'No. It's a disgrace. This wretched government, if only it had any guts, would have done something about all this, long ago! In some ways, of course, I'm really better out of it.'

'Much.'

'Oh, I don't know, dear. It's easy enough for *you* to say that, but . . .' She shook her head and pursed her lips. 'No. I just don't know what I'm going to do from now on, and that's the truth of it. Take a dose, I shouldn't wonder.'

'Or take a bus,' suggested Malcolm, whose sympathy was still a little dented.

'A bus!' said Daisy. 'What—with *my* knees? That shows how very little *you* understand. If you don't mind me saying.'

'Conductors are usually quite good, you know, about helping people on and off.' Phoebe, too, could be tart on occasion.

'Yes, I know, dear, I know.' Daisy sounded weary but propitiating. 'Even if most of them *are* as black as your hat.'

'The black ones are often the best.'

'Oh, I know that, too, of course.' Daisy spent the next three minutes staring out of the window. 'My word! Just look at that creature there! She must think she's on the beach —did you ever see such a brazen sight?' It was a June day and the woman, Phoebe noted, was wearing a perfectly respectable sundress. 'The silly ass! I'd better direct her to the Strand—if not the South of France!' She gave a bark of hollow laughter; but after that remained untypically silent for a while.

'Anyway, it was very good of you to accompany me,' she

observed eventually, still somewhat grudgingly.

'We were glad to be able to do it.' The short respite had regenerated Malcolm, and he said nothing about the amount of inconvenience created by their taking the day off.

'I'm only thankful that your mother and uncle didn't come. Let alone your brother.'

'Dan would have been very willing to do so. And I'm sure Andrew doesn't know the first thing about it.'

'He soon will, I suppose.'

'I don't see why.'

'Don't you?' The silence hung, provocative. 'No. I couldn't have borne it. They'd probably have agreed with everything they heard. Oh, they mightn't have said so outright, not to me, but . . . you can always tell with those two.' It wasn't so much that she had forgotten Andrew as that she simply didn't consider him worth the bothering with. 'Always bleating such damn fool things as, "Well, at our age, Daisy," or "*Anno Domini*, you know, plain *Anno Domini* . . ."' (She had put on her contemptuously falsetto voice.) '*Why?* That's what I don't understand. And why should I let myself be lumped together with that pair? Why should I let myself be made over into *their* image? Especially by your mother! "At our age, Daisy! At our age, Daisy!" Unimaginative and blinkered and boring—that's what it is. Besides, of course, being utterly untrue.'

Malcolm held his tongue. No wonder she was upset. The ignominy, in Daisy's eyes, of hearing her age discussed in court. Not merely mentioned. Discussed.

Bandied about.

The ignominy. The irrelevance.

Five years older than the century!

(And she had tried to claim—in a stricken, barely recognizable voice and in dogged refutation of the printed evidence—that she was twenty years younger than it!)

No wonder she had cried.

But didn't she realize that there were other forms of violation besides that one? Malcolm smiled to himself a little grimly—and postponed the ordeal of trying to educate her. 'Well, here we are at last! Dear old Notting Hill.'

'You can't say dear old Hendon Central,' muttered his aunt; wanting to express something, but certainly not pleasure, nor even strong relief, at their arrival.

'Dear old Hendon Central,' said Malcolm.

'Ha! Central!' exclaimed Daisy. 'I always like a good joke! Don't you?' She added, with deep scorn: 'It's so far off the map that even Columbus couldn't have found it.'

Malcolm laughed—with genuine amusement. 'I do like the idea of Queen Isabella of Spain saying, "Go, Sir Christopher; discover Hendon Central!" Perhaps that's what he was really looking for when he stumbled across America and had to be content with that.'

But Daisy was not amused.

'You're very callow,' she remarked, coldly. 'You have no idea what it's like, having to drag your knees over all those pavements. I always said it was suburbia.'

She paused a moment, before adding the ultimate withering refinement.

'These days I call it Lost Horizon.'

19

And this was more or less the refrain of the whole afternoon and evening. Not that Daisy didn't enjoy herself. After a sandwich and three cups of generously laced tea she needed very little encouragement to put her feet up—on a pouffe —with her shoelaces undone and her coat placed on her lap and covering her ankles. Then, with her head lolling back against a wing of the armchair and her *Woman's Own* half-fallen from her grasp, she was almost instantly asleep— though this was something she would later on deny. 'No, dear, I just had my eyes closed. It's very soothing to the retinas.' ('Snoring must help them, too,' whispered Phoebe to Malcolm.) Afterwards, they had their supper at a Spaghetti House and then went to the Odeon, where they saw *The Great Gatsby*. Daisy didn't care for the story very much, but she enjoyed the dresses and the tunes of the twenties and several times started humming an accompaniment in her own inimitable, slightly off-key but robust manner—much to the annoyance of the audience and the embarrassment of her companions. What was amazing was the way she could apparently quite forget her troubles for long periods at a time, be chuckling and zestful and totally caught up in the moment, and then revert to her grumbles with a disconcerting suddenness—only to be whisked back into merriment some moments later with an equally unexpected shift of the mercury. One instant she was nearly dancing along the pavement between them, saying ' "The Great Gatsby", did they call that? Well, give me "The Great Victor Herbert" *any* day—la-da-da-da-da—da-da—da-da,' (trilling 'The Blue Danube' by Strauss); and the next, sitting over milky coffee in a Greek restaurant, declaring, apropos of nothing that had just been said, 'No, it's no good. I shall simply have to get away from that place. My mind is totally made up.'

'But, Daisy, you can't! Where else would you go?'

Malcolm was more horrified than Phoebe: he knew at first hand (at least, to the extent that it was *he* who'd always had to see to the packing and unpacking, the placating of formerly benign, now shrilly indignant, landladies) the long and dismal trek from one bed-and-breakfast place to another, a month here, six weeks there, sometimes merely a fortnight, have you got a room on the ground floor, she's not too good on stairs, oh yes perfectly all right in every other way, have you by any chance some slightly thicker curtains that won't let in the daylight too early in the morning? The smiles and sweetness and stoicism at the beginning, on both sides, the final vituperative exchanges.

'You're all right where you are,' he added slowly, trying to introduce a hypnotic note that would force her to agree with him.

But of course she was never all right where she was; it was always the place where she'd been before, no matter what sort of hell-hole she'd thought it at the time, in which she'd been at her most comfortable and happy. 'I was well off then,' she would say. 'I can't think whatever persuaded me to leave,'—the implication being, although she never actually put it into words, that it was *you* who'd been responsible for that persuasion.

No good reminding her of draughts and noisy radio-playing neighbours and the foul and stinking lavatory (sometimes puddles of urine at its base) and the bath she couldn't get out of and the light and heating which suddenly went off if she had forgotten to put more money in the meter and the proprietress who kept knocking on the door wanting to know what was the *meaning* of those loud remarks she was always making in the hallway, sometimes to a passing tenant but just as often into thin air . . . 'Yes, dear,' she'd say, 'yet there are always minor inconveniences; in this life you just have to learn to accept them uncomplainingly.' But this didactic, sweetly pitying turn towards philosophy was invariably retrospective, as it were; never actual and of any help.

However, if you said to her, 'Well, Daisy, it certainly wasn't *me* who wanted you to move,' she would reply at once, 'No, dear, of course it wasn't; did I ever suggest for one moment that it was?' in the sort of humouring tone that intimated she was reluctant to apportion blame and, anyway, you'd learned your lesson.

And the worst thing about this was, that you never quite *knew* if she believed in her own little fantasy or not. You were inclined to consider that she did.

Malcolm said now, 'I thought you were happy living with Mother and Dan.'

Indeed she had now been there for more than two years. It was amazing; the sort of staggering information you usually came across only in the *Guinness Book of Records*.

'Oh—*happy*? I don't look for *happiness* these days. At best, a little pleasure here and there. While I had the car, perhaps, it was—almost—bearable.'

'But you've got everything you need. It's clean and comfortable and . . . well, knowing what Dan's like, I don't suppose it costs you very much. And Mother waits on you hand and foot. There's companionship whenever you want it. What more could you possibly ask for?'

'A little life,' said Daisy, crushingly.

'Good God, you can't have everything!' said Malcolm, with impatience.

Phoebe, being ten years younger than Malcolm, was always inclined to match her own tone to his. 'You know what the only other answer would be, Daisy, don't you?'

'A dose.'

'No—don't be so silly. A home.'

'That's all I want: a real home, with laughter and talk and stimulation; where things *go on*. Like this one. I shouldn't have thought that that was too much to ask for.'

She seemed to have forgotten for the moment that they were sitting in a restaurant; and it was hard to know whether she was wilfully misunderstanding or not—making a poignant little bid for commiseration, and popularity.

'What I meant was,' said Phoebe, with conscious brutality, 'a home for elderly people.' She couldn't, even at that point, quite bring herself to say old.

Daisy stared at her.

Then slowly she turned her eyes on Malcolm. 'Does that happen to be your opinion, too?'

'You've got to learn to realize, Daisy, when you're well off.'

'A home for elderly people?'

'A home with your brother- and sister-in-law; who care for you and feel concerned.'

'Pish!'

'It's true.'

'Codswallop!'

He smiled and attempted to put his hand upon hers; but she withdrew it. 'It's neither pish nor codswallop. And you know very well that it isn't.'

'Is that your last word?'

'My very last.'

'In that case, if you won't help me, I shall have to find somebody who will.' She spoke with dignified simplicity; strong under the weight of disillusion, her faith in human nature by no means totally destroyed. 'I used to think that you two were one in a million.' She smiled a little sadly. 'I've often told you so. But . . .' (with a stoical shake of the head) 'now I shall just need to look about me for some other friends.'

And what's more, thought Malcolm, she would probably find them. She went into a milk bar and five minutes later a perfect stranger—usually male and usually young—was buying her coffee, offering her cigarettes, exclaiming at her reminiscences, being delighted by her vitality, bemoaning her misfortunes. Oh, yes, at a first meeting, even at a second or a third, Daisy could be charming—with the additional fascination of seeming to be far more sinned against than sinning. And because, in her own words, her victims (sic) always appeared to make a bee-line for her, Malcolm saw her as a sort of vampire bee, who thrived on youthful, idealistic blood; a vampire bee he still couldn't help but feel protective towards—and even fond of—despite the many times he himself had been stung by it, and with an accumulatively debilitating effect.

The analogy was not perfect. The sting was retractable. Her victim was the sucker.

She arose from the table. She picked up her shopping basket, with the *Daily Telegraph* which she had found abandoned at the Spaghetti House now lying on top of it, covering her handbag, letter-writing materials and library books. She also took her stick in hand; then drew herself up to her full height—far more impressive than it should have been.

'Thank you for your hospitality. Perhaps you would now direct me to the bus?'

'Oh, don't be such a fool, Daisy. You don't really think we'd let you go home by bus?—even if there was still one running, which I doubt. Of course we'll drive you home.' He had brought his own car, not hers.

It was the quietest journey, in her company, that they had ever had. Occasionally she sniffed. She sometimes cleared her throat. To any question she replied just briefly and in exceedingly clipped tones; and only once did she address them at length.

'And I've got many other friends already, as a matter of fact. There's Edgar and Vera. Bill. Countless students from the School of English—literally—at the very least, four or five.' (Descendants of Félix and Homayoun.) 'Madge Fairweather. And I don't know if I've ever mentioned Mr Patrick, the man who does my hair. Well, he—the salt of the earth, if ever anybody was—*he* (I tell you this right now, quite openly and in all sincerity) *he* would do anything for me. Absolutely anything.'

She added: 'And there's your father, too. I'm sure he would be heartbroken—heartbroken!—if news should ever reach his ears . . . I mean, of my being treated shabbily.'

In some ways that was the most surprising remark, not simply of the evening, but of the whole day.

20

But she should never have given up the flat—large and inconvenient and uneconomical though it was. She could have taken in a lodger, couldn't she? It was the biggest mistake of her life, and they were fools who had counselled her! Sell up—find yourself a nice room—buy an annuity. Oh, how could she have been persuaded by them?

Yet, of course, she *hadn't* been. She had chosen to forget that. She had nearly always made her own decisions.

No, the truth was—after Marie had died she could hardly wait to get away from Marie's flat. Every inch of it was a reminder. Even during the brief period that she had remained, there were several occasions when she'd thought she'd heard a call from Marie's bedroom; several occasions when she'd actually been on the point of hurrying in.

Why, there was even one time, she remembered— unawares, she had been sitting at the piano—when she'd suddenly turned her head, fully expecting Marie to be about to walk into the room . . . and this despite the fact that Marie had been bedridden for the previous twelve months; dependent on a wheelchair for several years before that.

There'd even been the start of a silly welcoming grin upon her face.

People had often said to her that Marie should go into a hospital, that Daisy couldn't be expected to look after an invalid old lady, day and night, without assistance and without a break. But Daisy didn't look upon Marie as an old lady—merely as someone who'd been born about a quarter of a century earlier than herself and was therefore all the richer in wisdom and experience. Indeed, she hardly even looked upon her as an invalid, because the part of her that really mattered was just as lively and as loving as it had ever been, despite the limbs that now wouldn't function, the lungs that now had trouble. Marie in a ward for geriatrics—it was unthinkable. She had dismissed all such advice impatiently; and it was now the greatest comfort of her life that she had done so.

Even of those last times there were so many happy memories. For instance, she had frequently invited a few close friends in for a 'party'; they would play charades at Marie's bedside. But in the final months this got to be too tiring and gradually Daisy came to rely less and less on other people. She was ever thinking up fresh ways to entertain her. She prepared monologues in the manner of Ruth Draper. She taught herself some simple—and even not so simple— conjuring tricks; for one performance she actually acquired a live rabbit! She learned to do things with playing cards, too. And Marie liked it when she mimed to the gramophone or danced an elaborate tango. For this Daisy bought a special string of beads and sometimes held a rose between her teeth.

Her props were inventive. The tramp's costume, for example, could almost have been loaned by the great Charlie himself—though it was not as Charlie that she scored perhaps her most popular and oft-repeated success; *that* was as Burlington Bertie, from Bow.

Yet their entertainments were not always so rumbustious; piano-playing (with the doors kept open)—board games —even simple flower-arranging.

And it was certainly the one period in her life when Daisy became quite housewifely—those wartime and post-war years. (Partly, maybe, it was in atonement for the few months of marriage when, despite her husband's own precarious health, she hadn't really *cared*. She could have coped with sickness very well—but not with that unexpectedly weak-kneed mentality which had accompanied it so much of the time.) Now she read recipe books by the dozen and did everything she could to tempt a jaded appetite.

Marie particularly liked a certain walnut layer-cake. Even towards the end, when such food was totally out of the question, Daisy baked a fresh one every week—to have in the tin, 'just in case,' she always told herself. She usually gave it to the cleaning woman to take home.

A few weeks before she died Marie had a mild stroke and became senile; although, again, Daisy never referred to it as that. She had simply 'withdrawn a little . . . to get ready'. Daisy tried to see it in the light of a retreat—with leafy, dappled, rosemary-scented walks—and she still vehemently insisted upon nursing her. She carried on with daily readings, too: no longer *Vice Versa* or *The Diary of a Nobody* or *Cranford* but now mainly poetry: on the offchance that some of it might penetrate and—along with gentle images—bring gentle dreams. She also read, aloud, the Book of Common Prayer and she still played the piano: Tchaikovsky, Mendelssohn, Brahms—the more tranquil, tuneful, tender passages.

Later, when she moved, she had the piano put into a furniture respository—that and several of the larger pieces which she couldn't take with her but which she couldn't bear to sell. Afterwards she used to exasperate the men at John Bayes because she was so often wanting to go and look at her things to make sure they were all right; she would sometimes spend most of an afternoon either in dusting and polishing or else just sitting by them ruminating—once she even arranged for old Mr Matthews to go and tune the piano there. But in the end her hands became too arthritic for her to believe that, even if she found a place where she'd be allowed to have the piano, she would ever be able to play it again in the manner that it should be played; and her attempted recitals at the repository grew ever more frustrating and inept.

Besides which, the cost of storage seemed to mount in an iniquitous fashion almost every year.

So one day, in a fit of browned-off devil-may-care reckless-ness (which she very soon regretted), she had everything sent to the auction rooms; and then realized, when it was far too late, that even that string of beads and the tramp's outfit (together with a large box of photographs—nearly all the photographs that she possessed) had been included in the transfer.

It was as though most of the evidence that there had ever been this period in her life had now quite gone: a little foretaste of one's proper death, when times remembered, finally, only by oneself are . . . finally . . . forgotten.

A death, indeed, of more than just oneself.

But at least she gave the men at John Bayes half an hour of *hell*; and that helped to prevent her from feebly breaking down upon the sudden, shattering realization of her loss.

21

'Shall I give you a hand, dear, with the washing up?'

'It's all right, thank you, I can manage.'

'I thought you looked a trifle peaked.'

'Yes, I don't feel at my best.'

'You try to do too much. They should have called you Martha—not Marsha. Shall I sit down and keep you company?'

'It's up to you.'

Daisy pulled out a stool and perched herself uncomfortably. She didn't feel her sister-in-law's reply had been precisely gracious but for some time now Marsha had been showing signs of irritability. The poor old thing was running down, thought Daisy. Fading.

Also, she'd noticed, Marsha was beginning to repeat herself. And Dan was starting to do it, too—it must be infectious! Of course, they had so little, both of them, to exercise their minds. You only had to listen to one of their conversations; it didn't matter when. They were all, equally, pathetic.

'Forgive me for harping on it, dear, but you do appear a bit under the weather. Shall I go and get you some tonic? There's quite a nice man at Boots. I'm sure he'd recommend something.'

'No, thank you, Daisy; it will pass, I daresay. It's just that there doesn't seem very much to look forward to, any more.'

'Oh, you're right, dear. Yes, you're so right. We should make up a theatre party one of these evenings. That's what we should do.'

'Oh, there isn't anything worth seeing at the theatre. And it's all so expensive, anyway.'

'Well, we must think of *something*, that's clear.' Daisy decided she must try and jolly her up a bit. 'Daisy, you're a tonic,' people had so often cried. 'A real tonic!' They'd have been surprised, then, to hear her talking about some bottle of coloured water from Boots, when all she had to do was just pull out her own cork, up-end herself—and pour!

Yes. It wasn't like her to be nearly letting the side down.

'Marsha, you've got to enjoy yourself!' she said, firmly. 'It's later than you think. It's later than anybody thinks —except anybody who *does* think! Tomorrow we could all be dead! That idiot Carter could have pressed the wrong button. That dolt in the Kremlin could have done the same thing. So before I walk out of here I'm going to make you laugh—somehow—if it's the very last thing I do. Would you like me to topple off my stool?'

'Not very much.'

'Well, thank heaven for small mercies! I could throw a custard pie.'

'There aren't any. And if there were you'd only make a mess.'

'All of life's a mess—what difference is a little custard pie going to make? But you shouldn't be afraid of mess. I'm not. I welcome it. I go out and dabble my hands in it and swirl it all about me.'

'That must be nice. I hope you wash them afterwards.'

Daisy said, 'I know that was a joke, dear, but it's symptomatic: you're much too concerned with washing your hands. Not even Christ always washed his hands before lunch. And he knew something about the things that matter. Not pernicketiness. Not washed floors which you're frightened to death to let anybody walk across as soon as they're done. Not rubbish tied up in neat little parcels which are good enough to give away for Christmas. No. Jesus Christ certainly wasn't an old maid. Not in any shape or form!'

'Are you saying that I am?'

'No, dear. Why should you think that? You know, you shouldn't always be so ready to imagine criticism. It's a definite fault. Nobody's criticizing you.'

'Well, if you did say I was an old maid, it would be quite true, anyway. I know that. But I can't help thinking that things must have been a little easier in those days.'

'How? Easier?'

'You didn't have to worry so much about keeping up standards.'

'Flying the flag.'

'I don't enjoy having to be an old maid.'

'Nobody *has* to be anything, you know,' said Daisy consolingly.

'Oh, yes, they do. Life just pushes you into things—without your really noticing.' She paused. 'I don't suppose that anyone ever *sets out* to be a nag.'

Yet she said that more to the washing-up water than to Daisy; and Daisy didn't hear.

'I haven't made you laugh yet, have I? At any rate, not properly.'

'But you're certainly right about one thing, Daisy. It *is* later than you think.'

'And I'm right about another: however late it is, it's never *too* late.'

Marsha just proceeded, steadily, with the remainder of the lunch things. Daisy hated to see anyone unhappy.

'You can always turn over a new leaf.'

'What? At our age?'

'Oh, at any age! At any age! What has age got to do with it, anyway?' She controlled herself with difficulty and just as though she were being rewarded for this a piece of inspiration came to her. 'In fact, the older you are, the more of an achievement! Anyone can do *anything* when they're young. But when you're old you start collecting feathers in your cap. Real feathers. I know that I shall.'

As she said this, Daisy slipped down from her stool —though somewhat awkwardly; even in the short while she'd been perching on it, one of her knees had badly stiffened. Nevertheless she left her stick lying where she'd put it, along one edge of the table.

'We'll just show 'em, dear, shall we? The two of us together? We'll show 'em!'

'Show 'em what, Daisy?'

' "Every time it rains, it rains . . . pennies from heaven." '

For the first half dozen words Marsha, with her attention still directed towards the sink and the draining board, didn't even realize that Daisy was singing. She had missed both the stance—and the tune. Only that well-known phrase alerted her. She turned her head and gave Daisy a brief, apparently encouraging smile, but then continued with her work, hoping that she'd soon stop.

' "Don't you know each cloud contains . . . pennies from heaven?" '

Now—along with the familiar tune which had, albeit rather flatly, finally caught up with its lyric—Marsha saw, out of the corner of her eye, that there was also movement to accompany the words. Good God, she was actually dancing! (Or doing what from Daisy's viewpoint seemed to pass for dancing.) Why couldn't she just leave her alone? Marsha felt that she was close to bursting into tears.

' "You'll find your fortune falling . . . all over town. Be sure that your umbrella . . . is upside down." '

Now Daisy was nearly at her elbow. Marsha purposely hadn't looked round but she would have sensed it anyway, even if she hadn't heard.

And then she felt one of her sleeves being tugged—as if by a tiresome and persistent child.

Oh, this was too much. This was just too much.

Really, Daisy! Go away! Stop it!

'Now come on, dear. *You*'ve got to sing it, too.'

'No, don't be silly. I can't. I don't know the words.'

' "Trade them for a package of . . . sunshine and flowers. If you want the things you love . . . you must have showers. So when you hear it thunder . . . don't run under . . . a tree. There'll be pennies from heaven for you . . . and . . . me!" '

All the time, the importuning hand remained on Marsha's sleeve—and plucked it, more or less in rhythm to the song. Marsha bit her lip; and felt her lunch gradually turning to lead.

Daisy said, 'And it isn't bad advice, dear, is it? Now then; your turn. Remember we're in partnership!'—a deluge of washing-up water caught her across the lower part of her face and heavily spattered the front of her blouse.

There was a startled silence. Even a stunned one. Daisy regained her balance, blinked rapidly and rubbed her eyes.

'By Jove!' she cried. 'For a moment I thought it was raining pennies from heaven! But *they* wouldn't taste like soapsuds, would they? When you do enter into a part, dear, you certainly give it everything you've got! Well done, Mrs Siddons! A very fine achievement.'

Marsha—thoroughly contrite and appalled—was already busy with a tea-towel. Her exasperation had gone. Indeed, because Daisy was chuckling, she couldn't help laughing a little herself.

'There! I told you I'd make you laugh.'

'I just can't think how it happened. Somehow my hand must have slipped.'

'Now you mustn't detract from your achievements!' Daisy pretended to be stern. 'Anybody else's. Never your own.'

'Oh. I think you've got achievement on the brain, Daisy.'

'Yes, I have! So now tell me what you consider to be your greatest achievement—apart from this.'

Of course, she was quite sure of the answer even before she'd put the question; and if she hadn't wanted so much to cheer her up—consolidate that progress already made—she wouldn't have asked it. 'My children,' Marsha would say. All those fond complacent mothers were exactly the same. As though there was anything to be proud of in doing what the rabbits did oftener and with a great deal less fuss. But she felt

in sufficiently high spirits this afternoon to encourage anything even remotely positive.

'My greatest achievement?' Marsha scarcely hesitated;
three seconds at most. 'Snipping the condoms,' she smiled.

'*What* was that, dear?' Yet this time Daisy actually had
heard.

'Yes. Didn't you know? Andrew never wanted a second
child. And I was quite determined that we should have one.'
After all, there'd been nothing much else to salvage from the
marriage.'

'And so you . . . ?'

'Yes. One day when Andrew was at work. He had three or
four packets in his drawer. I just took my scissors, and very
carefully—'

Daisy suddenly raised her hands above her head and gave a
triumphal clap. 'So Malcolm really is your greatest achievement! He really is! Does he know?'

'Of course he does. I thought everybody did. Except
—possibly—Andrew.'

But Daisy's amusement was first-time genuine.

'What ever did he say?' she asked.

'Andrew?' Marsha's smile was speedily displaced. 'Oh, he
wasn't pleased at all when I told him—told him I was
pregnant. No, not at all. His first reaction was—well, not
very chivalrous, to say the least.'

'He swore?'

'No. Oh, well, perhaps—I can't remember. But he implied—'

'What did he imply, dear?'

'He implied that it wasn't his baby.'

'Oh! What a brute! How like a man! Always so ready to
think that he's been deceived! My word, though—he must
have been in quite a stew!'

'Yes, he was.'

'How lucky that Malcolm is the spit and image.'

'I suppose so.'

'But what a hoot!' Daisy's enjoyment of the joke was
irresistible. Soon the two of them were laughing together
uninhibitedly. It set them on very good terms with one

another; and even as much as two days later Daisy was still intermittently chortling. 'Yes, that was *quite* an achievement! I never knew you had it in you! I think we'll have to call you Snip. Miss Snip, the Barber's Daughter. How do you do, Miss Snip? Well done! I really must congratulate you.'

22

'Hello, Andrew. Turned up again like the bad penny, I see. How are you? Where's Myra?'

'Hello, Aunt Daisy. I'm all right.' He stood up but seemed uncertain whether just to take her hand or kiss her cheek or do both. In the end he did neither. He merely waited for her to sit down and then did so himself. 'Unfortunately, Myra couldn't make it. She's not up to much at the moment.'

'She wasn't up to much last time, if I remember rightly. I haven't seen her in donkey's years.'

'Myra's always been a bit on the sickly side.'

'She enjoys bad health—as people used to say. Yes. Poor Myra. She's never been up to much, has she? Where are the boys, then? In the garden?'

'No, they haven't come today. You know how it is with young people now—always off somewhere with their friends. Once they've turned sixteen they're very seldom at home. You hardly see them.'

'Nor does their grandmother.'

'Yes, I know. We keep inviting her to come and stay. Always tells us that she can't leave you and Uncle Dan!'

'Hmm. Probably can't see the huge advantage of Harrow over Hendon, more like it! *Even* Hendon, perhaps I ought to say. You should take her off to the sea with you for a few days. Must be aeons since she had a break.'

'Well, yes, but unfortunately that's easier said than done . . . Excuse me, Aunt Daisy. Perhaps I'll go and see if she needs some assistance.'

'No, sit down again. Finish your cigarette. Perhaps you'd like to offer me one?—I seem to have left my own packet upstairs. No, if I know your mother, the last thing she'll want is for someone to be getting under her feet in the kitchen.' She chuckled. 'What's the matter, though? Scared of a few minutes alone with your mad Aunt Daisy? You suddenly remind me of your father.'

Andrew, uncertain how to answer this, perhaps wisely didn't try to. He lit her cigarette, passed her an ashtray and then resumed his seat.

'Be brave. Dan will be back quite shortly, I daresay. At least I hope he will! Trust *him* not to have known there was no sherry in the house! I could have told him, if he'd only asked. I don't think, dear, your children are awfully good to their grandmother, if you want the honest truth.'

'She doesn't bother very much with them, either. It's reciprocal.'

'I don't think that you're so marvellous yourself, come to that. And as for Myra; well, she's a complete write-off, if ever I saw one. I hope you don't mind my mentioning these things?'

'Well, yes, as a matter of fact, I do. I don't feel it's any of your business.'

'Whose business is it, then?'

'Just ours and Mother's.'

'And will you and she be conducting it this afternoon —despite the absence of those other board members? Would you like me to raise certain items for the agenda over lunch and then leave you to discuss them as you do the washing up?'

'No, thank you very much. And would you mind changing the subject, please?'

'Yes, if you like. I suppose you think this Thatcher woman is the bee's knees? I shouldn't be at all surprised.'

'I like Margaret Thatcher, yes. I think she's highly admirable. She'll do a good job.'

'Pish!'

There was a long silence. Daisy drummed her fingers on the arm of her chair.

'You know I had to sell my car, I suppose? That was over a year ago.'

'I did hear something to that effect—yes.'

'You could do with selling your own car, if you ask me. Why didn't you walk with Dan just now to the shop?'

'As a matter of fact . . . I had a bit of a stitch for some reason.'

'Ah. I thought so. You're very overweight.'

'What's that book you brought down with you? Is it any good?'

'*Don Quixote*. It's my bible. One of them! What are you now—forty-five? Not that it matters, of course. Except that it does, you know. In one sense.'

'I happen to have just turned forty-three. Well—a month or two ago,' he amended, defensively.

She received this news with a raising of the eyebrows and a pursing of the lips. She put out her cigarette.

'I thought your birthday was in March.'

'The very end of it.'

'And with all that flesh that you carry . . . aren't you frightened at all for your heart?'

'Only when I'm with you.'

She smiled.

'No, but, seriously,' she said, 'the forties are a notoriously dangerous age. I mean—for men. Only the other day I heard of someone who was . . . well, he was also just forty-three, funnily enough. Enjoyed a good game of tennis in the morning—but he was quite used to playing it, of course —must have been in better shape than you. In the afternoon he suddenly keeled over. Dead. No warning whatsoever. Bonk! That was a Sunday, too.'

'I'm sorry to hear of it,' said Andrew.

'But the point is, dear—have you decided yet on the things that are really important to you. That's what I'm anxious to know.'

'Yes. Margaret Thatcher. The winner of the Derby. The state of the stock market.' He said this with not the glimmer of a smile.

Daisy laughed; and looked upon him far more kindly. 'Yes. You *are* your father's son.' As clearly as his brother was—though in a different way. In actual appearance, Andrew was a Stormont.

'You think so?'

'I hear that you're his favourite, too. His and his new wife's.' (Of thirty-five years' standing.)

'Just as Malcolm is his mother's.'

'Well, yes, there may be something in that, too.'

There was a pause. This moment of better feeling between them was precariously balanced.

Andrew spoke about the weather.

'It looks as though we might be in for a heatwave,' was his conclusion.

Daisy nodded her agreement. 'What's more, a break by the sea wouldn't do you any harm, either, I daresay. As for Myra—well, I should have thought she was positively crying out for one; what with all that poor health which she enjoys.'

'She does *not* enjoy it.'

'Exactly. That's the very thing I'm saying. A holiday would set her up.'

'I think that's Uncle Dan back, isn't it?'

Daisy had heard neither Dan—nor Andrew.

'But . . . don't you have any discipline at all, then, over those two boys of yours? In my day they wouldn't have been allowed just to go off like that—no, certainly not—not when it was a question of visiting their grandmother. (I'll wager that they get to see *her* mother a little more often! Any takers, I wonder?) And did you know she's made you all a lemon meringue pie? Not that I'm advising you, Andrew, to eat more than the smallest mouthful. But all the same I think it's very sad. I wonder if you'd like to give me another of those cigarettes, dear? They're rather small, aren't they?'

Andrew merely said, as he offered her the packet: 'Myra's mother died, Aunt Daisy. In 1970 or thereabouts.'

Although his tone was reasonably expressionless something in his eyes indicated that he felt this to be a fair point.

Daisy commiserated—genuinely. She wanted to hear the details. She was sorry that Marsha had never told her. She would have sent some flowers.

But then her flow of sympathy reverted into its original channel.

'Anyhow . . . we don't want to split hairs. Do we? The principle remains the same.'

Dan, who had been briefly sidetracked into the downstairs cloakroom, entered the lounge at last. The bottle he carried was still wrapped in its tissue paper.

'Sorry to have been so long. That was quite a queue! Anyway, Andrew, I see you've been in good hands during my absence. Never a dull moment while Daisy's around! What have the two of you been nattering about?'

'Oh,' said Daisy, with a careless laugh. 'Nothing very much. We've just been setting the world to rights—haven't we, dear? But, yes, I think you could say that I've been managing to keep him tolerably entertained. I have my uses.'

Marsha came in.

'Dinner's on the table, everyone.'

'Ah, Marsha. Just in time to join us for a sherry,' said Dan. 'I was going to bring you yours in the kitchen.'

'No, no. Everything will get cold. You've got to come at once.'

'Oh. Right you are, madam.' Dan put down the bottle, still in its tissue paper. 'Well, never mind. It won't come to any great harm, I suppose.'

Daisy stared from one to the other of them—and then at the bottle—with incredulous disgust. 'Well, who can be surprised that Andrew wanted to divorce her?' she asked, in an undertone.

'What was that, Daisy?'

'Only my little joke, dear. And I daresay you were much better off for it, anyway. I think that new dress is *most* becoming. At least—I don't believe I've ever seen it before, have I?'

'Not more than a dozen times.'

Marsha went ahead, into the dining-room.

Daisy adjusted her hearing-aid. She said to Andrew, as he held the door open for her: 'Oh, my word—that was a close shave. Did you see the old-fashioned look she gave me? Pure cut-throat! But thank God—if there's one quality I do possess—that quality is tact. I may get into things; but I always get out of them, too. Hallelujah! Anyway, she probably didn't hear me, if the truth be known. These days she's nearly as deaf as I am. Dan, as well. Poor old things. You've just got to make allowances for both of them—whatever you do, try not to forget that, dear. You'll find it makes things easier. I do.'

It was one of the longest exit lines that even she had ever delivered—especially while a gentleman held the door for her.

'Come on, old girl,' said Dan. 'Beep, beep! Beep, beep! You're causing an obstruction.'

23

But Marsha had heard.

And was she better off for it—as the old witch had then had the nerve to try and tell her?

Was she?

Well, at first it hadn't been so bad. Sometimes, she remembered now, she had actually sung at the beginning of a bright new day (who could say what might be just around the corner?) and danced gaily through the small, bare flat, while whirling an excited Malcolm.

Nor had she forgotten the sense of accomplishment she'd found in making a home out of something other than wedding presents and parental generosity—the sense of freedom. Before, when not accompanied by her own mother or by Andrew's, she had usually been directed round the stores by a fiancé who, even then, had seemed a little penny-pinching and rather too concerned with the opinions of other people —'I've heard that Mrs Chin wouldn't give a thank-you these days for anything made out of walnut,' he had said, decisively, when Marsha had admired a very pretty wardrobe. Now, however, Malcolm and she scoured the second-hand shops (by this time Andrew had chosen to go to boarding school) and generally celebrated the discovery of any small bargain by having their tea in a café, which really they couldn't afford. And Malcolm often saved up his pocket money, too, to surprise her with something which he considered pretty, either for the mantelpiece in the drawing-room or for the one in her own bedroom. On the whole, that was a rather happy time.

But even then the loneliness had been apparent; especially after Malcolm had been tucked up in his bed on those frequent, very long evenings when there was only the wireless or her library book for company. Nobody with whom to talk over the endless frustrations or the little excitements of the day (which even a child as sympathetic as Malcolm couldn't be expected always to find interesting)—nobody with whom it was any longer possible to try to laugh over the trivial, unmemorable things that in fact made up the fabric of a life. Even her own mother's interest in what were, after all, her only two grandchildren appeared at times a little superficial—not at all what a husband's would have been, or should have been.

It might have seemed less lonely, of course, if only she had enjoyed her job at the flower shop.

She did have boyfriends; naturally; in those immediately postwar years she was still quite young. And one of them had even promised to marry her—well, actually, there had been two, but she had really believed in the first—the moment that his wife would give him a divorce. Yet she quickly realized that a woman in her thirties, even in her very early thirties, with two growing children and hardly any money, was not a likely candidate for remarriage. The day she faced up to that was the day that middle age first took on a shape, in earnest, and the distance to it didn't seem so far.

And though the boyfriends still came (and went) they weren't any more the fancied pathway to a secure, companionable future but only a means of staving off her awareness that no such future now existed. Films, drinks and cuddles were still fun, of course, but with every year that passed, she thought she grew a little more frenzied about the pleasure she attempted to derive from them.

In the late nineteen-forties, her mother suggested that she

might go to a marriage bureau. Over the years she went to several. The nervousness, the disappointment, the frustration . . . the boredom. Occasionally, however, you met someone who gave you just enough hope to keep on going; although more often you vowed to yourself that never again . . . no, never again. It was pitiful, some of the types you met: she remembered the man with the appalling stammer and the constant rivulet of saliva running from a corner of his mouth.

And yet you did go on—for the mere fact, often, that you felt so desperate and were afraid to stop.

Surprisingly, though, the early nineteen-fifties brought with them a comradeship and a contentment that were to last for more than a decade and that were to provide not merely the most fulfilling period of her later life but even of her earlier life as well—though it was only towards the end of this peaceful, pleasant time that she fully came to realize it. Another divorcée had moved into the flat above; and an equally nice woman, whose husband was nearly always away, into the one immediately below—there were just four flats in the building, one on every floor. Her own home became the common meeting ground. Virtually every evening either Beryl or Joan or both of them would come in for a gossip and a cup of tea and stay at least an hour—usually twice or three times as long. Joan worked in a film studio—she was assistant to the art director—and Beryl in a handmade-chocolate shop. And it was so lovely to hear of their day-to-day experiences, and to be able to tell them yours. The laughs they had. It was almost like being at school again, only *there* Marsha had never had two such very close friends. She discovered for practically the first time in her life the deep pleasure that there was in having women friends—as opposed to men friends—who really knew, and cared, what you were talking about; who didn't make demands; and with whom you could simply be yourself. Malcolm, as he grew older, was usually there as well, and sometimes, even, the pleasant elderly couple in the downstairs flat (they and the wife's dotty sister) might drop in for half an hour or so, but essentially it was a trio, and it was lovely, being part of a trio.

Eventually Marsha worked in the same chocolate shop as

Beryl; but that was when that halcyon period was drawing to its end. Their rents were to have been put up startlingly; the whole of Paddington Street was beginning to acquire a gloss; they all had to look for alternative accomodation. In the process, they were scattered. Things were never the same again.

She lost her two friends, and she lost Malcolm. She went to Golders Green; he shared a house in Dulwich with some fellow students. It seemed the natural time for a break: 'Obviously I can't stay with you for ever.' He was then nearly twenty-four. She had always wanted him to marry and to provide her with grandchildren (Andrew's, she had often said, would never give her half the pleasure) but she hadn't really allowed herself to think about the time when he'd be old enough to do so. And as he pointed out with such unarguable logic, a one-bedroomed flat was a whole lot cheaper than a two-bedroomed flat; and she wouldn't want to make another move in just a year or two.

She wouldn't have cared. Honestly. It would have been worth it. And the further move would even have given her something more to do; something more to occupy her mind.

But she hadn't said that; she hadn't wanted to become the possessive kind of mother. And since, in reality, she had always been the possessive kind of mother, this decision to let him go was naturally a hard one. It hurt, far more than the separation from her husband, and in a different way even more than the separation from her friends.

At first she saw Beryl and Joan reasonably often; but the gaps between their meetings gradually grew longer. By the time, three years later, that she gave up her flat in Golders Green and went to live with her mother, now a charmingly eccentric old lady, she hardly even spoke to them on the phone more than six times a year. And when she did, it was sometimes difficult to think what she could say.

Joan had married again; Beryl's husband had given up his life in repertory and on tour; times had changed.

Times were always changing.

Oh, how she wished that she too could have remarried: somebody chatty and understanding, but strong and protective. Andrew had very soon found someone else. For a long time now he had been rather well off. (This didn't reflect itself in the alimony which he paid her, but it was something, she supposed, that after all this time she still got alimony at all.) She often felt bitter about two things: firstly, that it was always so easy for a man, unencumbered and earning well, to find himself another mate; and secondly, that it was now Janet, not she, who was reaping the benefit of all those early years of struggle. She didn't know if Andrew was still a stick-in-the-mud; perhaps he was, though now there couldn't, financially, be any need for it; yet she herself had certainly become one—at first through force of circumstance but finally through inclination—and she very much resented this. She had become rather shy, and nervous of the world.

People said she had grown hard.

But she had so much hated being alone. When her mother died, she had gone to share the flat of another woman—she'd seen the advert on a board; and after that, of another. They had not got on: in both cases the bickering had been interminable; she had grown hard only in watching out for her own rights. But at least it had been better than being alone (she had told herself afterwards, when she was alone). She had ended up back in that same block in Golders Green.

And now she bickered with Daisy—and even with Dan. There were times when she almost felt like strangling the pair of them. So was she better off? She might just as well, it seemed to her, have tried to hold on to Andrew (he'd probably grown easier with age, she thought) even though the greatest mistake of her life was in ever having married him, in not having realized that, with patience, she could have done so very much better for herself. (She didn't even see a lot of Malcolm any more.) It was ironic, too, that it should have been the one time she'd actually held out against her mother, who all through her life had made so many unfortunate decisions on her behalf—together, of course, with the good ones and always with the very best of motives . . . But if only, as a young woman or a child, she could have gone to RADA or to one of the other theatrical schools . . . (a younger cousin, not nearly her equal in looks, nor with nearly so sweet a voice, had become quite famous as an actress and a film star) . . . well, then, who knew how different her whole life might have been, how full of colour and satisfaction and abiding love, how full of stimulation and of *point*? Who knew, who knew? It was true, as Daisy had once said and she had never since forgotten, that she'd been dealt a very good hand at birth: and if only she'd been given the skill with which to play it she could have been amongst the very happiest of mortals. But as it was . . .

As it was . . .

It was too late. Too late.

Some forty, fifty years too late.

But then, of course, if she had gone on with Andrew she would never have met Joan: she would never have met Beryl.

It was necessary to remind herself.

24

'It's amazing,' said Joan. 'The days when you're working and haven't got one minute to call your own, you can reorganize your own life and everybody else's without turning a hair; the days when you're free, it becomes a major expedition to go out and buy a birthday card. I bought a birthday card this evening. It was just before the shops closed. I swear, I'd been working up to it all day. I'd better not tell you what I'd *intended* doing with my time.'

'Oh, go on, though; tell us!' cried Marsha.

'I'd *intended* to give the flat its weekly clean; get up-to-date with the ironing; and turn out the kitchen drawers. And that was just to start with!'

'But you've certainly baked a scrumptious cake,' said Beryl.

'And I'm sure that just being able to relax for once in a while must have done you the world of good,' said Marsha.

'Who's been relaxing? I've used up every ounce of energy I had in thinking what a dreadful waste of time it's all been. A whole day preparing to go out and buy a birthday card! And if I'd been just a couple of minutes later—I'd have missed even that!'

'I hope it's for somebody special,' said Marsha.

'My sister. And you know, of course, how my sister and I get on! But I'd never have heard the last of it if she'd thought that I'd forgotten!'

'Well, anyway, thank God, *I* didn't have the day off,' said Beryl. 'At least I managed to drop in and see Uncle on my way home.'

'The brooch?' smiled Marsha.

'What else?' said Beryl.

'So is it *there* or is it *here* at the moment?' asked Joan. 'Forgive me—but I do lose track.'

'Who doesn't? *I* lose track. Uncle loses track. "Oh, is it with me this month?" he says. "Well, I hope so," I tell him, "otherwise it's damned well lost." And Raymond's coming home on Sunday.'

'Oh, for how long?'

'Just two days.'

'But is it the first thing he always says, then?—"Darling, where's the brooch?" '

'No, of course not. Yet I just couldn't look him in the eye if it wasn't there. I'd go all shifty and stammer. He'd think there was another man. The family heirloom! His great-great-grandmother's diamond brooch! The pride of the Rochdales! With Uncle in Praed Street.'

'Oh,' said Joan, 'I bet that he must have some idea of it.'

'No—none at all. I swear not. The shock would kill him. We'd be in the divorce courts before lunch.'

'Come and join the party!'

'But if you've got the brooch,' said Marsha, 'how on earth are you going to give him lunch?'

'Well, Uncle asked the same question. I think he was going to offer to lend me a couple of quid!'

'Well, you know, my love, you've only got to ask . . .'

'Yes, I do know. But only as a last resort. I made myself that vow.'

'Oh, now that's silly. What are friends for?'

Marsha opened her handbag; Beryl shut it again.

'But if you won't let me lend you something, how can I tell you that I finally bought that dress today?—the one that I've had my eye on for such ages.'

'You didn't!'

'I did! At last I took the plunge.'

'Well, go and put it on then!'

'Shall I?'

'Yes!'

'At once!'

She went out, but with the drawing-room door ajar and her bedroom one as well, she could still hear most of the conversation.

'Malcolm, some more cake?' said Joan.

'Yes, please!'

'What's the homework?' asked Beryl.

Haud facile emergunt quorum virtutibus opstat
Res augusta domi.

'Pardon?'

'It means—I've got a crib—difficult indeed is it for those to emerge from obscurity whose noble qualities are cramped by narrow means at home.'

'Who said that? Your mother?'

'Well—Juvenal before her. He also said: Your prayer must be that you may have a sound mind in a sound body. Pray for a bold spirit, free from all dread of death; that reckons the closing scene of life among Nature's kindly boons.'

'This man was obviously a laugh a minute,' declared Joan.

'Death alone discloses how very small are the puny bodies of men.'

'The poor man's Bob Hope. Well, personally I think it disgusting that the taxpayer's money should all go on such frivolity.'

When Marsha came back in the new dress there were ten minutes of admiration, of feeling the material, exclaiming at the lining, trying out the effect of various scarves.

Then she said, 'I think my little boy, with his grubby knees and all that hair which needs cutting so badly, had better pack up now and go and have his bath. The water's good and hot. And, darling, don't forget your toenails.'

'Oh, Mummy! Must you?'

'I'll come in later on and say goodnight.'

' "Oh, Mummy!" ' Joan and Beryl quietly chorused, when the door was closed.

'Grubby knees,' observed Beryl, 'and prayers for a bold spirit, free from all dread of death!'

'The headmaster thinks he's doing extremely well,' said Marsha, proudly. She told them again of several of the encouraging comments he had made at a recent interview. 'And nearly every night, what's more, he does the washing up.'

'Isn't he a pet?' said Joan. 'I could eat every inch of him.' She and Malcolm sometimes went to the pictures together. 'Let's all go and see *The Robe* next Saturday. It's at the Odeon. How about it, you two? My treat, of course.'

In fact, it was just an average sort of evening; no different in essentials to a thousand others—and indeed it might have been an amalgam of several. But for some reason this was the evening that Marsha remembered that Sunday night in Hendon, nearly thirty years later, as she lay there sleepless in the dark; sleepless and moist-eyed.

She remembered it as the evening when, after Joan and Beryl had gone and she was tucking Malcolm up in bed, he'd said to her: 'They're very pretty, aren't they?'

'Yes, darling. Very.'

Joan—the most glamorous and sophisticated of the three, who took an hour every morning to apply her make-up and to do her hair and who left a trail of scent behind her on the dismal stairs.

Beryl—often scruffy and slightly tomboyish, yet with a much more delicate type of beauty, stunning when she wore a particular black dress and took more than usual pains with her appearance; Beryl with her white skin and her sparkling eyes and her chignon.'

'I shouldn't think there are many ordinary homes where you get *three* such pretty women who spend so much time together!'

'Oh, *darling*. I shall tell them what you say.'

'No. Don't.'

But naturally she did.

Yet where were they now?

Beryl, still living in Wimbledon, with Raymond and their daughter? (No, *she,* of course, would be a woman of forty by this time. How absurd!) She'd totally lost touch.

And Joan—dead half a dozen years ago; of cancer.

'I bought a birthday card this evening. It was a real expedition. It took me all day to work up to it!'

25

Dan was out. Marsha wanted a bath. A large spider sat beneath the taps. Marsha gave a little scream, and ran to find Daisy—who was in her bedroom, with her coat on, packing the day's needs into her shopping basket.

'And I can't flush him down the plughole,' she cried, with a shudder. 'He's so big. It would seem like murder.'

'And he might come back to haunt you?'

'Don't!'

'Anyway, you're quite right, dear. What's he ever done to you that you should do that to him?'

'It's not what he *has* done. It's more what he *might* do!'

'Exactly, dear.' Daisy took from her basket yesterday's copy of the *Financial Times*, purloined from the bank. She made a roll of it and waved it over her head. 'Excalibur! Right, then—on our way! Daisy the Fearless Spider-Catcher!'

'Shall I wait for you here?'

'No, you shall not! You can't push me into the front line, coward, and then turn down a place in the rear!' They proceeded to the bathroom, Daisy fierily twirling her sword rousingly chanting the Battle Hymn of the Republic.

'Oh, what a beauty! What a monster! I believe he's staring right back—and thinking the selfsame thing about me! He says he doesn't admire my hat very much. Oh, my word, but isn't he *leggy*! And fat! And almost blacker than a bus conductor!'

Daisy gazed at him with the admiration that one experienced duellist might feel for another, and then prodded him with Excalibur. He scuttled off across the porcelain.

'Oh, Daisy, I do appreciate this. I'll make you a special supper, as a reward.'

'Not that I've quite earned it yet! But . . . Now, the trick is, of course'—Daisy unrolled the paper and tried to flatten it against her coat—'the trick is to get him on to this, then lift him up and carry him over to the window. He'll think he's on a flying carpet! He'll dream of Turkish delight! Will you open the window, dear?'

Marsha did so; she opened it as wide as it would possibly go.

The paper was now spread carefully in the bath. 'She stoops to conquer!' said Daisy. 'Pass me that backbrush, will you, dear? I'm going to tickle his butt again.' The spider was induced to go the right way. 'Gen up on your investments,' Daisy advised him.

'You're very brave!' said Marsha.

'Now stand well back, Pearl White!'

'I shall! I am!'

With the spider at the centre of the double spread Daisy picked the paper up at either end.

'Got it!' she said.

But her balance wasn't good. The paper buckled. The spider dropped to the floor and scurried back to Marsha.

Marsha screamed.

'It's all right, dear. He won't hurt you. He's heading for the skirting-board.'

'If he disappears, I'll never *dare* come in here again!'

Marsha was pressed up againt the wall, ready at any moment to dash through the open door.

But it wasn't easy keeping track of him: the lino was black and white squared.

'Now you see him—now you don't!'

'There he is, Daisy.'

'Ah, yes. That's a good chap.' Daisy went down on her knees, holding on to the washbasin with one hand and the side of the bath with the other; then retrieved the plastic toothmug which she had previously set upon the floor. 'Now just sit still for a moment while your Aunt Daisy comes for you. There, there; nobody's going to harm you; even the hairs of *your* head must be numbered, somewhere, I suppose. Sing him a lullaby or something.'

'I can't!'

'Oh, well, never mind. Now gently—very gently—does it. Oh! There he goes again! But he's coming this way. Stout fellow! Over here, dear, and park yourself inside the garage; this nice, yellow, shiny garage. Good Lord, Marsha! What a creature of intelligence and charm! An officer and a gentleman! Even if he does tickle!' (Daisy had clapped the flat of her hand across the top of the toothmug.) 'Ugh! I don't think I like that! Stop it! Please!'

'Hold on, though, Daisy. Hold on, for dear life!'

'You'll have to help me up.'

'Don't drop it!'

'It's a bomb! If I drop it we're done for!'

Marsha managed to haul her to her feet. She hadn't known she'd have such strength.

The bomb remained intact, its lid still shakily in place.

'Carefully, now, Daisy. Don't stumble.'

' "Rock-a-bye-baby on the tree top . . ." *Somebody*'s got to sing to it, wee frightened mite. His poor little heart must be thudding fit to burst!'

'So's mine.'

Daisy arrived at the window—Marsha beside her, with her hands beneath her elbows.

'Here we are, then,' cried Daisy. 'Don't forget to pull the ripcord! There he goes, dear. And remember, now, you've got to fall properly. Don't crack your head on the concrete.'

They couldn't see what was his fate below.

'Oh, thank you, Daisy. What a relief! You've saved my life.'

'I quite believe you, dear. You're white as a sheet. What you need now is a small drop of something to bring back the colour to your cheeks.'

'Oh, we could both do with a small drop of something! Even if it is only ten o'clock in the morning! Let's see if there's a little whisky in the cupboard.'

'My word! A nip of whisky at ten o'clock in the morning (yes, there is, dear). What decadence! What fun! I'm going to put the flags out. What a real little adventure we've both been having! I quite enjoyed myself, in fact.'

They made their way downstairs. Daisy had collected her shopping basket and her walking stick and her gloves. The *Financial Times* was back in place.

'Yes, a real little adventure,' she said. 'Do you know (that phrase of mine reminded me) I actually did put the flags out once. Quite literally, I mean . . . Well, one flag, at any rate.'

26

On a Friday night in the summer of 1942, when Marie lost the glass both from her bedroom and the sitting-room windows, there was a direct hit on a block of flats some fifty yards away. The following afternoon Daisy came home from the ambulance station with a skinny, trembling six year old, whom she carried wrapped up in an eiderdown.

'Like Cleopatra in her carpet! Except that this one's called Jimmy and he's suffering from shock. I said we'd take him in for a day or two, till things got sorted out. In fact, I insisted upon it; scooped him up from under their wet noses while they were still just wiggling and waggling in the wind.'

Marie didn't stop to ask questions. She instantly took the

child and fed him and bathed him and put him to bed. She sang to him while he was in his bath—'Ta-ra-ra-boom-de-ay! Ta-ra-ra-boom-de-ay!'—poking her finger in his navel on every 'boom'. It was the only thing which elicited any smiles from him at all.

Afterwards, Daisy told her what had happened.

'His uncle was head porter at the flats—this poor mite was on a visit there with his mother and two sisters. The mother and sisters were killed outright; the uncle died in hospital. Jimmy escaped unhurt. But when they brought him into the station—it was the first thing that I saw of him—he was crying out that he wanted his mummy, where had they taken his mummy, why couldn't he go and see her? He spent the night on a couch, alternately dozing and sobbing.'

She broke off. Suddenly she shook her fist at the boarded window.

'Oh, blast and curse every last one of them!' she cried. 'For ever and ever!'

'What's going to become of him?' Marie asked.

'It seems that there's a father somewhere. No one's managed to find him yet.' But now that the gleam had gone from her eyes she was left looking merely tired. 'God, though, what a night! Edgware Road and Marble Arch; Paddington, St John's Wood. Gas mains, water mains. Blood everywhere. Fire. People having hysterics. Bedlam isn't the word for it!'

Then, surprisingly, Daisy gave a chuckle.

'But you should just have seen me, last night, hacking my way through all the red tape!'

She picked up her glass (it was whisky, which Marie, herself almost a tee-totaller and strongly opposed to the black market, had nevertheless paid an exorbitant price for); she sipped, and savoured it carefully.

'You see, I had a girl in the ambulance,' she said at last. 'She died on the way to hospital. And the hospital authorities wouldn't take her in! They just wouldn't! Well! I wasn't going to stand for that. I told them it was impossible to drive around with a corpse—all four bunks, of course, would most certainly be needed! "So simply throw it in the gutter," I said, "if that's the very best that you can do!" My dear, you should have seen their faces. I can assure you they were well worth seeing! I wish I'd had a camera.'

'But, Daisy, won't there be repercussions?'

'Oh, just let there be!' cried Daisy. '*I'm* ready for them. All I know is: I was driving back to where I was wanted, and those four bunks were hardly ever empty.'

She sat for a long time cradling the whisky and gazing up at the Pissarro reproduction. In some ways she was quite enjoying this war; she knew it, and she made no bones about it. She felt alive and useful and at her best. Even the red tape was fun to be able to snip against. 'Daisy,' people would say, 'you just don't care *who* you cock a snook at, do you? You haven't one ounce of fear in your whole body!'

Well, the first part was true; the second certainly wasn't.

She was afraid of the bombs—the heart-stoppingly loud and drawn-out screams they made; the chilling pause before the crashes. She was afraid of the anti-aircraft barrage, when she wasn't in the ambulance: many nights, on her short walk home (she *refused* to run), she was convinced that she was going to be hit by the shrapnel. She was afraid, constantly, that there were live people buried underneath the rubble who had been somehow missed by the rescue squads; she was always imagining she could hear a whimper or a movement or—nearly as bad—the plaintive miaow of a cat coming from recently bombed sites; and on dozens of occasions, even when she knew it was probably just neurotic and the workings of her over-strained mind (God, how tired she was for so much of the time—how tired they all were), she was up there scrabbling amongst the piles of debris, feverishly tearing at bricks and stones and timbers and exhorting passers-by to do the same. She sometimes dreamed, during the few snatches of sleep she did get—on average, just three or four hours a day—that she was slowly being buried alive.

She was afraid of going batty.

She was afraid of anything happening to Marie.

But—despite all these fears—despite the fact that people everywhere were being cut down in their prime, or even before they reached their prime, and that to die prematurely in old age was just as much of an obscenity—she did have to admit that war in some way suited her. It was utterly selfish, but there it was. She enjoyed the comradeship; she enjoyed the grumbles; she enjoyed knowing that a fresh egg would never again taste so good as it tasted then; the awareness and the urgency.

She enjoyed, amidst all the bungling and hysterics and overstretched nerves, the expression of people's resilience and courage.

'Do you know, my dear, what I saw today? There's a whopping crater in the Edgware Road: the second time they've had a hit in the same spot. And somebody's planted a Union Jack right in the middle of it. Well, it really brought the tears to my eyes. I felt like jumping down from the ambulance and standing there and saluting it. I jolly well wish I had!'

Marie nodded. 'You'd better go back tomorrow, then. And Jimmy and I will come with you.'

'But did you know that there are lots of small flags flying now from broken windows all over London? Well, we ourselves have just been blooded. I've a pretty good mind to buy one tomorrow and hang it out of *this* window.'

But the next day was Sunday and so the purchase had to be postponed. The three of them went to church in the morning. The vicar preached about the necessity to forgive and the sin of passing judgement. He spoke about motes and beams. It was a brave but not a popular sermon and there were mutterings both during it and after amongst people standing outside the church in the sunshine. Daisy contributed her own few mutterings but kept them brief and reasonably restrained; partly because of Marie—more because of Jimmy.

On the Monday Jimmy helped her to fasten their own paper flag from the window.

His father had still not been found.

'Marie.' Daisy was drinking some Bovril and eating a sandwich before she went on duty. 'What if they don't find him?' she said, slowly. 'What if he's been killed? I've been wondering, you know, whether possibly, in that case . . . whether we ourselves . . . ?'

'*You*, perhaps, Daisy. They'd never let me. Remember, I

do happen to be in my seventy-third year.'

Daisy didn't say much more about it then but all that night it stayed in her mind—as it had been in her mind, indeed, all of that day, and a lot of the previous one as well. Before she finally went to the station, she looked in on him. He was asleep. One cheek was resting against the small teddy bear which she'd bought at the same time as the Union Jack and he was smiling, very gently. A hank of reddish-brown hair had fallen across his forehead and she brushed it back into place with her fingertips—she had witnessed that very scene perhaps a dozen times at the pictures. She stooped and kissed his freckled nose. He turned over and sighed and murmured, 'Mummy . . .' He was fully asleep. Marie was in the other room. 'Yes, darling,' whispered Daisy. 'Mummy's here.' She had never said 'darling' to anyone; and yet it came quite naturally. With the back of her fingers she massaged the large red patch on his cheek—she knew that it would quickly fade, but half hoped that she was going to wake him. She decided that she also had time to fetch him an apple—to place beside his pillow, for the morning. She imagined the three of them in ten years' time: Jimmy then sixteen, tall and broad-shouldered and doing well at school, despite the glint of pure mischief which remained in his green-flecked eyes; she and his 'Gran' feeling so proud of him as they watched him go up to the rostrum to collect his prize: that far-off, peaceful, peacetime speech day. She imagined him running on the sands (he was younger again now) and the two of them side-by-side on their knees building a castle with a swirling brown moat. 'Rudolf Rassendyll swimming across to rescue the Prisoner of Zenda!'—she flicked two fingers through the sandy water. She imagined them in the Chamber of Horrors, at *Peter Pan* and *Where the Rainbow Ends*; she pictured them eating their sandwiches together outside the Tower of London. Later, of course, there'd be a time when Marie was no longer there. Then they'd be even greater friends, the pair of them. They'd go everywhere together and he would look down on her from his vast height and call her the midget and appoint himself her protector. (Though she'd be very quick to point out to him that *she* had never had any need of a protector!) What fun it would be. What fun! She loved him very much already—had done so, she thought, right from the minute she'd set eyes on him.

Only some of this, in fact, passed through her mind while she actually stood at his bedside; a nucleus which she gradually added to during the course of that night—like a gaily coloured patchwork quilt to be spread out warmly beneath the grim realities of the wounds that had to be bound up, the various forms of suffering that had to be allayed. Somehow, she knew, she would arrange it! Somehow she would arrange it—whatever they might say about the desirability of a father's influence in bringing up a child! She saw already that she would probably have to contend with a lot of interfering old biddies. Well, she would! My goodness. They'd be sorry in the end that they had ever drawn their swords out of their scabbards!

It came as a real shock to realize suddenly that she was almost hoping for the death of an unknown man; and for the absence, too, of any caring family. (But she herself would be so much better than any caring family!) She tried, after that, to push these dreams from her mind.

But with only partial success.

It was as well, however, that at least she made the effort, for the following day the news came through, just before she left the station—and while she'd been getting ready actually to run the short way home—that Jimmy's father had at long last been discovered; and was every bit as anxious for a speedy reunion with his son as even Jimmy himself could be for a reunion with his father.

Part Four

27

A few days later Daisy sent a 'thank you' for her weekend: a travelling chess set and a lace-edged handkerchief. Inside the set was a further small card—'From one outsider to another. All FRILs must stick together!' Andrew was mystified; but didn't mention it to Marsha. Instead, one evening before leaving work, he telephoned for enlightenment.

'I rang to thank you, Daisy, for the present.'

'Marsha thanked me for it yesterday.'

'What on earth are FRILs?'

'Florence-Ridden-In-Laws.'

'I should have known, of course.'

'I'm thinking of setting up a society. Would you like to join?' She offered the inducements of a free blowpipe—a set of darts dipped in poison—and a club tie. 'Grand introductory offer. Can never be repeated.'

'Why not?'

'Yes, you're right, of course. Why not? Wax effigies and pins. Unlimited supply.'

'Poor Florence. One begins almost to feel sorry for her. She hasn't got a hope.'

'I know, dear. Hopeless,' she agreed.

'Membership is going to be a little small, isn't it?'

'Select.'

'Very. Just you and me and Erica.'

'Good heavens! Not Erica. She was long ago made over in the image of Florence. She's one of *them*, now. Insufferable.'

'Well, where does Marsha fit in? What about Henry?'

'We reclaimed them.' She added—with the air of someone determined to be fair: 'Up to a point, I mean.'

'What are the aims of this society? Is there an annual dinner?'

She took up the latter question first. 'Oh, yes, of course. Every few weeks or so.'

'I could be interested.'

About a week after that—without any accompanying note —a FRILs membership card arrived at his office. It had been beautifully and painstakingly executed in black ink and for a fraction of a second, as he drew it from its typewritten envelope, he felt puzzled: he thought it was a wedding invitation.

By the second post that morning came some equally well-produced literature: 'A Statement of Further Aims'. It was all extremely juvenile, but at odd moments throughout the day Andrew took time off from his work to jot down additional objectives or regulations or suggestions for passwords, and it was often noticed that he had a broad grin on his face, while he appeared to be doing a lot of vacant staring through the window. At lunchtime one of his colleagues said, 'What's happened, old man? You seem to be in a dream today.'

'Oh, nothing. I'm sorry.'

'Well, don't apologize. It makes you almost human.'

When he telephoned her that evening, to share the fruits of his preoccupation, he asked another question. 'Oh—by the way—when does the first annual dinner come up? I've got a note in my diary that it's on Tuesday of next week—at your place. Can that be right?'

There was a pause, before she answered: 'The right date; the wrong location.'

'Oh. I thought according to the rules of the society that it had to be somewhere private.'

'No, no, on the contrary,' she said. 'We just have to go in disguise, that's all. I myself shall wear a beard and an eyepatch.'

He seemed uncertain but said eventually: 'Well, just so long as you don't expect *me* to wear a frock.' His tone was slightly sullen.

'I warn you—I'd certainly lose interest if you did. But I'll bring one along if you like and it's up to you whether or not you put it on.'

The following Tuesday it was Marsha whom he telephoned.

This was the first time he'd ever done so for such a reason—and as he sat there, preparing to lift the receiver, he felt nervous.

That was silly: he didn't think Marsha would ask him awkward questions. She knew nothing about his work and never wanted to know. (Oh, at the beginning, maybe, she had shown a certain curiosity, but her enquiries had been childish in the extreme and she had seldom seemed to remember even the very simple things that he *had* tried to explain. Three times in the first week she had asked him precisely the same question—and with a look of such lively interest and intelligence—it had infuriated him.)

Of course, what she did want to know, always, was whom he'd lunched with, what he'd eaten, what his companions had eaten, what they'd spoken about; she seemed almost passionately interested in the social lives of everyone he worked with—their state of health, their wives' and children's states of health, their leisure activities, their servant problems, their grocery bills—just as she must have assumed (to begin with) that he would be passionately interested in every small exchange of her own day: she told him of her telephone conversations, of her encounters at the shops or on her way to the shops, of the afternoons spent with her mother, of her lunchtime visits to the cinema (when admission prices were cheaper and she went with her little packet of sandwiches and one or other of her equally garrulous friends). And soon—God help him!—there'd be the baby talk, as well.

For even though she must have realized by now that he *wasn't* passionately interested, still it rolled out each evening, the full saga of her unmomentous day, as though this had indeed been history in the making and no power on earth could ever stop it. The end to the saga would only see the start to the questions (if he was still sitting there—which as often as not, of course, he wasn't): 'Did you have a long wait for your bus today? Who did you sit next to—anybody interesting—no glamorous stranger who tried to move her thigh too close to yours? (And that reminds me: I saw the *handsomest* man I've set eyes on in a long while, at the bacon counter in

Cullen's. Then I went and stood next to him by the biscuits.) Was Walter Jennings late again today?'

He had once told her—*once*—that Walter Jennings had been nearly an hour late in arriving and had got into trouble with the Colonel. Apart from that, this man might never have been late in his entire life, for all she knew—a paragon of punctuality. (Actually, he wasn't.) But perhaps once a week, almost without fail, and with a mischievous, elbow-nudging twinkle in her eye, she would ask him: 'Was Walter Jennings late again today?' He always thought that maybe the very next time she asked it he would really shout at her, but somehow, no matter how his stomach might screw up, even in advance, in sheer anticipation, that moment hadn't yet arrived. Instinctively he knew it would be killing something if it did; in her; perhaps in him, as well.

But for all her questions—or, rather, for all his answers —she apparently couldn't get it into her little head that the people in his office were just as monosyllabic as he wished to make them out to be; that his place of work was a bastion of dignity and seriousness—no fit subject for tattle. In short, he would have hoped that Ignorance would produce Awe. The fact that it didn't was disappointing.

Yet it was no reason at all for him to feel nervous—sitting at his desk waiting to ask the woman on the switchboard to get him his own number.

28

He suddenly wondered if he ought to do it from a call-box. But he hadn't spoken to Daisy from a call-box. It was absurd if he was going to allow himself to become paranoid.

'Marsha?'

'Yes. Who did you think it was—Mae West?'

'No, I didn't think it was Mae West. I thought that—just conceivably—it could have been Mary.'

'Oh, you fibber! You know she hardly ever answers the phone, and that her voice sounds just like Dracula's. (Lordy! I hope that she can't hear me!) But you always say "Marsha?" in that way—always.'

'Nonsense! How often do I ring?'

'Come up and see me sometime.'

'What?'

'Oh, by the way—who's speaking, please? I'm sure I ought to have asked.'

'Don't be a bloody fool.'

'Crosspatch! I was only laughing at you a very *little* bit.'

'Well, I sometimes wish you wouldn't.'

'Sorry! I've got a perfectly straight face now—not a dimple anywhere.'

'Right; now the reason that I telephoned—

'Darling, what causes dimples? Why do some people have them and others not?'

'Marsha,' he said, with a sigh. 'I have no idea what causes dimples.'

There was a brief pause. 'It isn't a riddle. I suddenly wondered, that's all. Don't you ever wonder about these things? I find them interesting. This morning I saw a man with a cleft in his chin. It was oddly attractive, somehow.'

'I'm sure that it was.' He still used the same exaggerated patience.

'Andrew, has it ever occurred to you that it's only men who have cleft chins? I wonder why that is. Or do you think I've got it wrong? But I've never seen a woman who has one.'

'I've got to confess, Marsha, that I've never considered the problem in depth.'

'It must make it difficult to shave.'

'Perhaps.' Was there ever a greater preventative to— what?—a husband's dining with another woman—than a wife who just wouldn't give him the opportunity to tell her he wouldn't be dining with *her*?

Was there ever a greater inducement?

'Why are you phoning from a public call-box?'

'What?'

'Why aren't you phoning from the office?'

143

'Oh, I don't know. It's lunchtime. I was out. I saw this box. Does it matter?'

'No, of course not. It makes life more exciting. For a wild moment when I heard button A being pressed I even had time to think it might be somebody tall, dark and handsome, his heart aflame with love. That gorgeous man I told you about whom I almost held hands with over the biscuit tins. It's just as well I didn't. The biscuits would have crumbled. The glass lids would have shattered. Cullen's would have sent you a simply *hair-raising* bill.'

'Why me? Not him?' Even in his own ears his voice sounded so aggrieved that it might actually have happened.

(Was it possible that she *had* really spoken to this man? Could that have been one conversation which she'd not in fact passed on? She was perfectly capable—dear heaven knew —of speaking to anybody.)

'I don't know. Life is unfair. You poor darling. And I even poked fun at you just now—when you were being so sweet and so impulsive. Aren't I a beast?'

'Impulsive?'

'Yes. You saw a phone-box and you thought of me. Who feels the need of any tall, dark stranger? Not I—quoth the raven!'

'You never mentioned that this man was dark.'

That was an imbecilic thing to say. This conversation was absurd.

'I thought you didn't like dark men,' he said. 'You always led me on to believe . . . well, the fairer the better.'

'Yes, of course, darling.'

'What does that mean? "Of course"? That you were only saying it because you thought you had to?'

'No, no. I just meant—it's the exception that proves the rule. There's really no comparison. I *much* prefer blond men.'

He felt mollified; and was vaguely annoyed with himself when he realized that he did so. 'Then as long as we've got that one sorted out . . .' He ended on a rather surly note.

'Now you can tell me about *your* preferences,' she suggested, blithely. 'Was that the reason why you telephoned?'

29

Yes, this whole conversation was absurd, and he hadn't got the time for it. It had been all right, of course, before they were married—even quite charming, quite sweet really, when it hadn't been embarrassing or trotted out in public. But didn't she realize, now, that things had changed? In less than six months she would be the mother of a baby. It was almost impossible to imagine; in some ways she was still such an utter baby herself. Of course—Daisy was right—her mother was to blame; had never treated her as anything else but a baby, a thoroughly spoilt one at that. Yet this was really no excuse. It was high time she started to grow up.

'Marsha, do you realize just how long we've been talking and that there's a great queue of people waiting to use this box?' It was indeed true that there was a woman and a child standing outside.

'Oh, let them wait!' she cried gaily.

'And what's more I shan't have any time for lunch.'

'Oh, gracious. You've got to eat, Andy! You'd better go at once!'

She waited for him to say goodbye. Yet, paradoxically, now that he had the opportunity, he experienced some slight difficulty in broaching what he had to. (Any less moral man, he told himself, would have found no difficulty at all.) 'Oh, well. Perhaps there isn't all that rush. They can wait a minute longer.'

'But it's not them I'm thinking about! It's you and your lunch!'

'Well, I daresay I'll manage to grab something.'

'But if you "grab" something you know it will only give you indigestion. It always does.' Perversely, too, he found her solicitude, in such a situation, extremely irritating.

But perhaps that even helped.

'I'm afraid, Marsha, I'll be home a little late this evening.

Annoyingly, I've got to stay on at the office.'

'Oh, you poor love!' she answered. 'I hate that Colonel Chin! But do you know roughly how late? I'd better ask Mary to hold back dinner.'

'No, don't do that. Don't even wait up. I may not get in till around midnight.'

'Oh, *Andrew*!'

He was totally unprepared for such a wail. 'What's the matter?'

'But do you *have* to stay so long?'

'Of course I do.'

'There's no way out?'

'Of course not.'

She gave a sigh.

'Oh, this is the first time that's it's ever happened, for God's sake.'

Some women's husbands, he thought—sailors, for instance—were away from home for months on end. Even commercial travellers could escape for six whole days a week.

'You can't think how boring it is,' she said, 'just sitting here hour after hour on my own. Sometimes I don't even know how I survive each night till nearly seven without screaming or something.'

She was strangling him; she was trying to hold him in a net; to fasten him with shackles. Such a terrifying display of naked anguish! And over what? In the name of pity—over what? Did she really think that other husbands didn't need to work late at the office? He had never realized she was so neurotic; so frankly pitiable.

'You know how much I always loathe my own company!' she said. (*He* heard it as a whine.)

'I can't see why. I think it's grand to be alone. I'd give my right arm sometimes—I swear I would—just to get a bit of solitude.'

'It's easy to see that you're not left on your own for ten hours every day!'

'And nor are you! There's always Mary you can go and talk to. Go and talk to her this evening.'

'Oh, I keep telling you! Mary doesn't approve of me. She

146

always stands so stiffly when I'm there and won't say one little word more than she has to!'

'Then why don't you just tell her to sit down? It might make all the difference!'

'Oh, don't be silly! And what a change of tune that is! Last time, you said that I was too familiar and small wonder she felt no respect!'

He ignored this. 'Of course, you know what the real trouble is, don't you? It was Mater who found her for us. I daresay you'd have thought her quite delightful if *your* mother had recommended her.'

Someone suddenly rapped on the window with the edge of a coin. He turned his head in a fury and scowled at the offender. The woman's air of pleading quickly faded; it left her looking cowed. He felt a fleeting sense of power.

He realized that Marsha had been saying something but didn't ask her to repeat it. 'Anyway, why not go and spend an hour or two with your mother?'

'I've already seen her once today.'

'Well, what's that got to do with it? You're always telling me how lovely she is—or she's always telling me how lovely she is—one or the other.' But he didn't want them to begin on that again; not this minute. 'Or what about going to the pictures—that Jean Harlow film you were talking about?' Hell. Did he really have to arrange every slightest detail of her life. At least, when he'd been living with Mater, that was one burden which he'd never had to bear. Aimlessness was a thing he couldn't tolerate.

'I don't *want* to go to the pictures. Not on my own. And in the evenings there isn't anybody else.'

Of course, it would be much better, he supposed, once they'd got the baby. She'd then have something to keep her occupied and there'd be no more of this awful nonsense about looking for a job. There *was*, possibly, something to be said for babies after all.

(He was glad he'd had the forethought to start on one quickly.)

'And a fat lot you'd care,' she muttered, 'if I were picked up or attacked or raped or something!'

147

First the sulks—and then the tears.

He said, before these latter should appear:

'I'm afraid I can't talk any longer. I'm going to put the phone down now.'

'Good! But I want to tell you something before you do. I would be very *glad* to be picked up! Very!'

'Yes,' he said; he couldn't leave her to suppose that she had had the last word. 'I should think you would—at over four months pregnant!'

'And I do prefer dark men, tall, dark, very dark men—'

He slammed down the receiver—annoyed that even so he hadn't done it quite fast enough; stood there for a moment; tried to gather his composure. A man in his middle twenties, with a long quivering nose and a carnation in his buttonhole, pulled open the glass door. 'Here, you know, I do think it's a bit thick . . .'

'Oh, go to hell!' said Andrew. He pushed his way out of the box and left the other man staring after him with a deeply offended and slightly uncertain expression. 'I've a good mind to go after him and make him take that back,' he said to a small but sympathetic group which had gathered around. 'There's one thing, anyway. With hair like that, you can tell that he's not English.'

'Swedish or something?' suggested an onlooker. 'He was big enough for that.'

'No; he sounded like a German, to me.'

'Well, that explains it, then.'

Some five years later, the man with the carnation, engaged in his first real, unsimulated experience of hand-to-hand combat, had a fleeting image of Andrew striding arrogantly off into Threadneedle Street, the very second before he managed to lunge home his bayonet.

30

Andrew took a ten-minute detour before arriving at the restaurant where he normally ate lunch. By that time he had composed himself sufficiently to stave off the certainty of his meal providing indigestion. He felt a mixture of reactions: guilt, indignation, despair, excitement. But—chiefly—he felt that it served her right. This ultimate conclusion was helped along by two further circumstances. The first was that Johnson and Haley were still at their usual table, eating pudding and that after they had strongly recommended the chicken curry (but, as he discovered—because *today* he wasn't worrying about his waistline—recommended it with complete justification) they proceeded with their conversation. Johnson, apparently, was at present having problems at home and was soliciting advice. Was divorce simply the public admission of total failure—and the ruin of a man's life—or was it in fact the lesser of two evils? Harry Johnson had been married for ten years and was thirty-eight years old. Ironically, this was just the sort of conversation which Marsha would have revelled in and which she dreamed that he engaged in every lunchtime. What sustenance it would have given her! Even for himself there was a certain balm—more than a certain balm—along with the embarrassment. Despite the chicken curry, and the rather good-looking apple charlotte, Johnson's eyes grew intermittently watery; though at least he was still enough of a man, thank God, to let it go no further than *that*. They heard about his wife's selfishness —and nerve-racking mannerisms—and utter lack of self-knowledge. He wished, he wished—oh, how he wished, he said—that he had never got married. He had tried to make a go of things; nobody could say he hadn't; and there *were* the two kids, of course (though this appeared to Andrew to be a strictly neutral statement); but what would he not give—ten years of his life at least!—to find himself at twenty-five and a bachelor again? How he wished that he had never married. 'Oh, yes, I forgot—she snores; sometimes she even snores.' They all agreed that a woman snoring was like a woman smoking in the street—or drinking to excess—or using masculine-type language. 'And if she sneezes once, you know for a *fact* that she will sneeze at least a half dozen times—even during meals. Unless you've lived with it you just can't *imagine* . . . Oh, no, it isn't like the films would try to have you think.' Well, this was a further point they could all safely agree upon, and Haley even hankered a little for his own bachelor days as well. 'I'm not saying that there aren't certain compensations about marriage—obviously there are, aren't there?—and I'm not talking just about the mended socks, either, if the two of you can follow my drift—get my meaning, do you?—but all the same . . .' There then followed a list of buts that were like honey to Johnson (more like bitter-sweet marmalade to Andrew). Johnson was invigorated. 'The first year was more or less all right,' he said, 'until she started having children, but when that happened—well, I can tell you—the honeymoon was over all right, the honeymoon was over.' Andrew said, lugubriously, 'Marsha's expecting a baby next March.' 'Is she? You never told us!' said Haley. 'Congratulations, you old dog! You certainly didn't let the grass grow under *your* feet, did you?' And Johnson said, 'Yes, congratulations, Poynton! Well done! But you just take my advice and make the most of it, while it still seems like a little bit of heaven; while she still thinks that you're the one and only boy in the world—and vice versa.' 'Good God!' said Andrew. They quite misunderstood his meaning; they believed he wasn't yet ready to face their vision of reality.

'Oh, God,' he thought.

Well, that was the first thing which confirmed to him that he had nothing whatever to reproach himself for—that if anything, indeed, he had been a model of restraint and husbandly forbearance. The second thing happened just half an hour later, when he got back to the office. The dumpy, middle-aged spinster on the switchboard gave him, with a very friendly smile but a look of some bewilderment, a message which she had taken for him in his absence.

'Oh, Mr Poynton, your wife phoned. She said did you want a cold tray left out for you tonight?—but only to ring back if the answer was yes. She said to thank you for your kind, impulsive call. And—now what was it, the other thing?—I've got it written down somewhere, to make sure that I'd got it exactly right. Ah, yes, here we are. "Also," she says, "with lots of black hair on the backs of their hands." That's precisely how she worded it—of course I read it back. "Lots of black hair on the backs of their hands." She said you'd be sure to understand.' There was a slightly intrigued question mark apparent in Miss Eggling's eyes.

Andrew was furious. It was as much as he could to to thank her. It was as much as he could do not to slam his office door. It was as much as he could do not to cry out, 'Oh, fuck that woman! Fuck her! Fuck her! Fuck her!'

He might then have had a hard job explaining that, no, he hadn't meant Miss Eggling.

31

They met at seven o'clock at Simpson's. Andrew had wondered about the element of risk involved in taking her somewhere so well-known—and somewhere so large—but, on the other hand, if they were going to be seen it could just as easily be (more easily) at one of the smaller, currently more fashionable spots (he wanted it to be somewhere nice, somewhere impressive) and who did he know that ever went to Simpson's? He had thought about it very carefully. At the worst, he could always say, with the sort of confident nonchalance that would come from knowing he only spoke the truth, 'Oh, Jones—Smith—Robinson, I think you know my sister-in-law, Mrs Stormont.' And they would see at once that she was a good ten years older than he was (although, admittedly, people always imagined him as twenty-six or twenty-seven) and ridiculously small when set against himself; and they would infer, of course, that it was merely the most innocent of family business that was being enacted. And was it really so much more than that, anyway? Surely, in all fairness, the FRIL Society could scarcely be classified as anything *other* than family business; the thought rather tickled him. And certainly, as Simpson's wasn't one of those candlelit and *intimate* new places, nobody could possibly consider it at all a strange venue for the sorting out of one's family affairs—for the necessary entertainment of one's sister-in-law. Could they?

And if they did, he suddenly thought, while waiting a little nervously just outside the main entrance—and if they did —well, what the heck; he felt reckless; he remembered only too clearly all the occurrences of that day's lunch hour. He wasn't looking forward to returning home. Not tonight. Nor tomorrow. Nor the day after that.

And Marsha had said that *she* was bored. Good God. She hardly knew the meaning of the word. *She* could spend her days at the cinema; or drinking coffee; or nattering on the telephone; or doing practically any damn-fool thing she wanted to. *She* wasn't tied to a job she hated; eight hours a day; day in, day out, for only a few years short of another half-century; literally decades of endless repetition and endless tedium, for the sake of bringing up a family he hadn't even got yet and didn't even want much. Twelve bus journeys a week, in all sorts of weather and under all sorts of unfavourable conditions; six hundred in a year; six thousand in a decade. Christ! Two weeks every year in Bexhill or Brighton or Bournemouth. Uncountable evenings and weekends—right up to the end of his life, indeed (and on the whole his family was long-lived!—and so was hers!)— listening or not listening to that endlessly unrolling saga, the minutiae of all their days . . . Unbearable. Unbearable. (Later, at Dunkirk, he would remember this awareness of his boredom and some of the things which lay behind it; but by then what he remembered, with uncomprehending remorse and aching wistfulness, was wholly irretrievable, anyway.) No. He thought he wouldn't much mind if he never went home again. Here I am, everybody. Come and take a look at me. Ask me what I'm doing here. Go and tell my wife.

Go and tell my mother-in-law.

'Hello! Penny for them!' He actually gave a start, before he quickly remembered to raise his bowler hat.

Andrew had booked a table for half-past-seven. They sat in a solidly comfortable ante-room and sipped the sherries that a waiter brought them, for which Andrew felt nigglingly that he had overtipped. It threatened to blight his evening.

'I see that you did come in disguise,' said Daisy.

'Of course.'

'As what?'

'I don't know.' He was aware that this exchange—especially on his own part—was not *incredibly* scintillating. Might it almost be classified as the conversation of a poor fish?

'Well, aren't you going to ask me, then, what I meant?'

'No, because I'm sure that you're going to tell me.' That was better. He had the feeling that it mightn't be wholly original—though with any luck, of course, she might think that it was—but, yes, it was certainly better.

She chuckled. 'Then you're perfectly right, my friend! You obviously know women! I thought you'd come in disguise as . . . well, do you want to guess?'

'No.'

'The Prince of Wales.'

'The Prince of Wales!'

'Yes, you've got quite a look of him, you know. Hasn't anybody ever told you? Of course, you're very much bigger —and broader—got shoulders on you, haven't you, and I do like to see a man with shoulders on him, most women do—but otherwise there's a most uncanny resemblance. I've always admired the Prince of Wales. Must be a bit of a gay dog—if everything one hears about him is **true**! Probably leads his parents a frightful dance! And what I **say** is: good luck to him if he does!'

No one had ever mentioned any likeness to the Prince of Wales and Andrew was surprised, though on the whole, he thought, not displeased. There was a mirror over Daisy's head; richly gilded and with cherubs. He stood up briefly and inspected himself, smiling foolishly, hoping that nobody but Daisy would notice.

'It must be the colour of the hair,' he said modestly, reseating himself.

Daisy let that pass. 'You know, it's got a very nice sheen —your hair. I suppose that you use Brilliantine or some such muck.'

'No. I use nothing.'

'Really?'

They both sat and thought about this. It had the air of an achievement.

'I always brush it, though,' he admitted, 'vigorously.' (At least, it wasn't an admission; he thought the adverb—it was an adverb, wasn't it?—kept it from being that: added an aura of rugged masculinity. He had chosen it with care.)

'Ah, so that's the secret? I'm not at all surprised. And your brown suit complements it perfectly. I think you know how to put yourself across: a most valuable art—which remarkably few men appear to possess, if you ask for my opinion.'

'Do you mean that?'

'Of course I do.' Daisy was looking rather pensively into her sherry glass. It happened to be empty.

'To be brutally frank with you: I wasn't sure that a brown suit was quite the thing to wear tonight to Simpson's. Naturally I couldn't ask Marsha. But I didn't want to put on the pinstripe trousers and the black coat, because I had the the feeling that you might think them a little on the dull side.'

'Oh, I can't tell you how I hate a uniform—any kind of uniform! Sheer anathema! (That's probably why I chucked in nursing!) Andrew, I take off my hat to you! How could you possibly have known: my one particular *bête noire*? I raise my glass to you! I drink to your sagacity!'

He smiled.

'That disconcerting smile!'

'Daisy, your glass is empty.'

'Is it? Yes, so it is.'

'Would you like another?'

'Oh, do you really think I ought? Are *you* going to?' she asked.

'Yes! Why not?'

'Why not, indeed? Let's throw caution to the winds! Our bonnets over the windmill! (See what a shocking influence you are!) Let's eat, drink and be merry, for tomorrow we . . . Lord, we know what we are, but know not what we may be. They say the owl was a baker's daughter.'

He looked at her, extremely puzzled.

She leant forward and patted his knee. 'Don't worry. I haven't gone quite addlepated—not yet. It's just that I don't think one should ever say die.'

The waiter glanced up from serving another couple on the far side of the room. Andrew tried to catch his eye; was even, for a moment, rather glad of the diversion.

'And don't worry, either,' Daisy added; 'I'm not going to be frightfully expensive. In fact, I would suggest that we went Dutch, if I didn't fear that you'd take offence.'

'Of course I should take offence,' he replied at once; and very truthfully.

'I'm sure you would—and quite right, too!' said Daisy, with the same sincerity. 'I think that I know you, Andrew, almost as well as you know me! But I'll tell you what we'll do. We'll both have steaming bowls of bread and milk. Very nourishing and most delicious. And it would show that we're both just a little bit different, too—have minds of our own—don't merely follow the common herd . . .'

'Ugh!' He gave a humorous shudder. 'You mustn't think I don't appreciate your motives—I really do, Daisy—though for tonight they're quite unnecessary; but I don't think much of your solution. Of all the things that I can't stand, one of them is bread and milk.'

'Yes, I know, dear. It doesn't surprise me in the least. I can't abide it, either.' She signalled, successfully, for the waiter.

'No. To hell with the expense! Tonight we'll be a couple of beefeaters! We'll pretend that we've been given the freedom of the Tower!'

' "Oh, she walks the bloody Tower with 'er 'ead tucked underneath 'er arm!" '

Andrew considered, indulgently, that they hardly needed their second sherries—either of them. Despite a somewhat shaky start, he couldn't remember now when he had last felt in such good form; anyway, he thought, certainly not since the weekend when she had stayed with them.

32

While they were drinking their sherry. Daisy asked:

'Now who do you think *I*'ve come in disguise as? And the answer, I warn you in advance, is *not* Frankenstein's monster. Neither is it Shirley Temple—which some might say was almost the same thing.'

He felt a little awkward, suddenly conscious that he was late in complimenting her on her appearance. But, in fact, he hadn't really taken it in. He had been vaguely aware that she looked all right, yet his mind had been too full of other things; and, besides, as he'd made clear before, she wasn't at all of the same type as Marsha: Marsha, who had to be assured about her hair, the angle of her hat, her stocking seams, the lack of creases in her dress, the proper handbag, the most appropriate ear-rings . . . and so on, and so on, *ad infinitum*. (*Ad nauseam*.) You couldn't simply say to Marsha, 'You look very nice,' and leave it at that. 'Do I really pass mustard?' she would ask. 'You wouldn't let me look a frump? I'd so hate to disgrace you. You don't think that I ought to change?' And this—as likely as not—when they were already fifteen minutes late.

'You look very nice,' he said to Daisy. She had on a dark green thing—silk, wasn't it?—with long sleeves and a high collar and black court shoes. But whereas Marsha would have carried an evening bag scarcely large enough to take a compact, Daisy had what was by comparison a holdall. Yet now he came to think about it, he did believe that there was something slightly different about her from the way that he remembered.

Well, she was wearing make-up, of course—she was wearing a little more, he fancied, than Marsha had applied for her (on either the Saturday or the Sunday) and his first conscious thought was that perhaps it looked a little crude, until he checked himself and realized that Daisy's personality just didn't go with the delicate English rose idea, and that she probably needed rather bolder strokes than most women, to do full justice to it.

'Come on,' she said. 'You haven't guessed yet.'

'I can't.'

'No such word.'

'Mary Pickford?' It was the first name that came into his mind.

'You mean—Mary Pickford in her heyday?'

'Yes.'

'The world's sweetheart?'

He nodded. He supposed that she was—if Daisy said so.

'Well, I can see why you should think so. To an extent. It must be this infernal wig.'

He almost choked.

'Wig?'

'You silly ass,' she said. 'You didn't think that all these curls had sprung up overnight?'

He *knew* that there had been something different.

'You see, I've decided to follow Marsha's good advice. I'm letting my own hair grow, but in the meantime . . . Why do you look so disbelieving? Have I got to take it off and prove it to you?'

And she was really—yes, she was really—he would have sworn that she was really going to do it.

'No! No!' He jerked up his free hand as if physically to restrain her. 'Of course I believe you.'

He looked about him, quickly and surreptitiously, and got out his handkerchief with which to wipe his face.

'It suits you awfully well. Er . . . what a lark. You really are a card, Daisy.' That nauseating word, but for the moment he couldn't think of any other to improve upon it.

He sipped some more of his sherry. An awful thought had come to him. The make-up somehow seemed extra heavy now that he knew the black hair was a wig. 'Good God!' he asked himself. 'Will people think that she's a painted woman?' He looked around him again, hurriedly, to see if people had that sort of look upon their faces.

On the whole, he thought, they hadn't.

'I'll tell you, if you like, the one thing I admired about Mary Pickford.' Daisy gave her rather throaty laugh.

'Why? Is she dead, then?' Andrew felt surprised.

'No, no. Good heavens, no, dear. But by now he's past his best. He used to be such a swashbuckler. So athletic—glorious—in his prime.'

'She's not . . . ! She never was . . . !' Andrew hadn't once seen Mary Pickford, it was true, but no one had ever mentioned to him that Mary Pickford was a man. The world's sweetheart? Daisy *must* be teasing him. Or was he just naïve? Visions of men trying to pass themselves off as women, of pansies, child molesters, the Marquis de Sade swept exotically before his eyes—he had no knowledge of any of them (except for what a prefect had once asked him to do at school; but naturally he hadn't complied; and Dawson, anyway, had later been expelled). 'Daisy, why do you call him "her"?'

She looked at him enquiringly.

'I mean her "him"?'

'What on earth is the good fellow talking about?' she asked the room at large. For a moment he was very much afraid the room at large might answer.

'You said that he was so athletic—glorious—in his prime. Mary Pickford.'

'No, you silly ass! Douglas Fairbanks. Her husband.' It was the best joke which she'd heard in a long time. He wasn't sure that he himself came out of it with too much credit —though he pretended to join her in her laughter. He hoped that he was just as good a sport as the next man. (But how could *any* living soul want to dress up as a woman?)

'If you're not Mary Pickford, who are you, then?'

'Catherine the Great! Empress of all the Russias! I should have hoped that it was rather obvious!'

All he knew about Catherine the Great—and this again came from school, though not from any history lesson—was her apparently insatiable sexual appetite. He shifted a little uncomfortably; and wondered, not for the first time, whether he might not have bitten off a little more than he could chew.

But by then it was half past seven and their table was ready; things improved again after that. When they were seated and had chosen their dinner—both the food and the drink (*that* was always a slightly tricky part, the selection of the wine, but Daisy had simplified his task enormously, by declaring that she'd rather have some cider; Marsha would have said, 'You choose; pick me something nice; surprise me,' and would probably have chirruped to the wine waiter, 'We don't really know a thing!' or have giggled when he had to sample and pronounce); when their napkins were unfolded and their devilled whitebait in front of them and Daisy had picked holes in all the women's hats (her own was shoved into her handbag); when all this had taken place, she said, with fork poised to attack, 'Well, don't we make a most impressive couple—the Empress Catherine the Great and His Royal Highness the Prince of Wales? No wonder that every eye in the place is turned towards us!'

He ascertained, quite quickly, that it wasn't.

'Figuratively speaking, I meant to say, of course.'

'Of course!'

'I see that you're beginning to speak my language!'

'I thought that I'd been doing that for some time.'

'I mean—like a native,' she added hastily, and with what she regarded as a touch of inspiration. 'This is very good.'

'Yes, isn't it? The waiter must have recognized me.'

'HRH?'

He nodded. 'A bit of a gay dog! Mind you,' he said, more seriously, 'it does seem that I'll have to settle down a bit as soon as I come to the throne.'

'Yes, I know, dear. It's almost a pity. But I think you'll make a first-rate king. One in a million. Shakespeare wrote a play about you, of course: *Henry IV*, Parts 1 and 2: that's when you sowed all your wild oats. And *Henry V*. That's where you smashed the Frogs at Agincourt and showed the whole world who was who! You really put us English on the map! I think that we should drink a toast to it!'

They did; but in water; their cider hadn't yet arrived.

'And you gave that silly ass St Joan what for! Or was that a bit after your time—it may have been. Though silly ass or not, I think she had her points.' Daisy suddenly looked grim. 'And I'm sorry that she ended up the way she did. Who wouldn't be? The fiends! Oh, the fiends!' She rapped her fork upon the table—twice—and this abrupt transition in her mood was really rather shocking. Her voice quivered and he had the impression that under all the make-up she had gone quite white. 'How I'd like to have them here in front of me this moment! My word, but I'd give them a piece of my mind!'

To distract her, he said rather hurriedly what he'd been about to say when they somehow hit the royal road to Agincourt and—where else? Rouen?

'But imagine anyone actually being able to lead Queen Mary a dance! Queen *Mary*!'

His success was undeniable, thank God; though it was really himself, rather than God, that Andrew now applauded. Daisy stepped down from her pile of faggots and—entirely genuine as had been the force and passion of her empathy —instantly threw it aside, with a rich chuckle.

'He's got her firmly wrapped around his little finger!' she opined. 'The thoroughgoing rascal!'

'Can we be speaking of the same Queen Mary?'

'I can, at any rate.'

'Do you know whom she reminds me of?'

'Florence.'

'I mean, whom else she reminds me of?'

'Well, as long as you aren't going to say *me* . . .'

'My own mother—that's whom. Mater.'

Daisy stared at him, incredulous.

'The man who jumped from a frying pan,' she said, at last. 'You ought to have been billed at the circus! "Death-defying leap into a ring of fire!" How could anyone have been so reckless? How could anyone have been so unfortunate?'

He shrugged.

'Or short-sighted? Not to mention blind!'

'The thing is, of course—I married Marsha, not her mother.' He spoke a little pompously; he was suddenly mindful of a forgotten code of honour.

Their best red beef and Yorkshire pudding came; their peas, their cauliflower, their roast potatoes. Also, the cider.

' "If the Dons sight Devon, I'll quit the port o' Heaven," ' said Daisy. 'Oh, no, it comes from Somerset! Same thing! What was your father like?'

'I never knew him. He met my mother very late in life. He died only a few months after their marriage.'

'In self-defence, I suppose?'

They smiled.

'What was his profession?'

'Like mine. The Stock Exchange.'

'Did he hate it as much as you do?'

'Mater would never tell me, even if he did. But perhaps we're alike in some ways. Apparently he enjoyed racing.'

'I meant to ask you about that,' said Daisy.

'What?'

'Well, I know nothing—truly not the first thing—about the sport of kings. But I've always thought I'd find it fascinating if ever I met someone who wouldn't mind talking about it to an ignoramus like myself.'

'Oh, I could talk about it till the cows came home,' laughed Andrew, 'to *anybody*—although there aren't many that I know who are really very interested. In fact,' he added, with a sudden, rather childlike, rather forlorn honesty, 'there aren't *any* that I know who are *at all* interested. Unfortunately I just don't seem to move in those circles.'

He hesitated.

'So be careful what you may unleash!'

'Oh, I was never in my life careful about anything like that,' boasted Daisy.

So by and large he had a lovely evening—certainly among

161

the twenty best of his existence, he considered afterwards.

He wouldn't have been able to enumerate the other nineteen.

33

And there were other almost equally good evenings—one about every eight weeks to begin with, soon becoming one about every six, one about every four. Marsha grew more and more accustomed to Andrew having to work late or spending the odd evening alone with his mother or with some schoolfriend whom he had happened to bump into in the street. (He never brought them home.) Once he spent a whole evening at a Turkish bath, hoping to sweat out a rotten cold which she hadn't even noticed that he had. She grew increasingly accustomed to these periodic absences of his; and finally didn't even care very much—just accepted his announcement with a casual shrug. By then she had a baby, of course, which (despite making her very depressed at the start) had soon introduced into her life the sort of interest which Andrew had hoped and foreseen that it would. When young Andrew was a few months old she dismissed the nanny and insisted on looking after him herself without one—although it was Mary, naturally, who saw to the bulk of his washing and even prepared most of his meals. But it was Marsha who fed him and changed his nappy and played games with him and bathed him and took him out for walks; and talked to him, talked to him endlessly—even when he slept. Young Andrew seemed to provide the kind of companionship that old Andrew so often didn't; and this, of course, brought benefits to all—or, anyway, that was how Andrew was inclined to put it to himself. For one thing, Marsha no longer bombarded him either with questions or with recitals. (Once, indeed, he had even said: 'Got a bit of news for you today! Walter was an hour and twenty minutes late this morning!' 'Oh—and what happened?' 'The Colonel seemed to swallow his excuse.' 'Well, I should think so, too—would you like to come and say goodnight to Andy?' He even had to tell her the nature of the excuse, without her asking; and after all this time Marsha's reaction to his little anecdote, when he had only hoped to give her pleasure, was somewhat anti-climatic, to say the least.) For another thing—more importantly, perhaps—she was obviously kept busy enough not to have suspicions. At times he was surprised, even mildly contemptuous, at the fact that she suspected nothing; but it was undeniably convenient—especially when he knew that he was taking risks. She *might* have phoned the office, and Miss Eggling *might* unwittingly have made some fateful revelation; Mater might equally unknowingly have disclosed intrigue; there was always the chance that somebody—a schoolfriend of Marsha's, maybe—might have seen him out with Daisy; the pitfalls were innumerable. But for a young man who in the past had so often prided himself on never running risks, on coolly and responsibly taking into account all eventualities and then trying to provide for them, there was now a certain charm in the thought of his own reckless-ness; the very knowledge that he was walking on a tightrope unexpectedly added piquancy and excitement—perhaps the greatest excitement of the whole affair. And he came gradual-ly to realize that he had never known himself before. (Other-wise, of course, upon leaving the frying pan he would have taken much better care where he landed.) Now he did know himself and he was not displeased with what he found. Allied to his sense of moral obligation and to his utter reliability, to the self-evident maturity contained in his policy of always planning for the morrow, was his awareness that he was also a man who enjoyed living dangerously; who liked to spice his plain and wholesome diet with adventure.

A bit of a romantic. A bit of an unknown quantity.

A bit of a gay dog.

It was especially satisfying because Marsha had several times in the past called him stuffy. The charge had wounded him a little: because he was fair-minded, he had wondered if it might contain an element of justice. Now at last he knew the answer.

And if either of them was stuffy—dull—a bore—it was certainly not him. No, my dear Marsha; it was certainly not him! He would have liked to bring her attention to one of her own favourite maxims: people who live in glass houses . . .

For Daisy didn't find him dull. And Daisy was the arbiter, the enemy, of dullness—and damnably well qualified to be so! Why, her interests weren't at all those of an ordinary woman—she was rare and splendid—even if he did have to admit that from time to time she might inhabit a house which had one or two panes of glass in it, somewhere in its construction. But in her case, of course, this only added to her charm: such occasional glimpses of glass reminded you that she'd got femininity!

In fact, he had never seen the *actual* house where she lived—or, at any rate, not from the inside. (She had a middle-floor flat in Swiss Cottage, more or less self-contained, although she had to share a bathroom with the couple who lived upstairs.) She was very old fashioned about inviting him in, and he respected her for that, despite the fact that it would have saved him quite a lot of expense if she could sometimes have cooked them dinner. But apart from the moral aspect of the thing (no, very much tied up with it) Daisy's landlord himself lived on the ground floor, and even as it was, it seemed, was trying to find good reason to get rid of her—simply because she always insisted on her rights and attempted to make him carry out repairs which he would have been happier ducking out of. The man was a villain; a profiteer; he was nothing but a fat idiot, to use Daisy's own terminology. And how like Daisy—how magnificently like Daisy—he felt proud of her—to snap and worry about his ankles and give him not one moment's rest until he'd been hounded and harried and threatened into carrying out his duties. The oaf! The bully! Andrew would have liked to come and punch him on the jaw; but was forced to admit that this might provide the wretch with the very lever he sought as a means of effecting Daisy's removal.

In a way this situation suited Andrew. As he knew, of

course, he had a remarkably strong sexual drive—what bit of a gay dog hadn't?—but he felt glad that he'd never descended to the level of somebody like Haley, who not only boasted over lunch about the sheer number of his love affairs but always seemed on the very brink of actually divulging *details*, guaranteed both to put Andrew off his dish of vegetables *and* to produce prolonged and nervous indigestion. Haley disgusted him—and so did Johnson, who was still very much shackled to his wife but endlessly self-pitying and unable either to find any partial solution to his troubles (like Haley) or else to show that he could take them squarely on the chin. ('For heaven's sake, have the courage of a man!' Andrew had several times wanted to tell him—and unless he could soon find some excuse to avoid their company altogether at lunchtimes, one of these days he might very well actually bring himself to do it!) Moreover, even forgetting the likes of Haley, he was glad to have it proved that he was master of his appetites. Despite great temptation he hadn't, in the last resort, been at all unfaithful to Marsha. He had preserved the sanctity of marriage.

So he never set foot in Daisy's house. They always went to a restaurant—though usually to a very much cheaper one than Simpson's. Eventually, in fact, they found their own special place, where after a while they came to be quite well known and to be greeted with friendliness: 'Good evening, sir, good evening, madam—we thought we'd soon be seeing you again!' It was in an alleyway close to Regent Street and was run by an Italian couple who were fat and sombre-clothed (especially the wife) but always very jolly; 'real people', as Daisy termed them, bestowing her second or third best accolade. Also, it was reasonable and the food was good, 'though madly fattening,' said Daisy, who never put on an ounce (the opposite of Marsha, who was constantly fussing about her weight), and they could afford to wash it down with plenty of Chianti. So they would usually sit for three or four hours—in their favourite corner booth, whenever possible —with either the Chianti still in front of them on the red-checked tablecloth, after they had finished eating, or else a large pot of coffee, and Daisy would lean back comfortably against the wooden partition and smoke cigarette after cigarette with the charming air of a catlike Venetian contessa —it was an *Italian* restaurant, he said, and he had quickly discarded her image of a Parisian Left-Bank intellectual. (Marsha, when she smoked, could nearly always be relied on to inhale the wrong way at least once in the course of a cigarette, and furthermore was singularly inept with a holder, and consequently often had nicotine upon her fingers. He himself seldom smoked a cigarette at all—people had told him that a pipe was a great deal healthier; incidentally, Daisy claimed, a pipe gave him a very manly jaw, provided sex appeal *and* dependability, and he supposed that it didn't cost very much to humour her.) Normally she got through at least twenty in an evening and it gave him simple pleasure, when she suddenly discovered that she had somehow reached the end of her packet, casually to produce a new one which he would lay on the table without comment. Yet she didn't even need to open it: he also carried his gold cigarette case on these occasions, always freshly filled. 'My word, what an escort!' she would say, or 'How you do think of everything!' or 'What made you guess that they'd be necessary?' *And* they're Abdullah, she would add, or De Reske Minor—or whatever might be the case; you always pick my favourite! She was such a strange mixture of someone who needed to be cared for and someone who could well look after herself (she forgot her cigarettes, but she could make plucky little fists at landlords) —of someone who had good, firm, even forceful opinions of her own and yet who nevertheless looked up to him for enlightenment and guidance (for what she herself had once termed 'the solidly masculine viewpoint'); he couldn't help but think her fascinating.

Specifically, the guidance she needed was often to do with business; she'd asked him to be her stockbroker. She had only a small amount of money but she trusted him to do his best with it. (Miracle worker, she sometimes called him.) He imagined that it had come from her parents—from her father anyway—more than from her husband; although he'd never, of course, had the indelicacy to ask. She had never once mentioned Henry; Andrew didn't mention him, either—not to her. Reading between the lines of what Marsha said about him (though Marsha had apparently been fond of him), dismissing out of hand all Florence's effusions, and relying mainly on his own instincts, objectively inspired by snapshots in the family album, he privately thought that Henry must have belonged to the species of 'poor fish'. Physically, at any rate, he had been a very poor specimen; Andrew had looked with some contempt at a photograph taken on the beach at Scarborough in 1929, when Henry had been much the same age as he himself was now. And even facially—well, not to put too fine a point on it, Andrew had thought that it was almost an effeminate face, weak and indeterminate; a 'pretty' face—rather similar to Marsha's, as a matter of fact—not quite decent on any man. No. He would never have said a thing to Daisy about it, obviously—nor yet to Marsha —but he rather suspected that Henry hadn't been a wholly decent type. Indeed, it wasn't a word which he'd apply to him at all. As 'decent' was the one adjective which, more than any other, Andrew hoped that people would use about himself after his death, he was aware that he was passing quite a judgement on this unknown brother-in-law of his. But the very fact that Daisy never mentioned him pointed up the soundness of that judgement. He believed that, short though it was, Daisy had probably led a brute of a life with him. Poor little thing! She was so small! *Brave* little thing! Whenever he thought about it, he wanted to enfold her in his arms and (despite everything) to let her feel the solid comfort of his strength. For—after all—what was the point of strength, if not to share it?

But though this form of guidance obviously involved discussing his work to some extent—and when he left the office that was precisely the last thing he normally wished for—he found that, strangely, he didn't at all mind talking shop with Daisy. It wasn't merely her quick grasp of things; or even the look of admiration so discernible in her gaze; it was more the impression of wistfulness she conveyed. If only she had been a man, she seemed to be saying, *she* would have chosen the Stock Exchange, too. What other job was so requisite of flair, imagination and boldness—a refusal just to play it safe and ape the common herd? He read this in her eyes, and it made him feel, if only temporarily, that after all, perhaps, he had a fine career. She could make things come alive, could Daisy. She could conjure up excitement.

They had a lot to talk about, too, in the way of politics; here guidance and enlightenment, of course, converged. There was, for instance, the death of the king and the accession of . . . himself! 'If ever his brother should try to depose him before the coronation,' cried Daisy, rather confusingly, 'we know exactly whom we could send to take his place! You'll have to swim the moat, of course; I'm sure that you *can* swim!' Well, certainly he could! Her confidence was not misplaced. 'Farewell to the sower of wild oats!' sighed Daisy. 'Hail to the sweet and sobered king!' That was in January. In March there came the German repudiation of the Locarno Treaty, and the return of its armed forces to the Rhineland. (There were a few harsh words spoken about Erica at this point.) In May, Italian troops occupied Addis Ababa—but Daisy and Andrew hadn't yet found their small Italian restaurant, and by the time that they had, in mid-July, the Civil War in Spain provided, politically, the chief topic of conversation. Their evening outings had now become monthly ones (if he'd been forced to give them up Andrew didn't know what he'd have done); but, even so, they'd only been to their new and regular meeting place five times when the newspapers and wireless finally announced the awful news: that King Edward, *their* Edward, was to abdicate, after a reign of merely three hundred and twenty-five days. As it happened, they met for the sixth time at that small restaurant exactly two days later—12th December—the day that his brother George had ascended the throne in his stead.

'But I take it I won't have to swim the moat now?'

It was a miscalculation. Although not solely on account of this remark, Daisy grew as outraged as she'd been when considering the fate of Joan of Arc. Perhaps she would have liked to see another female put there in the French girl's place.

'Poor fool! Poor sad fool! Been caught by a designing woman! Of course, one always knew that he would come to a sticky end. The signs were always there—for anyone able to read them, at least! Yes, I must say, I'm not at all surprised.'

Yet she was bitterly disappointed. Andrew was amazed that anyone could feel things—things which didn't directly concern themselves—half so vehemently as she did. In a way he was envious; he thought she might have the makings of a saint; yet it was all so very remote from his own experience —this fury and this passion—that he wasn't at all sure that, personally, he would have wanted such involvement; not in practice.

'Married *twice* before! I should have thought that that was warning enough for anyone—even the biggest fool out!'

Andrew felt a sneaking sympathy for him (which was utterly lacking in passion): that anyone could have fallen so swiftly from grace! So radical a change of circumstance!

'*And* American. And what's that silly pagan name that she rejoices in?—Wallis. *Wallis?* Does she think that she's a photographer's shop or something? Besides—she's not even good-looking. I can't imagine what he thinks he sees in her. She's bewitched him, that's what.'

From the way she almost glared at him across the table he could believe that he must indeed bear a strong resemblance to the king. The ex-king.

'Of course, one can see what *she* was after, all right. Very nice to be the Queen of England, I daresay. Very nice to get your hands on the crown jewels, stuff them quickly into all your pockets! Well, she jolly well underestimated *us*, didn't she—the people of Britain? The silly twat! How *like* an American! She probably thought she could bring her friends over here—if she has any, that is, which I very much doubt—and turn them all into dukes and earls and prime ministers and what not; the sheer and utter gall of it! Besides, she's old enough to be his mother.'

'Hardly!'

'Well, she looks it, anyway—which amounts to much the same thing. But what's the matter with you tonight? You're very quiet upon the subject. The cat got your tongue?' She gave a sharp laugh; a none too pleasant one. This was certainly a different Daisy.

169

He shrugged. 'No, obviously, I think it's just as appalling as you do.'

'Giving up a whole country—just for *love!*' She parodied and made it sound a rather filthy word.

'Unquestionably, he's a cad.'

And yet he *couldn't* help feeling slightly sorry for him —weak, caddish, a shirker of duty though the fellow had turned out to be. He wouldn't have expected to feel sorry for him. But it was all so final somehow—turning your back on a throne and a position of such authority and a people who had always worshipped you. And turning your back for what? —something that Haley (or was it Johnson?) had claimed couldn't last for more than eighteen months at the outside, that head-over-heels in love sensation, couldn't last whether or not you had to go to the office each day, to a job that you hated each day, or catch your bus each day and sit next to people with *colds* or *pimples* or *b.o.* each day; it was scientifically established, he had said. (Yes—Johnson.) So you'd be bound to regret it, bound to look back—or sideways —and wonder, in a particular moment of boredom and frustration, what you might have been doing *now* if your life had gone along that other road which everyone, yourself included probably, had always assumed that it would go along . . .

'Yet the thing is,' he said to Daisy, 'surely you have to feel sorry for someone who's made such a mess of his life? Especially when he's someone who began with so very much?' Andrew didn't add that somehow he found the whole thing strangely comforting. He even felt quite grateful to the man; although he would never have put it into those words —or realized that gratitude was what in fact he did feel. It just wouldn't have been decent.

And another thing which he didn't acknowledge, either to her or to himself, was his odd feeling of melancholy in the face of a love so deep and all-consuming that it could blind you to everything about you—everything—except your need to be with the beloved, to hold her and be held by her, no matter what the cost.

Even though it didn't last for more than eighteen

months . . . Even though this might be a scientifically proven fact . . .

He tried to imagine what it would be like, at the moment, to be poor Edward Windsor.

He tried to imagine what it would be like to be Wallis Simpson.

He saw Daisy looking at him and started slightly, with an unformulated sense of guilt. Perhaps he even blushed. 'But in a way,' he said defiantly, 'you do have to feel a little sorry for him.'

To his surprise, after a further pause, Daisy agreed with him.

'Yes, I know, dear.'

So evidently the ex-king wasn't quite beyond the pale. He hadn't joined company with her mother yet or her landlord, or Florence or Erica. Andrew was beginning to realize, with some amusement, what a very crowded territory it was, beyond the pale.

'And in a way, too, you could say . . .' (he felt emboldened by his small success) '. . . you could say that it was even quite romantic. Giving up everything for love!' Too late, he remembered that she herself had just used that same phrase; remembered the tone of voice in which she'd done so.

But again he was surprised by her.

'Yes, you're right, dear,' she said. 'Up to a point. Of course, you nearly always are. It would be a drab world if there wasn't any place in it to house the unexpected.'

He was delighted. It appeared that he even had authority over her most cantankerous mood. He felt like King Canute —well, King Canute on a successful day. (Of course, he had influence over Marsha, too, but *everybody* had influence over Marsha, so there wasn't a lot of true glory in that. Besides —Marsha would have sulked for ages.) Daisy was now all laughter and frivolity. 'Romance!' she said. She could even bring herself to use his own word, which he thought a second ago would have stuck in her craw, in company with 'lerve'. '*Romance!* Yes, I shall have to sing you something from *The Desert Song!*' (Well, he didn't care for that so much. Why did every woman he met feel this terrible need to *sing* to him?)

But she was only joking, thank God. When he gave Daisy her Christmas present—a copy of *Gone With The Wind*, the same thing that he'd bought for Marsha—he felt better pleased with her than ever.

'Awful bosh!' Daisy was later to designate it. (Though not to him; she *just* managed to save herself in time.)

But the minute Marsha finished it, she started to read it again.

34

1937 came . . . and more than half went. But now not only did they have their monthly evenings out: three times, as well, they went to the races. They saw the Derby; they spent a day at Ascot; they even went so far as Doncaster. (They had lunch on the train; *that* was an occasion.) But after the Derby he had to be careful and avoid the big races, in case someone at the office twigged. As it was, when he telephoned on Derby Day, Miss Eggling cried out skittishly, 'Now, Mr Poynton. Are you perfectly *sure* that you're reclining on a bed of sickness?' (They were all aware of his interest—though none of them took it very seriously, except when they wanted, they said, to have 'a bit of a flutter' and came sidling over for advice.) And he'd had to use a neighbour's telephone, as well, to evade the telltale rattle of the dropping coin; it was all quite risky.

But it was worth it. Apart from anything else, he won more than twenty pounds on a rank outsider at Doncaster. When they returned to King's Cross he bought Daisy a hat—though she herself had backed the same horse—a hat of the type that she couldn't just throw into a handbag (but would quite possibly never wear, other than when she was out with him!—well, never mind, he felt reckless; they both did!) Arriving home he gave Marsha three pounds for herself (he told her that he'd telephoned a bookmaker) and a guinea to put into the baby's post office account the following day.

The winner had been called Daisy's Lot; when Marsha asked its name, he saw no reason to try and hide it from her, though he let her think the horse had been a favourite and said he'd won six pounds upon it. (At that, she wanted to give him one of her own pounds back and, when he wouldn't take it, seemed disproportionately moved by his generosity; he felt both gratified and ashamed.)

'But Daisy's Lot,' she said, after all this. 'It must be meant as a reminder.'

'What of?'

'How like a man! You ask what of when you know that I've been meaning to ring Daisy for months and months and months! But the trouble is—as I also keep telling you!—I've got so bad a conscience now, that I just go on putting it off.'

'Yet she could as easily ring you. If she wanted.'

'Yes, she could. And especially, of course, since she hasn't yet seen Andy.' (She had stopped saying, 'congratulated us or sent him a present.') 'But the fact remains that we did say we'd invite her to spend another weekend here. And *that*, believe it or not, was getting on for two whole years ago!' At the moment—as it usually was, indeed—her *guilt* was uppermost, not her resentment.

'Well, I get the feeling that she's not much interested in babies,' he answered, rather lamely. But fortunately—since there was a perceptible note of approval in his voice and since, anyway, he suddenly thought that he'd made the same comment before (yes, he had—and hadn't she challenged him on it, fairly sharply?)—Marsha didn't hear.

'Sorry?'

'Nothing,' he murmured.

So she repeated *her* remark that had been uttered simultaneously with his. 'But I was just saying, too, that I've always thought of the Stormonts as being a very united sort of family.'

'Well, yes, maybe.' He spoke a little drily. 'But Daisy's something of an outcast.'

'I don't see why. What has she done?' She added with a little smile: 'After all—poor thing—she could hardly help old Henry's dying.'

Andrew thought: that's not what your mother tells herself, *I'll* be bound. But he kept this notion secret. He always enjoyed hearing Marsha talk about Daisy and he had no wish to introduce red herrings. For the same reason he didn't say: Well, she married him—those are good enough grounds in your mother's eyes to make an outcast of anyone. And he himself smiled a little, at the formulation of two such worthy thoughts for a member of the FRIL Society—though he certainly couldn't share the first of these with Daisy.

'Perhaps I'll write to her,' said Marsha.

'Well, just don't invite her for another weekend.'

'But I really don't understand this—it's the second time you've said it. I thought we all enjoyed ourselves; I truly did think so. I believed you'd found someone to play chess with.'

He shrugged. 'It was all right. Yes, then—whatever you think best.'

It wasn't of course that he was afraid of taking risks: this reluctance to have Daisy in the house. (Although you never quite knew with Daisy *what* she might be going to say next!) It was more that he liked to keep the different areas of his life distinct from one another—it was messy to let them overlap. (He had hesitated a very long time, for instance, before finally buying them both a copy of the same book.) And it would also be extremely difficult to have to sit there in the same room with her and keep remembering that he had met her only twice before—and that one of those occasions had merely been at his wedding! Artificial; wholly unnatural. Besides, he thought, rather vaguely—it would hardly be the act of a gentleman.

'Why don't you just have her to tea with you one after-noon? During the week, I mean. Or even to lunch. If that would salve your conscience.'

'Yes, I might do that.'

Then, suddenly, she giggled; and it occurred to him that recently he hadn't heard a great deal of that giggle. Perhaps, after all, she *was* growing up a little.

'Or why don't I just let sleeping dogs lie? The thing is—not counting that weekend—we never seemed to get on so awfully well together, Daisy and I. And, as you say, if she

174

wanted to keep in touch, it would be just as easy for her to do it as for me . . . Easier, really,' she added hazily, thinking that Daisy had no baby to keep her busy all the time.

'Exactly,' he said.

'It's funny, though. At one time I thought that she would *always* be turning up, be quite impossible to get rid of . . . We sometimes don't know people as well as we think we do, do we? Erica used to say she was a parasite.'

'Then that was exceedingly unkind and exceedingly un-fair.'

'Yes, I suppose that it may have been.'

He had spoken in a fairly controlled manner. But suddenly he said:

'Just who the hell does Erica think she is?'

Marsha stared at him in astonishment. He was aware that he had almost shouted. He was aware now that he was turning red. 'After all,' he mumbled, on his way out of the room, *'you're* always talking about people who live in glass houses . . . Isn't that so?'

'But Andrew.' She followed him out of the doorway; stood at the foot of the stairs. 'Erica isn't a parasite.'

'No, no. Perhaps she isn't. I don't know. But at least Daisy isn't foreign; she's living in her own country; if you see what I mean.' He didn't see at all clearly what he meant himself. He wasn't sure that he meant anything.

'Well, I don't. I thought that you liked Erica.'

'Oh, she's all right. She just . . . shouldn't make judge-ments, that's all. About her own people if she likes; not about the English.'

He went in the bathroom and locked the door; Marsha was perfectly capable of following him in there. He sluiced cold water over his face, and wished he hadn't said any of the things he had said. He was stupid to have come up here; he could have made a far easier escape into the cloakroom downstairs.

But when he came down he made a simple apology, said he couldn't imagine what had got into him, and that, yes, of course, he did like Erica; and then everything was all right again. Marsha wasn't very used to receiving apologies, and what largely accounted for this one was the lingering taste of his delightful day and his reluctance to spoil it all with bad behaviour. Marsha was almost as grateful for this unexpectedly contrite spirit as she had been earlier for his equally unexpected openhandedness. For the time being, she had quite forgotten Daisy.

Yet, later on, she said: 'You know, I really don't like losing touch with people. Not with anyone. A Christmas card just isn't enough, is it?'

She turned over then and settled for sleep, and Andrew decided that, next time he spoke to Daisy, he should perhaps rescind his suggestion—made right at the beginning—that she should stay away from Marsha.

35

'I hate,' she said, 'to be a damp squib, but I think I'd better go home, dear, if you don't mind.' It was barely eight o'clock. Her plate of cannelloni sat on the table more or less untasted; even the wine in her glass was just as he had poured it.

'But you can't,' he said. 'You know how I always look forward to seeing you! These evenings are my lifeline!' He was aware that he sounded peevish, but he couldn't help it. He loathed it when people got ill. If you had things planned it was always so . . . so irritatingly inconvenient. 'Are you sure that you're not just hungry?' he asked. 'Sometimes you simply don't realize it, but if you only tried to force a little food down you . . .'

'I should throw it up all over the floor!'

Oh, well, of course, if she was going to take that line about it . . . ! That put an entirely different complexion on the matter. He couldn't stand vulgarity.

'I'll go and settle up,' he told her, tonelessly. What he really couldn't understand was why, if she'd felt well enough to come and meet him in the first place and to let him order the meal . . . Then he remembered that, ironically, for the first time ever, he had ordered it before she came, since she could always be relied upon to be so punctual—unlike the vast majority of women—and it had seemed to him an efficient, thoughtful and rather masterful thing to do. And he knew how she enjoyed the cannelloni.

'I'm afraid the lady isn't feeling very well; we've got to leave. What do I owe you? We've hardly touched our meal.'

Mr Bertorelli appeared all wide-eyed sympathy and concern; he ran back into the kitchen to tell his wife and she, too, came and fussed. Oh, the poor signora, the poor signora —would she like to lie down, did she need some aspirin, was there anything that they could do? Typically, the one thing that they could have done . . . they didn't. Andrew's opinion of Italians fell. Surely the wine at least could be re-used, *would* be re-used . . . Even the cannelloni . . . It would just about serve them right, he thought, if he and Daisy never set foot in there again.

(And in fact they never did.)

'Are you fit to drive—or should I see if I can find a taxi and take you home in that?'

'I'll try to drive,' said Daisy. 'No, of *course* I can drive.'

He said—rapidly experiencing, to some extent, a return of his affection—'Well, if we do have to abandon the car half-way, at least it will be that much easier for you to pick it up, won't it, as soon as you feel better?'

They reached Swiss Cottage without incident, although she gave small groans from time to time, which—at the beginning—seemed to freeze him to the leather of his seat.

He left her with relief now, rather than with disappointment, but with renewed admiration for her spirit and a nagging conviction that he himself had acted less than admirably. He would ring her tomorrow, he decided—send flowers through Interflora—try to make it up to her; although he very much hoped that she didn't realize there was anything to make up for. She probably didn't: she was so incredibly independent and plucky; just as plucky as a man—more so in many cases. (He thought of Johnson.) As he walked home she rose higher in his esteem, with almost every footstep that increased the distance between them. All the bad luck that dogged her! She'd had a rotten childhood (thinking of her, he entirely forgot that he had, too); she'd had a rotten marriage (he forgot his own rotten marriage); she struggled valiantly to earn a rather meagre living through bringing physical relief to those who suffered but, even then, could never fully find the peace she merited, because her only sanctuary was turned into a place of torment by a brutish, bullying landlord. And yet she always came up smiling. She was . . .

And then it suddenly struck him.

She was . . .

. . . marvellous.

And he realized that he loved her.

Indeed, this was a suspicion he'd had many times before, but it had never quite developed into certainty, as it did on this occasion; and the further he went, the better he knew it. His step became sprightly, joyous. He tapped with his umbrella on the pavement, in time to a lively tune inside his head—he didn't know its name. When he reached a phone-box he suddenly considered ringing her, and had in fact even gone into the kiosk, grinning with anticipation, and started to pick through his money before it occurred to him that of course by now she'd probably be in bed—and maybe already asleep—he hoped so, anyway—and that his startling, splendid revelation could wait, impatient though he naturally was, until tomorrow. Tomorrow he would ring her. Tomorrow he would let her know that she was loved—important—that she wasn't all alone in the world, not any more. No, never, never again, an outcast. She would be the one he thought of whenever he had to put his arms around Marsha. (Well, even up to now, she often had been.) It wasn't very much, he knew, but it was something. It would be marvellous to realize you were loved—even at a distance—by somebody strong and protective and able to take care of things.

Surely? Yes, it must be marvellous.

And they would have their times together. Somehow—he would arrange it—they would have more time together than they did now.

'You need never again feel that you're unwanted!' He almost sang it, as he left the box, even if it *was* only inside his head.

'My *amour fou!*' French unquestionably seemed the right language, and though he didn't really know a lot of it, this was a phrase which swam into his mind and was undoubtedly applicable.

Amour, amour, amour. Not for nothing was it called the language of romance. *Mon amour fou!* He wondered what it meant.

(He would even ask Marsha! She had been to a finishing school in Switzerland.)

A parasite, indeed! A parasite! The utter *gall!*

He glanced at his watch—was gladdened by the contour of his strong, fine wrist. (What a wonderful world it undeniably was!) Laughingly, he had to look again to find out what the time was. Just a little after nine. He was amazed that so much could have happened in so very short a time! His whole life had changed.

He could even forgive the Italians.

He could even forgive the Germans.

With the tip of his umbrella, he tried to spear an empty crisp bag that had blown into his front garden—and felt like a failed park attendant, as he finally had to stoop to pick up the recalcitrant bit of rubbish. (Well, one couldn't expect success in absolutely *every* department!) He opened the front door, and called out, 'Marsha!'

It would be a nice surprise for her that he was early. He felt full of smiling magnanimity for everyone.

36

There was a silence inside the house, which—perhaps only because he hadn't expected it—had a strange, unnatural quality about it. Could Marsha still be at her mother's—and the baby with her, of course—because he had just remembered that this was Mary's weekly night off? And yet the hall light was on. (To discourage burglars?) But somehow it didn't *feel* like an empty house. 'Marsha!' he called again, and went to the base of the staircase—the drawing-room door was open and he could see that the room was unlit, unoccupied.

'Yes, Andrew. Coming! I'm coming.' It hardly sounded like her voice.

What was the matter with her? Had she gone to lie down with a headache and just been woken up, startled, out of a heavy doze?

Then why hadn't she simply called out, 'I'm up here, darling; I'm lying down?' But on the other hand, it occurred to him, she knew that he got impatient with her headaches —he felt instantly repentant.

Daisy unwell? Marsha unwell? It was a good job that at least one of the three of them was fit—and able to shoulder (and with some buoyancy, too) the exigencies of life!

But there *was* something wrong. His senses felt alert —receptive. He started up the narrow staircase, two stairs at a time, and was nearly half-way up when Marsha came out of the bedroom in her négligé, holding it around her to cover up her nakedness.

'I'm just out of the bath, Andy! You are home early! Sorry if I look a mess—I haven't done my hair.'

Even before she'd finished speaking, she had reached the topmost stair and was coming down.

'But this is so nice, darling! I'll pour you a drink. Have you had your supper?'

She seemed almost out of breath—but there wasn't the flush on her skin that she normally had following a bath (he hadn't realized he was so observant) and her face was still made up; though not, he thought, quite freshly. Besides, in place of the usual smell of talcum . . . He continued briskly up the staircase and pushed past her without ceremony. His umbrella briefly caught at, snagged, her négligé.

'Andrew! No!' But it was hardly louder than a whisper.

In less than three seconds he had got to the bedroom door.

The man was just pulling on his jacket and one of his shirt-ends still hung above his trouser-top.

At the same time, he was pushing his carelessly stockinged feet into his shoes, though as the two of them confronted each other all such frenzied movement halted.

There was a silence as total as there had been when he'd come into the house. As total—and as stunned.

He noticed that the man had hair on the backs of his hands—dark hair.

'Well?' he said.

'I'm awfully sorry,' said the man.

If he hit him, Andrew thought, he would probably fall against the dressing-table; there'd be broken glass and powder and creams and unguents all over the place—the carpet would be ruined. He didn't know whether to hit him or not; the man was smaller than he was, and also older —thirty-five?—forty?—but neither so much smaller nor so much older that there'd be any disgrace in his doing so. And it was the accepted code, wasn't it, to hit a man who'd just been making love to your wife? But now that such an unexpected thing had happened he felt almost as awkward as he did angry. Inadequate.

And he suddenly became aware of his umbrella. He threw it, threateningly, on to the rumpled bed—*his* bed. Simultaneously he realized that in his other hand he was still holding the empty crisp bag. He let it drop to the floor with an expression of distaste.

'Well?' he demanded again.

'Peter was just going,' said Marsha shakily, from her position near the door. 'Weren't you, Peter? Oh—' She added, without much expression: 'Peter Makins—Andrew Poynton.' Her mother would have been so proud of her.

'No. Peter was *not* just going,' corrected Andrew. 'Or, rather, he's now decided that he can stay a little longer, after all. Isn't that right?'

'Yes—indeed,' said the man. He then finished pulling on his jacket, as though suddenly released from a state of suspended animation.

'I think that he ought to go,' said Marsha. 'We may as well

try to be civilized about this.' Her voice was gaining in confidence.

The man indicated that he would like to sit down on the edge of the bed, the more easily to tie up his shoelaces. 'May I?' he asked.

'Good God!' said Andrew. 'You lie in it and on it and all over it, *with* my wife, and now you ask permission to sit on it, without her!'

It wasn't clear, from this, whether permission had, or had not, been granted. After a second or two, the man assumed that it had. They watched him rearrange one of his socks.

Although he'd been faintly pleased with his last retort, Andrew now felt somehow at a disadvantage. The word 'cuckold' came into his mind and the memory of a Ben Travers farce which he had recently taken Marsha to see at the Aldwych. His feeling of inadequacy—of the unfairness of it all—was compounded a moment later when he happened to glance up and catch sight of himself in the wardrobe mirror, unobstructed now by the hangdog form of his wife's lover. He saw his own hunched and menacing posture; he saw the unrelenting scowl upon his face; he saw the bowler hat upon his head.

He twitched it off, disgustedly, and flung that down as well, alongside the umbrella. The whole scene suddenly appeared to acquire a distancing, an unreal quality. He felt he wasn't quite a part of it.

'Would anybody like a cup of tea?' asked Marsha.

Unexpectedly, he was aware that he'd have loved a cup of tea. Hot and sweet and strong. He was aware, furthermore, that he was even hungry; that he had eaten hardly anything since lunch.

But he was damned if he was going to admit to any of this, damned if he was going to give her the opportunity of escaping to the kitchen, damned if the three of them were going to sit around politely, sipping tea, being 'civilized'. If there was one thing he knew clearly, it was this: that because he himself was about to suffer he would make them suffer with him.

'May I ask just how long this has been going on?' he

enquired coldly. He knew it sounded like a cliché, but at least it had some dignity and that was the chief thing to aim for at the moment. While he held on to his dignity he was in control of the situation.

'Since about half past seven,' said Marsha.

'This is only the third time,' the man told him.

'Only!'

'And—of course—it won't occur again. It was my fault, by the way. Your wife wasn't to blame.'

'Oh, quite the little gentleman!' he sneered.

'I wasn't trying to be gentlemanly.'

'No, you can say that again!' The shout was more effective than the sneer; or certainly it gave more solid satisfaction. 'And, my God, you're right! It won't occur again! Not ever!'

'Andrew!' cautioned Marsha, nervously. But he shook off her restraining hand with impatience.

'Do you think that—after what *you've* done—I haven't even got the right to raise my voice? Because—let me just tell you, woman—I don't care what the neighbours are going to think—they can think what they damned well like—and in all probability it won't be half as bad as you deserve!'

(And when I was pregnant, she thought bitterly, he didn't even want them to know that *he* had been to bed with me—let alone anybody else!) But, at this point, the baby began to cry.

'There!' said Marsha. 'I tried to stop you. And now see what you've done.'

It wasn't just reproach; it was anger. Good God! She hadn't even the intelligence to realize that the last thing *she* had any right to feel was anger.

'Stay where you are!' he ordered.

'No—I must go to him. He must be very frightened.'

And she went—she snatched her arm away, and went. Enraged, he was going to follow and *enforce* obedience; but suddenly, even in the midst of such a fury, he understood the foolishness of trying to do it, the utter pointlessness.

At once he felt deprived of impetus. Defeated. Depression started to crawl in.

He recognized the signs; and did his best to push it from him.

'Get out!' he said to the man—who'd now stood up again and was quietly putting on his tie. 'Get out, before I throw you down the stairs!'

As he came past him Makins paused—and said once more: 'I'm sorry. I'm sorry about all of this,' and shrugged, helplessly.

But Andrew made a fist and the man flinched. On the landing Makins hesitated, glanced towards the room where the baby's cries were coming from, decided to say nothing, and ran quickly down the stairs. At the bottom he looked up briefly, met Andrew's implacable gaze—and left the house without another word. Andrew stayed where he was for a minute, motionless, staring down at the closed door. Then he made his way, reluctantly, towards the lighted nursery.

37

The room was very small. Marsha sat on the only chair, between the window and the cot, her son's face turned against her breast, his cries now sounding rather weaker. She was rhythmically patting his back with one hand and making small cooing sounds of comfort, while her own tears provided a mute accompaniment to his. Andrew leant against the doorjamb and watched them.

'If you mean to say anything,' warned Marsha, 'please remember to keep your voice down.'

He continued silent.

'It probably doesn't matter, but he was the only one who really cared for me,' she said listlessly, after a long pause.

'What?' He genuinely hadn't heard her.

This time she managed to speak more clearly. 'I said that he was the only one who really cared for me.'

'*That* poor apology for a man? That filthy little whiner?'

'*You* haven't cared about me for ages now.'

'I don't know why you should say that.'

'I say it just because it's true. I think you've got a girlfriend that you see. I don't believe in all those evenings at the office.'

'How dare you accuse me of that? How dare you? Oh, just a frantic attempt, I suppose, to try and get yourself out of trouble! How despicable!'

'Anyway, I don't much care any more,' she said. 'Just don't shout, that's all.'

'You can check with the office—why don't you? Phone them and find out! In fact, I shall insist you do so!'

There was a pause. She went on comforting the baby.

He said: 'Was that the man who picked you up in Cullen's?'

'What?'

'Or the man, perhaps, that *you* picked up in Cullen's.' But she couldn't remember what he was referring to. Peter was somebody she had sat next to at the pictures on one occasion. Afterwards, they had recognized one another in Lyons; Eunice had had to dash off and Marsha had been buying rollmops. Marsha had smiled; Peter had asked if she'd enjoyed the film. They had gone upstairs to share a pot of tea and a plate of buttered toast. Andrew believed her—but what difference did it make? The Coventry Street Corner House over the toast, or Cullen's over the biscuit tins? There had probably been a long line of men; and all with black hair on the backs of their hands.

'*Have* there been others?'

'No, of course not!'

One of her tears must suddenly have dropped on to the baby's head, because he instantly stopped his own crying and gazed up at her; with vast surprise and patent interest.

'You're practically naked,' said Andrew, at last, in a tone of deep disgust.

She didn't answer. She tried to pull her négligé closer about her.

'And do you realize that you haven't even washed your hands?' The violent shudder that he gave was no mere piece of theatre. 'You slut! Why, just looking at you makes me feel that *I've* got to go and wash mine!'

And then, abruptly, Andrew turned and left—but not for

his ablutions. He walked straight down the stairs and out of the front door. Its slam provided another point of interest for the baby.

38

He strode blindly forwards; with resolution, yes, but almost without thought. He had no idea what time it was when he reached the house where Daisy lived. (It was, in fact, about eleven; he had stopped, very briefly, at a pub, to down two double whiskies.) He pressed his thumb against her bell and kept it there: five seconds, ten seconds, twenty. And then he stepped back—as far as the front gate—and waited for a light to show; he had forgotten that behind drawn curtains a light quite often didn't.

'Come on, come on, come *on*!' he cried impatiently. He had forgotten, too, that Daisy was unwell.

But one thing he had not forgotten was the landlord. Let Mr Queechy give a hint of trouble—just one *hint* of trouble, mind—and Andrew would knock him down senseless; would take great pleasure in so doing. He very much regretted, now, that he had not struck Makins; Makins, who had deserved to be castrated, let alone struck, but who had just slunk away like a miserable coward without a taste of punishment. He had meant to get revenge; had been deflected, or deflated. Now he needed to get revenge on someone; it hardly mattered whom. He *needed* to use his fists.

At last, a window was thrown up.

'Who is it? What do you want?'

'Daisy, it's me. Andrew. I love you.'

'What?'

'I—love—you!' He felt like Romeo. (He had never read the play, of course, but everyone knew about that balcony scene.) Or he felt like some hotblooded South American suitor serenading his sweetheart with a guitar. He thought that Daisy ought to have a rose between her teeth, or else behind her ear. She ought to have some castanets and be gaily stamping her feet, swaying to the rhythm of a—what? —flamenco. He recognized, even through his whisky, that she wasn't quite the type just to stand there, all patiently adoring, a demure and blushing Juliet, unemployed, for the duration of a serenade.

'What on earth's the matter with you? This is no time to play the giddy goat! Don't you know how *late* it is?'

'All I know, thank God, is that it isn't *too* late!'

'Are you drunk?'

'No!'

'Well, anyway. I was extremely sick when I got home tonight—violently—three times!' She stated this fact with relish, but, having extracted the last ounce of resonance from it, seemed about to draw her head in.

'Daisy, I must talk to you! It's imperative! Something has happened.'

'Then ring me tomorrow.' She added: 'But not too early!'

'It can't wait.'

'It will have to. You just don't understand. I feel at death's door.'

'So do I,' he said, urgently. 'Oh, so do I. I feel at death's door, too.'

And at that moment, as if on cue, as if between them they had used the proper incantation, the door, not death's door (just another door along the way), seemed magically to open.

'What in hell's name is going on out here?'

'Nothing,' called out Daisy. 'Nothing that need concern you, at any rate. This gentleman is just going.' She went on more appeasingly, but still with coldness, 'I'm sorry that you should have been disturbed. It isn't all that late, however.'

'No, it isn't!' said Andrew. 'It isn't all that late at all!' So *this* was the dreaded landlord, was it?

Suddenly the Latin lover had disappeared; the vengeful pugilist was once more in his place, clenching his fists and flexing his shoulders; he even did a little footwork.

'And I'll tell you something else. This gentleman is not just going. No, not at all. Not one bit of it. This gentleman,

187

Daisy, is coming up to tell you something else.' He had the strangest feeling that he'd said that once before, in this same situation or in one very similar. The night seemed full of echoes.

But just then the landlord stepped out from the dimly lit shadows of the hall to stand on the path beside him; and Andrew had a shock which caused him to forget all echoes. Although Daisy had often spoken of the man as a fat idiot, Andrew had somehow always assumed that she was speaking figuratively. Therefore he was totally unprepared for the twenty-odd-stone fat idiot whom he now had hastily to back away from, to avoid feeling hemmed in and stalk-like and gaspingly short of air.

Andrew unclenched his fists.

He had to terminate his fancy footwork.

'Clear off!' said the man, succinctly. 'Scram!' It seemed the ultimate humiliation—not only of his evening but also of his life. And Andrew turned away, moaning.

Yet even as he did so something in him suddenly reared up. Perhaps it was the alcohol, perhaps it was the largely dormant quality that would later get him mentioned in dispatches —would get him decorated, too. Whatever it was, anyhow, it provided a brand of defiance that balked hotly at defeat. And it made him cunning; nimble; reckless. He dodged around the great dressing-gowned lump of Daisy's landlord. He ran into the hallway. He quickly slammed the door. And he'd even shot home its two thick, heavy bolts before his enemy had fully realized what was happening. 'Where did he go?' requested Daisy.

In less than a minute, though, she knew—and not only by means of her landlord's violent imprecations. There was a knocking at her own door to complement the prolonged and vehement battering at the one downstairs. All the bells in the house rang in hideous orchestration. 'I shall call the police! I shall call the police! I am going to call the police!' She'd nodded and had the quiet good sense to close her window, but this refrain rose clearly, above all the rest of the cacophony.

Despite everything—Daisy laughed.

Lights all over the neighbourhood were being switched on; or curtains drawn back. Doors and windows opened everywhere.

'By God, *now* you've done it!' said Daisy, not without a hint of admiration, as she opened her own door.

'I don't care,' he said. 'Daisy, I'm leaving Marsha. I love you. I love you. And I want to marry you.'

For long seconds she just stood and stared at him. Her mouth was partly open and she hadn't wiped her make-up off before retiring—it was smeared and stale-looking and reminded him of Marsha earlier on. But there was more excuse, of course, in Daisy's case. She looked smaller than she usually did, more in need of protection than ever, in her striped pyjamas and her woollen dressing-gown, and with her small, bare feet protruding. He just stared back at her—with clenched lips—and waited. 'Well, either I'm batty or you are!' she said, finally. 'But I suppose that you'd better come in.' The door opened straight into her over-furnished sitting-room, every surface cluttered with photographs and bric-a-brac. He noticed, with a feeling of some shock, that this was also the room in which she slept: her divan bed was set into one corner, on the opposite side to the fireplace. Her clothes were strewn, unattractively, reprehensibly, over the back of a chair. He saw, before he quickly looked away, that her brassière and bloomers were right on the top of the pile; and that one of her stockings had fallen to the floor.

It wasn't quite the romantic setting he had visualized. It wasn't quite the romantic setting of his first proposal.

They stood inside the doorway.

'Now, then,' she said, 'what's all this nonsense?'

'I'm leaving Marsha.'

'Why?'

'We don't get on.'

'What happened then?'

'Happened?'

'You said something had happened.'

'Oh. I meant I'd finally made up my mind. That's all. I'd been thinking about it, of course, for a long while.'

'And for that you woke me up—and the whole of Swiss Cottage, too?'

He frowned; as though he found some difficulty in following her argument.

'This decision—has it anything to do with me?'

'Well, naturally it has. It has everything to do with you. I said just now I loved you. Didn't you *hear* me?'

Up till this point her questions had been brisk—even businesslike—performed against the unceasing staccato of hammerings and rings. But then she paused; she looked pleased; despite her previously unsmiling face—a face that still wasn't quite smiling—he could now see the satisfaction which she must have been feeling from the start; and which, after all, was unconcealable. It came into her eyes slowly but it grew there and it gradually filled them.

And this was all that he needed to find out; the rest could wait until tomorrow. He'd had his answer and the answer was the one he'd known it would be. (Well, *almost* known it would be.) He said, 'Are the couple who live upstairs at home?'

To Daisy it obviously seemed an irrelevant question, and he was sorry to see that it disturbed that look of satisfaction.

'Them? How should I know? I can't say that I listen out for them.'

But he'd been waiting for the sound of footsteps on the stairs; *theirs* going down, the landlord's coming up.

Daisy added sharply (and rather fatuously; people in love said very silly things!): 'In any case—you can't possibly sleep there tonight.'

'Well, naturally not! I was only wondering if anyone was going to open up the door to him. That's all.'

'Oh, yes, of course. I realized that.'

'While he's waiting round the front, don't you see, perhaps *I* can slip out round the back?'

'And what do you think's going to happen to me, as a result of all this?' The question very much surprised him.

'But what does it matter? We'll soon be getting married.'

'Ha!'

'What do you mean—ha?'

'Have you *any* idea at all how long a divorce would take?' Not just her tone—her very look—was back to the businesslike; he couldn't understand it. He thought as long as he lived he would never get to know a woman's mind. But he had to keep reminding himself: she wasn't well: she wasn't quite herself tonight.

'I shall start proceedings first thing in the morning,' he said. 'I might, you know . . . I might be able to find grounds.'

'And have you told Marsha that you intend to divorce her?'

'Not yet. Not in so many words.'

'Well, you don't take *many* people into your confidence, do you, Ague-Cheek?' The word of affection reassured him, even if her tone was still ironic. And then, as though it had only needed this little reassurance, he suddenly saw why she was angry with him.

'You think my presence here will compromise you? Of course! I've been a fool. I'll go downstairs at once and open the front door. They'll see then that there wouldn't even have been time . . . I'm sorry,' he repeated, 'yes, I've been a fool.'

'Yes,' said Daisy. 'Yes, you have.'

His hand was already on the doorknob. 'I would suggest,' she added, 'that when you get home you don't say anything about all this to Marsha.'

'But I shan't be going home. I plan to spend the night at a hotel.'

'I only hope that you haven't mentioned me in any way already—incriminatingly?'

'No, of course not. Did you think that I would?'

'I think that you must have had a row.'

'A small one,' he conceded.

'Go home and patch it up.'

'What!'

'I said go home and patch it up.'

'But you can't believe *that*'s why I've come here and asked you to marry me—just because Marsha and I have had a row?' He suddenly realized what the problem was: he saw she was being noble.

She confirmed it with her next words.

'I am not—I am *not*—a home wrecker!'

'No, of course you aren't. This would have happened, no matter what. I've told you: we're not suited. *You're* much more my type of woman. You're the one I want to be with.' Again, that gleam of satisfaction; even of delight; almost, it occurred to him, of *victory*! (But hadn't he known it all along—that she had wanted him?) 'In fact, Daisy, there's nothing that I wouldn't do for you.'

'Go home, then.'

'Yes. Your reputation.' He smiled. 'I shall spend the night in a hotel—tomorrow, I'll see about some lodgings.'

'I don't care what you do tomorrow. I'd advise you, though, just to go home. It's cheaper.'

'Well, it's certainly true that we've got to think about our future, Daisy. But—'

'Not *our* future,' she said crisply. 'And, Andrew, you must never come back here again—never. Don't even try to ring me. I want your promise.'

'What?'

'Besides, I shan't be here much longer—it's intolerable.' She gave one of those special snorts that he had never heard from anybody else—and would have found peculiarly unpleasant if he'd done so. In *her* it had always seemed quite charming. 'And after tonight I don't suppose I'll really have the choice, anyhow. One week, I'd say, at the outside.'

His hand was still on the doorknob. He glanced at it with some surprise, as though he couldn't understand even the workings of his own parts any more.

'I know that you won't be here much longer. We must obviously find you somewhere else. Temporarily. But if I'm not going to be allowed even to telephone you . . .' He shook his head, in bewilderment. 'I wouldn't want you ringing *me*, you see, too often. Miss Eggling would soon gossip.'

'Ague-Cheek, you don't understand,' she said. (How very right she was!) For the first time since they'd been talking in that room she reached out and made physical contact: the back of her hand fleetingly touched his cheek. 'You're a nice boy, Andrew, but I just don't love you. And I don't want ever to see you again—at least not for a long time, a year or two, maybe. For I repeat: I don't want to be a marriage-breaker. That was never my intention.'

'You don't love me?' he said.

'No.'

'But do you really mean that? You're not just making a martyr of yourself?'

'Me—a martyr! Sweet heaven forbid!' She even shuddered.

'I see.'

'But you really are a pleasant boy,' she repeated. 'We've had a lot of fun together—a lot of good times. A lot of nice dinners and a lot of intelligent conversations. You make a very good listener—did you know that? And an excellent guide on the racecourse, naturally.'

'But that's all? That's absolutely all?'

She pursed her lips and nodded.

'I see,' he said again.

They were silent for a while. It didn't occur to either of them that all the battering at the front door had apparently come to an end; that there was no more ringing of the bell.

'What will you do now, then?' he asked.

'Now?'

'I mean—if you can't stay on here? Or if you don't want to, anyway?' He had a vague, tenacious hope that if he simply went on talking she might change her mind—or that, somehow, he had merely got hold of the wrong end of the stick and that things would clarify themselves, reality would return, the fog would lift. In just a minute or so. She would suddenly break down, or weaken; explain her silly, well-intentioned motives. All would be well again.

If not—what could he do?

He couldn't just leave.

He had been so happy in the street. So very happy.

'Oh,' she said casually, 'there's some woman I know. I may go and share her flat. It's been on the cards for years now.'

'Where?'

'Fortune Green Road.'

'Quite close, then.' That somehow made it better. No. Why? 'You never mentioned it,' he said.

'I couldn't make up my mind. Not until now. Yet all this may have helped me do so. She's an older woman than I am, you see—much older. But she's a good woman . . . sane and steady and . . . serene. I feel that she might even have a beneficial influence upon me!' Daisy chuckled; that chuckle hadn't been so much in evidence this evening. 'You may believe it or not,' she allowed.

'It sounds a little dull to me.'

'Then in that case it *must* be dull!' she said. 'Very dull indeed. No, that was just my little joke, dear. Despite all that I've said—she isn't dull. Perhaps that's the truly incredible thing about her.'

'Ah.'

'The Italians have a word for it. I can't remember what, though.'

He nodded. There didn't seem a lot more left to say. He saw that, after all, there could be little point in hanging on.

'Well, then . . .' he mumbled.

It was like having to say goodbye to someone at a mainline station: that unbearable moment of parting, a parting that could last for ever. He remembered their jubilant, suspense-filled day at Doncaster—it seemed so very long ago: the way they'd lunched upon the train, played chess while they were coming home, drunk to the man who'd backed into her car the previous afternoon.

'Well, then . . .' she replied. She stood suddenly on tiptoe and kissed him on the cheek.

It was a brief kiss, but affectionate.

The only other time she'd done that was at the instant Daisy's Lot had passed the winning post. Then she'd thrown her arms around him, too. In retrospect, it seemed the consummation of their love.

No—only of his, of course. Only of his.

'Well, Daisy . . .'

They heard the slamming of car doors, almost without realizing they'd done so. But a minute afterwards the knocking on the main door was suddenly and dreadfully renewed. 'This is the police. I command you to open up, in the name of the Law!' The voice came through a megaphone.

'Quick!' said Daisy. 'Quick! Downstairs! Go out the back way—*I*'ll open up in front!'

'No!'

'Yes, yes! . . . Coming! Coming!' she called, while they were yet a long way from the bottom.

'But what will you say to them? What are you going to do?'

'Oh, never mind about that!' she whispered back, impatient. 'I'll think of something. *Coming*! Just go!' It was she who unlocked the back door, at the end of the tiled passageway; she who pushed him out of it into the dark. 'Coming, *coming*!' she'd called once more, across her shoulder, to cover the sound of the key being turned.

He'd have thought that they'd have heard it, anyway; he fully expected to step out into tensed and waiting arms —arms uniformed blue or dressing-gowned; or he expected *at least* to hear the thud of running feet. And he wouldn't have cared about it either, not in the slightest, he told himself. But as soon as he realized that there *wasn't* anybody waiting in ambush, that everyone was in fact still round the front of the house, his instinct to get away reasserted itself. From one back garden he climbed the fence into another; and from that into the one beyond—a further barking dog added his own chaotic mite to the disturbance. But even as he ran he was conscious of the sound of voices raised in altercation—and, amongst them, he was sure that he could make out Daisy's. He hoped, fervently, that she wasn't heaping up more troubles for herself. He had caught the note of fierceness.

During the next few days, indeed, he wanted and wanted to phone her. Several times, in fact, he had his hand on the receiver. But he couldn't do it. He just couldn't. He felt bound by that silly promise she had wanted him to give.

He scanned the local paper; yet to his frustration—and relief—found nothing there.

He never saw Daisy again. (One of his colleagues took over her business—which very soon afterwards, anyway, she placed in the hands of another firm.) He never knew what inspired extravagances she might have uttered that night to Mr Queechy or the police.

In later years, however, he used to hear about her from his

sons—uncharitably from one, with laughing tolerance from the other. And once, when he and Janet had called in briefly at Malcolm's (deliberately picking a time when he'd thought that Phoebe might be absent), the telephone rang and Malcolm shouted from the kitchen asking him to answer it. It was Daisy; he recognized her voice immediately. When Malcolm himself came to the phone Andrew whispered to him not to reveal his identity ('I met her once, you know,' he said to Janet; 'my God, how she could talk!') but he felt a little shaken, none the less, forcibly reminded of the miraculous escape he'd had that night some forty years before: not merely from the arms of the Law and the possibility of unimaginable embarrassment in court; nor from the arms of Daisy's obese and unattractive landlord; but more particularly, of course, from the arms of Daisy herself, who'd been bent on acquiring a luckless successor to poor old Henry—and who might, so *very* nearly, have cleverly managed to catch one, at that!

Part Five

39

It was a Saturday. Marsha was having lunch at Notting Hill but had left a cold meal in the fridge for her brother and sister-in-law, and some chicken soup in a saucepan on the stove. 'So all you've got to do is warm it up, very carefully,' she said to Dan. 'Only turn the heat on low, and remember to stir, so that the soup won't catch. I've put a lid on top of the saucepan, and the wooden spoon is lying across the lid. You may need a little salt and pepper. I rather wish I wasn't going.'

On departure she reminded him again. 'Whatever you do, Dan, check that you've turned the stove off properly. I haven't left a line of make-up, have I? Now, are you sure that I can trust you to do all that? . . . I hope it isn't going to rain.'

Daisy sat down in a peevish mood.

'Well, you'd suppose they could have asked us *all*. That would have been the *obvious* thing. The *decent* thing. But some people wouldn't know the decent thing if it jumped right out and spat at them!'

'Oh, I think I'm really quite thankful, old girl, to be stopping here at home.'

'Yes, you may be, dear, but I most certainly am not! After all, you were born a Stormont; *I* wasn't—praise the Lord!'

'Even poor Marsha didn't much want to go,' smiled Dan. 'Especially, of course, since she had to get our own meal ready first. It wasn't worth it, she said. But she could hardly get out of it this time: it must be a good five years since she last went. More.'

'You don't surprise me in the least,' said Daisy. 'How typical, how utterly predictable! One simply wouldn't credit it.'

She glared at what was set in front of her.

'In fact,' she said, 'I can't think why they didn't leave Marsha out of it altogether. Why didn't they just ask *me* and have done with it? Then we'd all have been satisfied. Except for one thing.'

'What?' Dan had the feeling that she might have said something that unfortunately required an answer.

'What? Well, that I don't suppose I'd have gone—naturally! There's only one way, in my view, to teach people like that not to be so casual; turn down all their invitations. What *is* this muck?' she asked. It was tinned macedoine, mixed up with salad cream. 'Is it vomit?'

'Omelette?'

Dan would *not* get himself a hearing-aid! No more would Marsha. They were both of them so stubborn: they had her own example, didn't they? In Dan's case, though, it was as much laziness as obstinacy. He would shrug equably and say, 'Oh, Daisy, what will any of it matter a hundred years from now?' It made her so angry. 'It's today that counts; today —today—today! What sort of fun do you suppose it is for me?' Yet even so Dan was marginally less irritating than his sister. At least *he* owned up to his defect. Sometimes.

'Talk about the deaf leading the deaf!' (You could! *They'd* never hear you!) 'I asked if this were vomit,' she enunciated, with almost poetic diction.

'Oh. One rather hopes it isn't,' answered Dan.

'Ah—*hope*,' she murmured, cryptically. 'Well, hope makes a good breakfast; but it's not much cop as a supper. Didn't you ever hear that proverb?' She didn't say where lunch fitted in, exactly. "All hope abandon, ye who enter here!" That one's particularly apt. Did Dante come from Hendon? Or—perhaps I should say—did Dante come *to* Hendon? Alderton Crescent. Number ten.'

She smiled at him, sweetly.

'Daisy's Inferno.'

Dan laughed. He said, 'Do you know, I was just thinking that it must be years and years since you and I last had a meal together in this room without Marsha?'

'Why? Have we ever?'

'No—perhaps not.' He relapsed into his normal silence, a shell-like cave of peace and gentle murmurings, from which he'd poke out his head amiably from time to time in the

sanguine yet unfounded expectation that he would not encounter difficulties.

Daisy gave a sigh. She said: 'There's always been Marsha.
There always will be Marsha. There always will be about to
be Marsha. For ever and ever, amen! And heaven help the lot
of us! But quite right, too—and very nice—and that's what *I*
say, dear, don't you?' It had seemed, for a moment, that Dan
might be on the point of raising some objection. 'Her
brother's keeper. Her sister-in-law's keeper. Tell me, dear,
did she always—as a child—show an exceptional interest in
going to the zoo?'

'But this can't be the first time that you've eaten in this
room without Marsha? Did you and Henry never dine here?
Oh, you must have.'

'I did come here once—I do seem vaguely to recall—there
was a cake, some sort of cake—but no, dear, I don't think
that I mean Henry—' she chuckled—'now why on earth,'
she said, 'should I remember that?'

40

'Then, Daisy, you must come to lunch!' Dan cried. 'Ah,
there's a box just over there.'

But his number was engaged.

He tried at a second box half-way up the hill and again
when they arrived at the Hampstead underground. 'I think
that she must be talking to Mother!' he laughed, uncertainly.

The uncertainty was not to do with whom Erica might or
might not be talking to; it was because he was now worrying
in case he'd acted somewhat rashly. People often told him he
was apt to be impulsive.

At Hendon Central there seemed little point in ringing up a
fourth time: the house was just five minutes from the station.
When they got there, Erica had finished on the telephone.

'Darling,' Dan called. 'Darling, we have a visitor!' He

attempted to radiate optimism, confidence and cheer: good-will toward all men and a reminder that it was the duty of God-fearing people everywhere to try to carry out the Ten Commandments. 'Darling, you'll never guess whom I've just met—Daisy, of all people! I've invited her to lunch! I hope we can do something with the loaves and fishes—I'm sure we can, knowing you!'

'Yes, the Germans always make excellent *hausfraus*,' nodded Daisy, encouragingly; 'at least, one's always heard they do—no matter what their *other* deficiencies may be,' she added, with a tactful lowering of the voice.

Erica arrived just then from the kitchen. She had heard Dan's cry and seemed to have responded to its silent plea. She kissed Daisy on both cheeks and held her warmly by the hand.

'Daisy, how marvellous to see you! How well you look! Marsha wasn't exaggerating, was she?'

'I don't know, dear. You'd better tell me what she said. Fit to take my place in the chair of honour at the chimpanzees' tea-party, no doubt!'

Dan laughed. 'My word, Daisy, it's not like you to fish. Or is it?'

It was the question mark which annoyed his sister-in-law. 'Oh, I do believe you've got fish on the brain!' she said, tartly. 'Or else it's water!'

'Why?' Dan felt quite bewildered by this change in mood.

'Well, you started off with *loaves* and fishes. And, as if that wasn't quite enough . . .' (Daisy's attempt at self-justification floundered) '. . . well, I shouldn't think poor Erica would even understand the reference! And why should she, indeed?'

'Oh, but I do understand the reference, Daisy; though it's more a question of ham and salad this particular lunchtime —and *that* will surely stretch. I hope that you like ham and salad?'

'Ham?'

'Yes, the Sabbath, you see. We're strictly kosher on a Saturday.'

But as it was now after one and the meal was ready and

Erica obviously hadn't enough *savoir-faire* to offer any guest a drink, they went straight in and took their seats at the table—some silly ass of a maid having already set another place.

'Speaking of such things,' said Daisy, aware of the visitor's obligation to entertain, 'do you ever encounter any anti-Semitism, dear? I mean, here in the backwaters, away from Oswald Mosley and that fearful gang.'

'No, not a great deal, Daisy, not in its more overt forms, anyway.'

'Well, I'm very pleased to hear it. I can't stand people who harbour that sort of prejudice, can you? Besides, dear, you don't look at all Jewish, you know.' Daisy smiled at her, reassuringly.

Then she put her head on one side and dispassionately considered Erica's appearance: fair hair (rather lifeless—not at all like Andrew's—clearly, she should brush it more!), too large a chin, heavy features that would quickly turn to fat—pretty enough in their way, she supposed, at least for the time being, if you didn't mind insipidity, or, not to put too fine a point on it, vacuity; an almost Junoesque figure that made poor Dan look even more of a spindleshanks than he already did; and—particularly unfortunate, of course—an aura of unEnglishness which somehow gave you the feeling that she wore traditional peasant costume and had her hair coiled up in braids and yodelled.

'Well, do I pass?' asked Erica, with a smile.

'Oh, yes! Through the eye of a needle! Every time!' Daisy cried.

She wondered, though, if she'd now gone slightly too far and speedily offset this small uncertainty by making a circle between her thumb and forefinger to indicate unqualified approval.

Erica laughed; amazed to hear such fulsomeness coming from such a quarter; and conscientiously added a new English idiom to her already large collection.

Similarly, Dan supposed the phrase to be an example of the latest slang; and secretly smiled at all his earlier apprehensions.

Yet, to get back on to safer ground, Daisy said again: 'No, I just can't abide the prejudices of narrow-minded people. I daresay I'm a bit off my noddle in that respect. But I truly can't.'

'Attagirl!' applauded Dan. 'That's our Daisy!' He discovered that he spoke with pride.

His sister-in-law felt gratified, but wanted to show that she could handle praise maturely—not letting it destroy impartiality.

'Mind you, dear, at the same time you do have to be fair and admit that in some neighbourhoods (take this one, for instance) while not condoning it, of course, you can better understand how people occasionally do feel twinges of anti-Semitism.'

'You can?' said Erica.

'Oh, yes. My word, you've only got to spend ten minutes in the Golders Green Road on a busy morning, being jostled and elbowed and all but trampled down by hoards of screeching, fur-clad matrons, most of them nearly bent double by the weight of diamond rings and noses and nail polish—particularly, I mean, Erica, when you're just a little shrimp like me, not a great big hulking thing like you, who can no doubt give every bit as good as you get—and make no mistake about it, dear, I admire it if you can, indeed I do—well, where was I now? . . . yes, *that*'s the kind of thing that really gets the Jews a bad name, if anything does.'

There was a silence. She gradually sensed that her audience was not, perhaps, one hundred per cent behind her.

'Not that I mean, you understand, that anything actually *does*. Necessarily. Or ought to. No.'

She suddenly spied a still better avenue of escape.

'Of course, I'm just telling you the type of thing so many people *say*; and, personally, I find it quite disgusting. Hit a man when he's down—give a dog a bad name—you know I don't approve of that! No. It's my own belief that it's not the fact of their *Jewishness* which is to blame. How could it be? I've met some extremely nice Jewish people in my time. No. I ascribe such vulgarity not to their being Jewish, these women, but to their being foreign. Continental. That's the truth of it. At most, you could say, if you really wanted to, that it's just a rather unfortunate combination.'

She nodded and smiled at the two of them, continued with her meal, and felt that she had handled that quite neatly.

There was a pause.

'This ham is *very* good,' she said, to keep the party going. (Honestly! Why did it all devolve on her?)

'I'm not at all ashamed of being Jewish,' said Erica, her pale face now looking slightly flushed. 'Nor of my being continental.'

'Good God, of course you're not,' said Dan.

Ye gods and little fishes! How could you possibly be expected to keep track of everything? Daisy had been so preoccupied with the fact that Erica was Jewish that she had momentarily forgotten that Erica was also foreign. And why did people have to be so sensitive? Daisy sighed; and, though feeling somewhat weary, girded herself anew.

'Why, there's absolutely *nothing* to be ashamed of,' she asseverated, just as emphatically as Dan. 'After all, you've only got to remember that Christ himself was a Jew.' Except that he'd succeeded in getting out of it, she added to herself, as one would naturally expect of somebody whose common sense and wisdom could never have been equalled. 'And although you couldn't say he was exactly continental—well, he certainly wasn't English, either; except perhaps in character, but that's a slightly different point.'

'I think I'd like to change the subject,' said Erica.

The trouble was, of course, Daisy had forgotten just how *common* Erica was. She herself couldn't have cared less about class, yet at the same time you had to remember it was always much more difficult to assess the background of a foreigner. Dan, if she remembered rightly, had met her in Wolverhampton—or was it Birkenhead, or maybe Wales?—working in a café. A café! And probably, too, a café for workmen—though there was nothing wrong with that, of course; workmen were the salt of the earth. Or could be. But in Hamburg—or Hanover or wherever it was—she'd been a shopgirl; and the two facts taken together were surely quite indicative. Not to mention this perfectly *awful* wallpaper, whose only merit was that it was slightly less dreadful than the curtains. And only someone essentially common would have taken her up on her silly little gaffe just now. Anyone with breeding would have laughed and spoken of the weather.

My word, but how she pitied Dan!

Well, that was what happened, of course, when your parents put you into hairnets!

'*Was* it Wolverhampton?'

It turned out, eventually, to have been Colchester.

It turned out, also, to have been a rather foolish enquiry. She had neither expected nor wanted a eulogy of Dan.

'Dear Daisy.' In reviewing the circumstances of that meeting in Colchester and in having a chance to speak of them again (at quite interminable length!) Erica appeared to have forgotten every difference of opinion. 'Did you know that Dan offered to marry me even without loving me? He felt sorry for me—that was all. This poor little refugee girl, he thought, a long way from her home. Wasn't that marvellous of him?'

Daisy didn't say anything. She stared down with great concentration at her plate; busied herself with the frenzied cutting of a piece of ham. She didn't think that it was marvellous of him. Rank stupidity is what *she* would have called it. Soft, sentimental tushery.

'You see, I just didn't realize,' mumbled Dan, who had himself been looking more at his plate than at anything else during the last five minutes or so, 'what an incredible prize I had managed to get hold of.'

'Aaahhh . . . ,' said Erica, gazing at her husband very lovingly across the table and reaching out to take his hand. If their guest was now to bring up her lunch, Daisy reflected, they would have only themselves to blame. Besides—it couldn't be anything but an improvement to the carpet.

It was not merely ill-bred. It was so lacking in all tact and sensitivity. And even if it could have been forgiven (which it certainly couldn't) in a pair of newlyweds, Dan and Erica had now been married for some three years. It was peculiarly revolting.

What where they trying to hide?

(Well, at least Andrew never carried on like that, she told herself gratefully. Daisy was seldom so fond of people as when she was away from them—with one or two quite notable exceptions. It was an attitude, as a matter of fact, that was usually reciprocal.)

Mercifully, however, before either Erica or Dan could reverently inform her that they had never exchanged a single cross word, the door was opened and dessert brought in. Well, there was nothing, unfortunately, so very merciful about *that*: stewed apples and custard. (No matter how you might try to call it *compote* and *crème anglaise*!) 'I'm afraid it's only very plain, Daisy. Had I known, of course . . .'

Dan then jumped up and fetched the cake, which he had left in its box on the hall table. 'A present for you, darling. Many happy returns!'

'Oh, is it your birthday?' Daisy asked, grudgingly.

'No, no. He always says that, whenever he gives me a present. And I do have many happy returns, don't I, Liebling? Many, many, many.'

'Yes, I see,' said Daisy. She then compressed her lips.

'Well, I think I don't have to open it to guess what's inside,' said Erica. 'And now I know just how you spent your morning. Bend down a moment.' (And she kissed his cheek.) 'Now, Daisy, I can tell you that you're certainly in for a big treat.'

'Oh, I thought that I'd just had it.'

They assumed this was a compliment to the ham and salad. Dan explained to Erica the story of the cake.

'Then Daisy shall have an especially large piece, to make up. And a piece to take home with her as well.'

Daisy interpreted this as confirmation of the hint that she was not required to stay to tea. The hint itself had been Dan's production of the cake so that it might be eaten for dessert.

Had she realized that this would be the case she would never have come so far out of her way merely for lunch. She seldom bothered with lunch, anyhow.

If people didn't like your company she much preferred them to tell you so, straightforwardly. But of course she'd never felt at home among the Stormonts. They'd never made her welcome. And all that she had wanted was to give some hope to Henry. Scarcely so very sinful an ambition, she would have thought. But, of course, in this life you were judged solely on your achievements, not on your intentions. They had always sought to push her out, right from the start.

'It's good, Daisy, isn't it?'

'Yes, quite good, thank you. I'll eat it, shall I, and then go?'

'Go?' exclaimed Erica. 'What, already?'

'I'd forgotten that I have an extra patient whom I have to see this afternoon.'

'Oh, what a shame!' said Dan. 'Our own little Miss Nightingale! But at least you'll stay and have some coffee?'

'Yes. I think that I can wait for coffee.' She was glad to see they had a modicum of conscience. 'But at the same time—I would rather, Dan, that you didn't try to compare me to Miss Nightingale.'

'The Lady with the Lamp?'

'I know who Miss Nightingale is.'

'I thought it was a compliment.'

'I can assure you,' said Daisy, 'I take it as very little compliment to be compared to a liar, a bully, a hypocrite, a busybody, an egoist, a betrayer . . .' She stopped, a trifle out of breath. 'And several other things, beside.'

Dan stared at her.

'I don't believe it!'

'Why not? It's true!'

'That wasn't how Kay Francis played her.'

Then, suddenly, Erica began to laugh. 'And this—an Englishwoman, too!' she exclaimed.

Daisy's eyes moved over to her, coldly.

'I'm sorry,' said Erica. 'Excuse me. I really know so little about her—whether she was good or bad or in between. I imagined she was good,' she added, with an evident attempt at appeasement. But she seemed almost under strain.

'The extent of people's ignorance,' said Daisy, 'never ceases to amaze me—hers, of course, included. I've met people who actually knew her. They tell me she'd say anything to put herself in a good light; but from all accounts she knew as little about her own motives as . . . well, as most other people know about them, I should say.'

'Poor woman,' said Erica.

'What do you mean—poor woman?'

'I mean that . . . all this seems a little . . . vitriolic. And she isn't here to defend herself. I don't understand why you should want to blacken her. After all, despite whatever failings she may have had, she must have done a lot of good as well.'

'Vitriolic, nothing! *I* don't want to blacken her. Why should I? But at the same time I just can't stand hypocrisy. And I feel nothing but scorn for so-called educated people who don't *know* themselves. "From the gods comes the saying: Know thyself." Well, that's perfectly true—as *I* can vouch for—and shall, I hope, until my dying day! "Know then thyself, presume not God to scan, The proper study of mankind is man." ' She glared at them both, and dared them to refute it.

Erica laughed again, nervously. 'Well, we certainly seem to have covered a lot of ground. I'm not quite certain how we got here.'

'It's funny,' said Daisy, 'that *her* first name was Florence, too. It's only just struck me.'

'Why? What do you mean by that?' asked Erica.

'Oh, nothing. Nothing at all.' Daisy looked round the upper part of the room and made a faint whistling noise through her teeth.

'The name of the film,' said Dan, '—I've been trying to remember—the name of that film was *The White Angel*. Isn't that right, darling?'

'It must be some reference to Dan's mother, I think.'

'Ha!' said Daisy.

'Oh, that reminds me,' said Dan. 'I tried to phone you a couple of times before we got here—but the number was engaged. We thought you were probably speaking to Mother. Has she got over the after-effects of the 'flu?'

The maid came in. 'Would you like your coffee served in here, madam, or in the drawing-room?'

'Oh, in the drawing-room, I think,' said Dan. 'Don't you, Erica?'

They moved into the drawing-room. Dan was glad of the diversion. 'These days a lot of people are calling it the lounge. I vote that we should do that, too. Think of the time that it would save! Lounge. Lounge. Lounge.'

'What did you mean by saying it's funny that *her* first name was Florence too?'

'Oh, Erica! For heaven's sake!' exclaimed Dan.

'Well, you may not care, Dan, but I certainly do! And I would have expected some support, indeed, when it happens to be your own mother who is being discussed. Nothing quite so general, now, as Jews *en masse* . . . Or quite so indefensible, perhaps, as Germans *en masse* . . .' Erica's hand shook slightly, as she poured the coffee.

'I really don't remember *what* I meant,' said Daisy. 'Nothing at all, most probably, if I know me. It's simply not important. It's just occurred to me: the last time that I sat in this room it was with Henry.'

'Was it really?' said Dan, looking at Erica in a very troubled fashion. 'Poor old Henry.'

She allowed them to think a little about that.

'What do you do with yourselves in the evenings?' she asked at last.

'Oh, nothing very much,' he answered.

'No. I didn't suppose that you did. Somehow.'

Conversation was desultory.

'Marsha's a very lively girl, isn't she? I'm a great admirer of Marsha's. You couldn't wish for anybody prettier.'

'Yes, Marsha's a grand girl, of course.'

'Not one of the most heavily endowed, up here,' (and Daisy tapped her forehead) 'but then tell me—these days, who is? Nobody that I know; anybody that you do? Oh, at the club perhaps, but that's a rather different kettle of fish. And at least Marsha doesn't *pretend*. That's one of the most refreshing things about her. She's always honest enough to be *herself*. Still . . . I do rather wonder sometimes if she'll manage to hold Andrew. Better not tell her that I ever said so!'

'But why, Daisy? Why on *earth*? I'm sure they're very happy.'

'Are you? Well, they certainly started on that infant fast enough, if that's any indication. They'll probably breed like rabbits supposing that they do stay together. When are *you* going to set your mind to it?' she said to Erica.

Erica didn't answer.

'But whatever made you say it?' persisted Dan, quickly. 'About Andrew and Marsha?'

'Only that he strikes me as having something more between the eyes than she has; and I've often thought that it must be pure hell for a man with any sort of spark in him to be chained to an uninteresting woman. Beauty isn't everything, you know. I'm willing to bet that it's not. Although I daresay that it helps,' she added, after a pause, looking at Erica reflectively.

Erica said, 'Can this be a record? You have insulted me; you have insulted your mother-in-law; you have insulted your sister-in-law. I don't know whether you've insulted Dan—but what is worse—far, far worse—you have actually managed to belittle him in front of me. I would have thought that was impossible. I believe that I should offer my congratulation.'

With which, she left the room.

There was a silence.

'That woman,' said Daisy, 'is paranoid. You should have her treated.' She looked at Dan—then raised her eyes, expressively, towards the ceiling. 'Well, *I* thought we were enjoying a pleasant hour or so of small talk. Didn't you?'

'Just something about a cake,' repeated Daisy. 'I can't remember any more than that, though. Can you, dear?'

'No,' said Dan, 'I can't. Would it have been a chocolate cake? Erica was always awfully fond of that.' He smiled; then gave a sigh.

'Penny for them,' offered Daisy.

'Oh, nothing. Nothing at all, really. I was only thinking: happy days . . .'

41

While dusting the shelves one day, taking the books down and giving them a bang—a job she normally tackled like an automaton, thinking about something else—Marsha came across a copy of a classic that she'd years before lent to Erica and then entirely forgotten. She gazed a moment at the soft, maroon, composition-leather cover; she opened it and looked at the flyleaf. Four-and-sixpence written in pencil, in figures just decipherable. At the bottom lefthand corner, a tiny printed sticker: 'The Delphian Arts, 6 Wilton Court, Marina, Bexhill-on-Sea'. She nearly cried.

She stood there and put the book to her nostrils and smelt the binding.

She had known how it would smell.

Twenty-five years ago, more or less. A quarter of a century. '55 had it been, or '56? August. The sun slanting into the small bookshop; the owner—a nice man with grey hair and kind eyes—talking about the excellent tea you got at Susan Throssil's; herself deliberating between a Pearl Buck, a Philip Gibbs and a Frances Parkinson Keyes.

'Here! Read something decent for a change!'

Malcolm had held up *Wuthering Heights*.

'I saw the film,' said Marsha. 'It was very sweet.'

'Well, read the book,' said Malcolm. 'You'll like it even better.'

'Oh, no. Jane Brontë. Isn't she a bit on the heavy side?'

'*Emily* Brontë. And there could never have been anyone less so. This book is as romantic as even you could wish for.'

'Well, darling, I'm not honestly too sure.' She looked for a minute at the opening paragraphs. 'Perhaps another time.'

'No nonsense. I'm buying it for you.'

It had been a perfect holiday. She remembered her first sight of the sea, from the train, near Eastbourne; she had felt like a child again. They had shared a box of Bassett's liquorice allsorts sitting on one of the seats along the front.

She didn't like *Wuthering Heights*. Indeed she only read the first two or three chapters of it—mercifully they were short —and then Malcolm relented. 'All right, go back to your Elinor Glyn,' he said. 'You're hopeless.' In fact, she went back to her Georgette Heyer.

She remembered another dose of culture—surprisingly, less painful. The film of *Hamlet* had been revived at the Playhouse. She wouldn't say that she enjoyed it, but—she wasn't bored. She rather sympathized with Gertrude; Gertrude, who had so much loved her son. Hamlet himself reminded her a great deal of Malcolm. Except that Hamlet was a bit older.

For there was no disguising the fact that Malcolm could sometimes be a little difficult, as well. Moody. Of course, he got that from his father. But several evenings he had gone off for lengthy walks on his own, along the beach, towards Hastings. Marsha wondered if he'd found himself a girl-friend, although he kept on denying it. (She wouldn't have minded, she told him; she'd just have liked to hear some details.) While he was away, she usually sat and talked with Mrs Anderson in her kitchen. She and Malcolm were quite her favourite visitors, the landlady had said, and, as always, Marsha never cared much for her own company. Sometimes, when they could get away, the Andersons sat on the beach with them. Mr Anderson had very white legs above his stocking tops and wore suspenders to hold those stockings up. His black lace-up shoes gleamed in the hot sunshine. He was in his fifties. He intimated, very nicely, that he fancied Marsha. On their last day in Bexhill, she let him go to bed with her. Surprisingly, he made a good lover; she wished she had discovered earlier. But it was not—she realized even then—it was not really very much of a conquest; though a small conquest, of course, was better than none at all. As one grew older one was thankful for even that.

But what a holiday it had been—perhaps the one she looked back on now with most affection. They hadn't done much: seen *Twinkle* at the White Rock Pavilion and another typical seaside show at the De La Warr. They'd been to the

Playhouse a second time and also to the Ritz (*Interrupted Melody*, she thought—or was that the following year? In any case, it had been a mistake to try and repeat it. Even the Andersons had packed up and gone to Aldershot.) They'd had their morning coffees and afternoon teas each day at one of three or four not dissimilar places—though mainly at Susan Throssil's (for its meringues) and *The Nell Gwynn* (for its flapjacks and macaroons, and the spruce young waiter with his white jacket and his very clean fingernails). And before bed they had wandered along to an ice-cream parlour on the front, for a cup of coffee and a wafer biscuit. It had been a fortnight of near-heaven—though perhaps while it was actually going on, she hadn't fully realized it. At the time, maybe, she had even been a little bored at odd moments, or positively disgruntled. (One morning when they'd been playing miniature golf, for instance; her senna pods just hadn't worked.) She castigated herself later, and got depressed, because she hadn't reminded herself, all the while, that she was happy. She hadn't really taken it in. Even a mere week after they'd left Bexhill, she had discovered, to her chagrin, that she couldn't remember the pattern of the wallpaper.

She had told Malcolm about this. She recalled that he had shrugged—disconcertingly mature for a boy of only fifteen. He said, 'It's always the same with a holiday. Good to look forward to—good to look back on—not so hot, maybe, while it's actually taking place.'

'But it shouldn't be like that!'

'Should or shouldn't doesn't come into it. Just is.'

It was meant to be comforting; she supposed it was, in a way; but it hurt her slightly, too. He must have seen this. He added rather quickly: 'Did you know that an awful lot of crack-ups occur during a holiday, or else immediately afterwards? People who've been hanging on up till then by just the skin of their teeth expect it to provide the perfect cure. Of course it doesn't—it can't. As the imperfections accumulate they blame themselves for allowing the first, which led to the second, and then on to the third, et cetera. Or else they believe they could have snapped the thread between those imperfections. . .' He shrugged again, and laughed. 'I think I sound like *Reader's Digest.*'

She didn't understand him; she found him rather frightening. (How could *she* have given birth to somebody like Malcolm, she wondered, touched by the very miracle of it, the awesome unpredictability.) 'But do you realize,' she said, returning to much easier things, 'that this time a month ago we'd have been sitting at our table by the window eating supper, with the Thompsons at their table on one side and Miss Price at hers on the other? Always with her bottle of Wincarnis and the pencil lines on the label? And you said that when she ran out of label she'd clearly have to stick on another one, lower down, and shouldn't we prolong our holiday to see whether she did?'

'Perhaps she'd patented a sliding label,' answered Malcolm, 'else, what had happened at the start?' It was an intriguing little mystery, which they both savoured.

But of course it hadn't really been so bad—returning to London. Joan was there. Beryl was there. In fact it had been a very happy homecoming. For one thing, she had bought them rather handsome presents. There had been the joy of giving those.

Also she had carried back with her a bag of macaroons and a bag of flapjacks—they had had a sort of party!

And she had made a little promise to herself: that no matter what had gone before, from then on she really *would* make the most of her life; she would do her best to appreciate every little experience, whether good or bad, and she would try to do something a little new, she would try to broaden her outlook just a teeny bit, each day.

She would even read *Wuthering Heights* . . . !

Yet she never had.

She'd never managed to get past those opening chapters.

And—now—she never would. She'd lost all impetus; she'd lost the urge; the feeling that she still had time.

No point in even trying.

For the greater the success—*now*—of course—the sharper the regret.

With a sigh, she was just about to replace the book when

she noticed something held between its pages. It was a postcard, unused, which on its rack outside the shop had made her laugh, and Malcolm had hurried back (without her knowing) and got it as a bookmark. 'Not quite suitable for Miss Brontë,' he had said, '—oh, I don't know—but eminently suitable for you.'

Two short-skirted bosomy blondes were gazing at a guard on sentry duty—of whom you only saw the back. One was confiding to the other:

'I do love the way they always stand erect!'

Somehow that card just seemed the final straw.

Mr Anderson, with his smooth white legs and his suspenders and his well-kept shoes (but had she ever known his Christian name?), had been the last, the very last, whom she had ever had. And she hadn't then been forty!—or, if she had, only just. And why was there nothing that ever told you: this is the last? The last time you'll ever hear your favourite tune; the last time that you'll ever have a bath—or a mackerel —or a lover. The last Christmas. The last book. And would it have been better, or worse, if you had known?

Marsha sat down, with a hand across her eyes—and wept.

42

One of the bitterest blows of Marsha's and Daisy's last years was the emigration of Malcolm to Canada. 'I always knew there was no good in that Phoebe-girl of his!' declared Daisy roundly, when she first heard of these intentions. (By which time it had been almost a *fait accompli*.) 'It's all her doing, of course,' she said to Marsha. 'The silly ass!'

Remembering the days when Daisy had so often referred to Phoebe as one in a million, Marsha was not greatly impressed by these claims to foresight. 'Nonsense,' she said, briskly. 'You used to think that Phoebe was the bee's knees.'

'That shows how very little *you* know about it!' answered

Daisy—as a prelude to a quantity of muttering on the subject of people whose poverty of language was such that they could only express themselves in clichés; she had forgotten that it was *she* who was in fact being quoted. But it was certainly true that, since the day of the court hearing, both Malcolm's and Phoebe's stock had fallen considerably with Daisy; and often whole weeks, even months, had gone by without their either seeing her or hearing from her; to their relief but also somewhat to their consternation.

'And who are you to talk about knees, anyway? If anyone's an expert on knees around here—having to drag them along these hard pavements the way that I do, shamefully—it's certainly not you! No! You were always interested in something higher up!'

Yet as she told this mainly to the wall, and Marsha didn't catch more than one word in every three, it fizzled out into just an angry murmuring, a Daisy-type sort of buzz and burble.

In any case, though Malcolm had somehow contrived to keep this from the household in Alderton Crescent, it was now nearly six months since Phoebe had walked out on him and soon afterwards married a widower from her office. ('Good riddance!' Daisy had said in a not-wholly-successful attempt at comforting her nephew, when she did learn. 'I can't imagine what the fool can see in her. Probably another of these weak-willed idiots who like to have their lives regimented by a bossy woman. Anyway, dear, in my opinion, you're well out of it and no mistake.' It was not in any way an accurate reading of the situation, but, even if it failed lamentably in its proper objective, at least it had the effect of cheering up Daisy herself—who very quickly came to believe it, and liked to imagine Phoebe giving hell to the widower's children, and the widower's children giving hell straight back again, with interest.)

They had been living together, on and off, for the best part of a dozen years. Malcolm was devastated. After she left, it seemed he couldn't settle to anything; a totally new way of life appeared to be the answer. He had friends in Canada, who suggested he might go and join them there.

There was a bitter-sweet corollary to this—well, fairly bitter for Marsha, and certainly rather sweet for her sister-in-law and brother. Andrew (or more probably Myra) quickly grew envious on reading Malcolm's accounts of the higher standard of living obtaining in Canada. They applied for entry there. It was refused: advertising men were far less in demand than architects. By then, however, the travelling bug had got them; they settled for Australia, which, they now let it be known, would have been their first choice all along, if they hadn't been swayed by their consideration for Malcolm. They went—Andrew, Myra and the two boys. Marsha dabbed her eyes at the dockside. Daisy said she felt that, after all, she might have been a little hasty in her judgement of Phoebe. 'She wasn't such a bad type, I believe, *au fond*. You know, dear, God moves in a mysterious way . . .' And Dan—to whom this was primarily addressed—said sympathetically, 'Oh, Lord, I'm sure that Myra is going to have a most difficult and testing voyage!'

'If that's true so is everybody else!'

'She's not up to much at the moment.'

'I'm afraid she never has been!'

Brother- and sister-in-law were never so united.

The fact of the matter—in Dan's case—was that he had once viewed Myra's hypochondria with tolerance and even sympathy, although he and Erica had always suspected that the reports of her stoicism came indirectly from the lady herself. When Erica had been discovered to have cancer, however, and Dan had been forced to witness what real courage could be in the face of real illness, his amusement at the varied trials of Myra had abruptly ceased.

Unfortunately, though, Andrew hadn't learned not to propagate these tales of his wife's saintliness until hearing some of the most uncharitable sentiments ever to issue from his uncle's lips.

But on the evening of the day they sailed, some neighbours to whom Marsha had spoken of the impending separation (while standing in a queue at the greengrocer's) called round to extend their condolences. They were a husband and wife who were not yet in their seventies, but unluckily, because they both seemed more infirm than Dan and spoke rather more loudly, Daisy rashly assumed that they were equally hard of hearing. In answer to their second round of polite enquiries after Andrew and Myra and the boys ('It must be such a wrench for you all; we know so well ourselves what it feels like to be left behind!'), while Marsha nodded gratefully and murmured, 'Yes; oh, *yes!*', Daisy gave a very sweet smile and told them, 'Poppycock!'

The visitors imagined they'd misheard—and then compounded their mistake by not asking her to repeat what she had said. They commiserated further, as though they hadn't already done so quite enough; and Daisy, like a child who'd been encouraged by its initial success, continued to whisper pertinent asides, masked—as she supposed—by her sister-in-law's flow of platitudes. Certainly Marsha carried on quite innocently and not even the hint of a smile came to poor Dan's face, to signify awareness of the witty enjoyment that so narrowly eluded him.

'Yes, that's right, we're heartily glad to be shot of them. We call them "the dear departed"—though there's much controversy about the adjective! They're only dear because they have departed, if you see what I mean. But then you'll fall into that same category yourselves in an hour's time—or six, more likely, from the way you both seem to have settled in! What did you *really* come here for? To find out what the curtains looked like from the inside? To scrounge a glass or two (or three or four) of free sherry?—well, you'd be lucky, in this household! Interfering old biddies. "*We* know what it's like to be left behind," indeed! Yes, I'll bet you do! Silly asses! Who do you suppose in their right minds would aim to take *you* along with them?'

She snorted. She looked up contemptuously from her own empty sherry glass and was then suddenly aware that everybody else had finished talking. How long ago? Panic-stricken, she wondered if perhaps she'd slightly overstepped the mark—swept away by her too lively sense of fun. Had she remembered to keep a hospitable smile in evidence? She said:

'Did you ever know such a woman as that silly ass Thatcher?'

She looked around expectantly. As a stock conversational gambit she had to acknowledge that it had usually met with more success.

43

Afterwards, Marsha physically assaulted her. Or very nearly. At one point she looked as though she actually meant to shake her. And she screamed like a fishwife. She dredged up every sin that Daisy was supposed to have committed in the last seven hundred and fifty years and told her that she was evil—*evil*! It was degrading and scaring and obscene. Daisy could hardly drag herself away from it all fast enough, but even then Marsha ran in front of her and barred the door like some terrible ogress, at least nine inches taller than she really was.

'We *can't* have her in this house!' the ogress cried to Dan. 'Put her out! Tonight! If *you* don't, *I* shall!'

Yes, it was frightening—frightening—the more so, of course, since she didn't know at all what Dan was thinking. His presence between them was possibly what had saved her from being struck—she admitted that; but all the same he appeared to be letting his demon-possessed sister rant on and on, almost as though he believed she might be justified in her attack. It was nightmarishly unimaginable . . . yet it really did seem that he aligned himself with Marsha.

Eventually, however, she was able to get to the stairs, because, she vaguely supposed, Dan must at least have mildly remonstrated with the vixen—and the moment she gained the potential sanctuary of her bedroom she wedged her fireside chair beneath the doorknob. Afterwards, she didn't know where she'd found the strength to do it.

Then she sat, trembling, on the edge of her bed and covered her face with her hands. It was only by the way her hands moved up and down that she suddenly realized how quickly and how deeply she was breathing.

But did you ever witness such a terrifying performance? The woman had gone quite literally berserk.

Did they really mean to throw her out—homeless—before she'd had the chance to try and arrange anything?

Of course she wouldn't want to stay; not after this; but she *would* have to arrange where she could go.

It was all so . . . extraordinary. What had she done? Just played the giddy goat a little and performed—let's face it—quite the funniest, most entertaining piece of nonsense that could have enlivened that dreary sitting-room in the last six thousand years. (Oh, beg its pardon: *lounge!*) If only the other participants had seen the delightful, madcap humour of it!

But what could you expect—in Hendon?

Oh, how they would have laughed about it at the club!

It was no good: she would have to get down there again, even if it *was* a question of two buses in each direction and of having to hang around late at night for God knew how many hours on windswept corners and hard pavements, waiting to be mugged and to have your handbag stolen from you—if not your very life and your shopping basket, too. And this was to say absolutely nothing, of course, about the likelihood of driving rain and the near-certainty of having to harangue a coal-black conductor for ringing the bell too soon, either while you were still standing there expecting to be hauled up on to the platform or else—much worse—at the moment when you were already nearly there, by dint of your own Herculean efforts, but still unhappily half-hanging over space, as if in preparation for some barbarous, and compulsory, ski jump. And even if by any chance you *were* able to wangle a lift back again, the outward journey was still quite enough, and more than enough, of an endurance test for anyone. For anyone!

But she would manage it somehow! She must! She must! There was no acceptable alternative.

And abruptly she brought her fists down on the bed, one on either side of her, in a despairing attempt to release even a little of her frustration. She suddenly felt so unloved, and isolated, and *homesick*. Homesick for the club; homesick for all those friends who were now either dead or living away from London but who would at once have understood her need; homesick, above all, for Marie.

She moved to her wooden upright chair beside the table and put her head down on her hands.

She really hadn't intended any harm. She'd never liked to hurt people, not even in the smallest way . . .

And half an hour later, Dan came up to see her.

44

He had to knock a long time before she realized he was there, and he quickly grew alarmed, calling out her name with mounting urgency, while trying to believe that she was merely sulking and hadn't had a stroke or heart attack. But Daisy, in fact—just before making her escape—had finally had the presence of mind to switch off her hearing-aid (and thus reduce the ogress—magnify her?—to a grotesquely moving mouth and set of dentures: almost Hogarthian) yet had afterwards forgotten, in all her misery, to switch it on again; in any case, what point? Eventually, however, she saw the rattling of the knob.

'Who is it? What do you want?'

'Ah—thank God! Daisy. Are you all right?'

'I said—who is it? Have you come to harass me again? I can't take any more of it—do you hear? I can't stand any fresh persecution.'

She added with the type of grim comicality that was almost second nature to her: 'Or even *stale*, come to that!'

'It's Dan. Please let me in, Daisy. Turn on your—'

'Go away! Don't think you can intimidate me by mere stealth and silence. This is my home; I'm sticking to it. I won't allow you to throw me out.'

'Turn on your hearing-aid!'

'Go away! I know that you're still there.'

She remembered her hearing-aid.

'Is it Dan?'

'I want to talk to you.'

'Are you alone?'

She had to repeat the question.

'You're quite sure of that? No she-devils lurking round the corner, waiting to lambaste me, push me down?'

'There's nobody up here but me.' Even she could hear the weariness.

She pulled away the chair—with a lot more difficulty than she'd had putting it there in the first place. Dan stood just inside the door—florid of complexion, decidely rather fat these days, and somehow a little absurd, breathing hard from his exertions and his apprehensions, but essentially exuding the air of kindliness, bewilderment and regret that was as characteristic of him as those brown Harris tweed jackets he always wore.

'Are you coming down to supper?' he asked; smiling; as though it had been just a normal sort of evening with no quarrels and no barricades.

'Do you think I could swallow a crumb? With *her*? That harridan downstairs? You must be as mad as she is.' Daisy glared at him defiantly.

'You know, old girl, it wasn't all her fault. You've got to come clean and own up.'

'Old girl? Come clean?' she said. 'Where do you manage to find these up-to-date expressions?'

'In fact, I rather think you should apologize.'

'It's not as if you even read much, is it? No. How often do I see you sitting with a book? Weren't you ever *taught* to appreciate good literature, I want to know. Your world must be a very barren one. Exceedingly. Not even the television. Only a wireless—which I daresay you can't hear!'

'Please, Daisy,' he said. 'Please, old girl.'

'A household without books! One shelf; maybe two! Small ones. Henry was just the same, of course. Thank God that *I* came from a background with a bit of culture. My father may not have been up to much in many ways, but . . . He was a schoolmaster. Did I ever tell you that?'

Dan didn't answer. But he met her gaze and held it, levelly, until she finally looked away from him—in irritation.

She sat down again upon the wooden chair and sighed, impatiently.

'*Apologize*? For what—I'd like to know? For nearly being beaten to a pulp?'

'What was that, Daisy?'

'Apologize for *what*?'

'Well, for one thing, for having lost her, as she says, another pair of friends. She thinks that they could have been good friends. You know how she loves to have people to talk to. And they're the only neighbours we've had since she's been here who've ever taken any interest.'

'Interest? They were almost peering into our account books.'

'And, I must say, they did seem rather pleasant people.'

'It's *next* time that they'll want to see the birth certificates!'

'But Marsha doesn't think, now, that they'll come again.'

'Why not? She can tell them I'm an actress, can't she? —that I was simply learning the lines for my new play. There! It isn't true—but at any rate it's inventive. Would you or she have ever thought of it? No, of course you wouldn't; that shows how very much you need me! And to make it more convincing I'll recite them Juliet. I can declaim the whole part—or as much of it as matters. "O Romeo, Romeo! wherefore art thou Romeo? Deny thy father and refuse thy name; or, if thou wilt not, be but sworn my love, and I'll no longer be a Capulet." Et cetera; et cetera. She can tell them that I'm Edith Evans; I'm sure *they*'ll never know the difference. And perhaps that way, when they do come again, we could even charge admission.' The prospect of it, for a moment, seemed quite to cheer her.

'I'd like to have been Juliet. Yes, I really would. But I wouldn't have messed things up like she did.'

Dan smiled, too—less dreamily than Daisy—and with relief.

'To begin with,' she went on, 'I'd never have swallowed

down that dose. No fear! Not even to end with, either!'

'That's right, my love. That's right. We could all get on so well together if only . . .'

There was a pause.

'If only what?' The smile had altogether faded.

Annoyed with himself, he answered slowly and with thought: 'Well, if only you were, occasionally, just a little more careful about some of the things you say . . . That's all.'

'No, it isn't.' She pursed her lips. 'You don't mean occasionally, do you?—you mean always. You don't mean *some* of the things, you mean all of the things. I've got to live in a strait-jacket. Is that your idea? Well, I can't do it. The strait-jackets of this world are for Marsha—perhaps even for yourself, too—I don't know. This afternoon I thought we understood each other.'

'And now?' Dan propped himself against the doorjamb, heavy with disappointment. He hadn't wholly grasped her meaning, but at least his ear seemed more attuned. 'And now?'

'And now? And now?' she parroted. 'We'd better *all* of us take a dose!—that's what—and now! Have done with it,' she said.

Dan breathed yet more heavily. 'If anyone in this family is in need of a strait-jacket, old girl, a lot of people would probably say it's neither me *nor* Marsha.'

'I see,' said Daisy, very quietly (for her). 'I see. So now you plan to have me certified, the pair of you?'

'Oh, don't be silly. Just come down for your supper. And don't say another word.'

'Ah ha! From censorship to complete suppression. That was fast. But I'm sorry. I can't eat in a strait-jacket. I can't reach for the condiments.'

The whole thing, indeed, was now going *much* too fast. She realized that. But as always on these occasions (things were often going too quickly for her, getting out of hand, when all she wanted out of life was interest, not speed) she was totally powerless to do anything but step on the accelerator.

'And possibly I'd be better off in an asylum. At least I

could stare at the white walls and perhaps find a modicum of entertainment *there*. At least it would get me away from this loonybin and its two keepers—who ought to be its inmates; it's a strange reversal. At least it would get me away from Erica's wallpapers! My God. I wouldn't use *those* to wipe my bottom with, let alone put them on display!'

She added: 'I apologize for the crudity. (Or should I say—pardon my French?) But there are some things which can positively drive you to it. Those wallpapers make up a good proportion of them.'

She added further: 'Credit where credit's due, though. This in here isn't actually so bad. You must both have had an off day.'

Dan's face had gone a deeper shade of red; and he spoke thickly, as though he were suddenly having trouble with his enunciation.

'All right, Daisy. If that's the way you feel.'

'Where are you going?'

'Downstairs.'

'Yes—just slope off! Why does nobody in this house ever stop to finish a conversation? That's what I'd like to know.'

'Downstairs—to telephone,' he added.

'That's nice,' said Daisy. 'Who's going to have the privilege of enjoying a stimulating exchange of ideas with you *this* time?'

'The doctor!' he exclaimed. 'I shall now do what I should have done years ago. But I hadn't then had the benefit of one of *your* stimulating ideas, you see, Daisy. I'm going to take the first steps towards having you committed!'

45

And he thought he really meant it, too. He certainly lurched downstairs in the enraged belief that the hall table, with the telephone upon it, was his proper destination. He even pulled out the correct directory. But by the time he'd taken his spectacle case out of his jacket pocket his vindictiveness —and therefore his momentum—was already on the wane. He held the unopened case an instant, weighing it absently in his palm, then returned it to his pocket; the A–D he replaced beside its bookend.

And as if in confirmation that he had thereby acted rightly, the telephone itself began to ring. For a moment he just stared at it, not fully sure that it was real.

He picked up the receiver as though partly in a dream. He intoned their number.

Marsha walked towards him, woodenly; coming from the lounge.

'I'd like to speak to Mrs Daisy Stormont. This is long distance.'

The woman's voice on the line sounded very clipped; Dan for some reason thought it was the operator. This didn't please her.

'I happen to be one of Mrs Stormont's nieces,' she explained, impatiently. 'You can tell her that it's Colleen.'

'Oh, my goodness.' Dan suddenly emerged out of his trance. 'You're speaking from Ireland.'

'No. Not from Ireland. We haven't lived in Ireland for years now. If it matters, I'm speaking from Bournemouth. Is Mrs Stormont there?'

But in fact she sounded quite relieved to hear her aunt could not come to the phone.

At first Dan wondered, though, if he might have made a mistake: at least it could have been a means of getting her to come downstairs. Then, almost immediately, he realized that he hadn't.

The woman's father—Daisy's brother—had just died.

The death had taken place in a nursing-home in Bournemouth. Dan offered his condolences. 'Had your father been very ill? I don't think Daisy knew about it.'

'No, he was hardly ill at all. He was lucky.' He'd been eighty-four years old. He'd had a fair crack of the whip. It was a blessing in disguise.

The funeral would be next Friday. The niece doubted that

Daisy would be able to come, but she and her sisters had supposed she ought to be given the opportunity. If she did come, the woman went on, she herself could put her up over the Thursday night but unfortunately she and her family had arranged to leave Bournemouth for the weekend early on the Friday afternoon. Would he make that very clear to her?

Dan also doubted that Daisy would be able to go, but he didn't reveal that. The niece's tone and manner did more than even her news—perhaps more than anything else within reason could have done—to arouse his feelings of partisanship for the woman who had just insulted his dead wife. He said: 'Yes, I should think she'd like to come. It would make a break for her.'

It occurred to him as he said it that it would also make a break for Marsha and for him.

'A break? That seems rather an odd choice of word, doesn't it?—under the circumstances.'

'I'm sorry. Could you repeat that?' He pressed the receiver more closely to his ear.

She did repeat it, more or less.

'I'm sorry,' he said again. 'Yes, you're right. I know that this is going to be a most unpleasant shock for her.'

He looked at Marsha. She, too, he could tell, had caught his feelings of hostility towards the woman on the phone. Or was that only wishful thinking?—she could certainly have heard little that the niece had actually said. But earlier Marsha had cried, 'I'd like to push her under a bus—I would, really—I mean it!', referring, of course, to Daisy. Any transference of that hostility, thought Dan—and so very speedily, at that—could only be a miracle.

'I'm really not sure how we're going to break it to her,' he said into the mouthpiece.

'Oh, she'll be all right,' said the woman. 'She's tough as old boots. Besides—they hadn't seen each other for donkey's years. There was no love lost between them. Not a jot.'

'Just the same. Their youth—their shared experience—'

'Oh, you'll forgive my saying so, of course, and perhaps

228

you know her better than I do, but I think that's pure malarky.'

It sounded like something her aunt might have said; and yet—not quite.

'Has she got your number?' asked Dan.

The niece repeated it three times. He couldn't get it right, though Marsha held the paper for him. In the end he pretended that he had. Her tone reminded him: long distance.

'Well, I hope that the funeral goes smoothly,' he said at last, 'and that afterwards you all have a nice weekend away, to get over it.' He winked at Marsha. He was glad he'd thought of that retort in time (it was the sort of thing that usually only occurred to him too late—and he knew that Daisy would appreciate it). 'At least it ought to make a break for you,' he said.

46

She *had* been rude, of course. She realized that. But they had deserved it in a way, with all their mealy-mouthings and their namby-pambiness of spirit. Nothing of any moment to say for themselves. And she hadn't known that they could hear—that was the point. Naturally, if one of them had only mentioned it, when they first came doddering into the room, none of this would ever have happened. It was a mix-up, a misunderstanding. You couldn't strictly say, she supposed, that it was anybody's fault.

And they had in fact talked—be fair—even if they hadn't *said* anything and even if scarcely any of it had been addressed to herself (which was remarkably impolite, as nobody with any pretensions to breeding would dare to deny for one moment). But it had hardly made the party swing, their conversation; it hadn't *quite* had that fizzing, champagne quality beloved of Noël Coward.

Some of the topics:

The weather here.

The weather in Australia.

The friend of the son of an acquaintance who had at one time emigrated there; or had at any rate *thought* about emigrating there—they seemed to recollect now that he might have changed his mind.

The eating of Christmas pudding in the summer.

August Bank Holiday in the winter.

Why had they moved it?

'What—Australia? I didn't know they had.'

(Daisy's own contribution; and by far the most amusing one of the whole session—apart from the monologue.)

'No, you big chump. The August Bank Holiday.' Marsha.

'It used to be on the first Monday of the month, you see. Now it's on the last.'

'Which month?'

'August.'

'Ah? How interesting.'

'Oh dear. I think you're teasing me. Have I been teaching my grandmother to suck eggs? Denny says I do it all the time! Don't you, dear?'

'Why is *Easter* never constant?' Marsha again. 'It's something I've so often wondered.'

None of them knew, of course. They waffled on ludicrously (was it the moon, was it the sun, could it be something to do with the tides?), no doubt believing that they sounded very intellectual. Naturally, though, they didn't dream of consulting *her*.

'Anyway, do any of us even know that they *keep* the August Bank Holiday in Australia?' Easter was dismissed, clearly, as being of somewhat less importance.

(Besides, that woman's grandmother would have gone right back to Boadicea! Earlier! To a time, probably, before they even *had* any eggs!)

'Well, I'll tell you what I'm going to do! I shall ask Andrew in my very first letter—I shall write it tomorrow—and let you know the moment I've received an answer!'

'Yes—he'd be the sort of person able to find out, wouldn't

he? Oh, how fascinating! And what fun to have someone dependable like that right across the globe, right on the other side of the world!'

'Yes,' said Daisy. She broke her vow of silence. 'Yes, indeed.'

'Oh dear, but only in a manner of speaking, I mean. Poor Mrs Poynton. We do know what you're going through. And wouldn't anyone—anyone who's ever been a mother? One dear fledgling leaving the nest, followed so very shortly by another. Oh, how you're going to miss them! It must be such a wrench for you all. We know so well ourselves what it feels like to be left behind.'

'Yes; oh, *yes!*' said Marsha, with a grateful nod.

'Poppycock!' muttered Daisy, with her sweetest smile.

No.

Hardly what you'd term a shindig!

Hardly what you'd term a satisfactory wake. (All of the lamentations. None of the merrymaking.)

How typical.

Yes, and how she despised that tepid sort of nothingness; that total lack of any finer feeling. The fact that people could fritter their lives away in such everlastingly paltry exchanges —oh, it was pitiable, just so utterly pitiable!

And yet . . .

Well, of course, that was precisely what it should be, wasn't it? Pitiable. Hadn't she been told by Marie, time and time again, that perhaps her greatest failing was her inability to suffer fools gladly?

'Everybody has his own special niche in life, Daisy, even those whom you dismiss as fools.' It was funny how Marie could say things like that, and somehow it was quite acceptable.

'Yes, dear, I know. But why does it always have to be around me? Why am I surrounded by these niches?'

'And God loves all of us, quite equally.'

'Yes, dear, I know that, too. I don't believe it—but I know it. (Seriously, though, don't you think he should really have just a few preferences tucked in here and there? For his own good, I mean—naturally—certainly not for *mine!*) But you should have been a vicar, Marie! So should I!—we've both of us missed our vocation! I should have liked more than anything to be able to push people in the right direction —wouldn't you? And I don't mean just the fools, either!'

Daisy chuckled again now, as she thought about it.

But Marie was right, of course.

And what were fools to do, then, if they didn't possess a talent for being entertaining?

Shun all invitations? Pay no calls?

'*Yes!*' cried Daisy; the irrepressible, the unsinkable. (But perhaps it wasn't quite so simple as all that—as even she felt bound to admit.)

All right. She *had* been rude. Unforgiveably rude. And those poor people hadn't deserved it. She confessed it all, freely and humbly. 'It's as true now, Marie, as it ever was. Truer! (Who ever said that we grew nicer or wiser with age? What an unconscionable ass *he* must have been! We mostly get aching bones and bunions, to emasculate intentions!) I've got so *very* little charity. I do realize, dear.' But perhaps she could do something as a peace-offering—write them a letter, buy them a packet of biscuits?

Yes. Yes, she must obviously do something of that sort. And it would please Marsha into the bargain. She had always done her best to please Marsha. She had never wanted to be a nuisance. One of her chief regrets, indeed, was provided by her demoralizing inability ever to be of any real use at times when Marsha seemed to be especially busy. You'd think that a club-woman who'd had her portrait painted by Augustus John, and been told that her fingertips felt like the brush of angels' wings, and who had been both the terror and the pride of her wartime colleagues and superiors, not to mention the beloved heroine, in the war before that one, of so many luckless lads in the trenches—you'd think that such a woman would at least know how to operate the washing machine, wouldn't you, without letting the soapy water flood on to the newly polished floor; or how to put away just two bottles of milk into the fridge without letting one of them slip from her grasp? She had felt so *sorry* for the poor soul, having to clear up after her on top of all her other chores.

(Of course, the washing machine was antediluvian; and why did the milk bottles have to be given a wipe, almost a baptism, before being fit to be placed in the fridge? But she had only pointed out these not unimportant things afterwards—well, a little afterwards—and she hadn't been thinking simply of her own good in any case. It certainly hadn't invalidated the sincerity of her apology, as they had somehow got it into their heads that it had. No. Why on earth should it? That's what she could never understand.)

However, she remembered saying once—or thinking once, she couldn't be quite sure—that Marsha should have been called Martha; a possible implication being that she, Daisy, had elected to play Mary. But what had she learned at the Master's feet? Not tolerance, it seemed. Not up to now. (Even that slippery milk bottle could still rankle!) Then how about forgiveness—if only in the hope that she herself might also be forgiven? There would never (she trusted!) be any more suitable occasion than this, both to sue for forgiveness and simultaneously to grant it.

And Daisy rose, while the spirit was still upon her. She would go downstairs—at once—and practise all the Christian virtues.

She would turn the other cheek.

She would not become as sounding brass, or as a tinkling cymbal.

And she would eat her supper at the same time.

(She hoped that it was something tasty.)

She left her bedroom and started down the stairs, holding on to the banister with one hand, supporting herself against the wall with the other. Below her, by the front door, Dan replaced the telephone receiver abruptly, with a satisfied smile and an almost mischievous look of daring. She had forgotten about his threatened phone call; or, rather, after a minute of reflection, had not paid it any serious attention; he had simply been upset. Now she saw that the row had been merely an excuse—wholly trumped up most likely. Now she saw how pleased they were to have found a way of removing her. It wasn't just his smile that announced this to her; it was also the manner in which Marsha was suddenly gazing up at her, as though at Lazarus taking everyone by surprise after a possible moment of eavesdropping; Marsha looked startled —shifty.

And little wonder, too. It was Marsha, of course, who was really at the bottom of all this. Dan was just her dupe; nondescript, weak-kneed, like the majority of men, good-natured in a way but at any time ready to surrender his integrity in exchange for a life of peace; no better than wet clay in the hands of an unscrupulous woman.

Yes, it was Marsha.

Daisy cried out vengefully, stern and uncompromising, as though Apollo's Oracle had suddenly been transported from Delphi and set down half-way up their stairs:

When the Himalayan peasant meets the he-bear in his pride,
He shouts to scare the monster, who will often turn aside.

Here, however, was the really telling bit:

But the she-bear thus accosted rends the peasant tooth and nail
For the female of the species is more deadly than the male!

She allowed those ringing words to fade majestically into the silence.

'There!' said the Oracle. 'How I wish that I had written that! Did you ever meet Kipling? Or—rather—did Kipling ever meet you? Oh, he knew what he was on about, that man!'

Marsha continued just to stand there and look stupid. *She* obviously didn't know what he was on about—nor what Daisy, speaking through him, was on about either.

'Oh, what's the use?' cried Daisy. 'Haven't you even heard of Kipling?'

How did you make contact with someone who hadn't even heard of Kipling?

Suddenly, she knew.

'You did realize, I suppose, that Andrew wanted to leave

234

home once and marry me instead?' The Oracle's words—and the medium's tone—had grown quite conversational.

Silence.

'What?' asked Marsha. 'I'm sorry. I don't understand you, Daisy. How old was he?'

Daisy affected a laugh. 'Good old Marsha! Running true to form! Always the one reliable question.'

'I mean—was it before or after he met Myra? I suppose it must have been before,' she added tonelessly.

'Your *husband*, idiot—your husband, not your son! I always thought it was a singularly daft idea, anyway. And very arrogant, as well. No doubt, it must have been Andrew's —how very like him!' She added: 'Your husband's—not your son's.'

She was holding court from the staircase. She hadn't come one step further down.

'I mean—how foolish. What happened when a letter arrived for Andrew Poynton, Esq.? Did they take it in turns to open them?—one for you and one for me. Oh, I forgot —your husband wasn't around long enough, was he, for it ever to become a major issue in your lives?'

She was, by now, actually enjoying herself.

'Somebody else got to him; somebody with less of a conscience than I had, obviously.' She shrugged. 'But I'll swear he never loved her more than he did me.'

Marsha's face looked old and very drawn, in a way that it hadn't looked earlier, when she had been filled with fiery anger. One of her legs had started trembling spasmodically —her shoe beat a light, involuntary tattoo against the carpet. But her voice remained reasonably steady, even if it sounded odd.

'But you don't know what you're saying, Daisy. You only met him once. Or maybe twice. You scarcely knew him.'

'No, dear. Correction. You were the one who scarcely knew him. He and I had quite a little love affair. He said I was the most exciting woman that he'd ever met. He said that he'd do *anything* for me. Anything. I told him to go home to you!'

Outside, in the crescent, a horn hooted—there was a

tremendous squealing of brakes—a dog barked; none of them was aware of it; not even Dan, who merely stood there looking at the floor.

'He was a nice lad,' said Daisy; 'but *I* didn't need him. Yet it was good to know I could have had him!'

She chuckled.

'Oh, I wasn't quite as beautiful as you—but there was something else I wasn't, either—and that was a poor fish, a poor, sad, little fish swimming all alone around her poor, sad, little bowl. You'd only been married such a short time, too; yet you obviously couldn't hold him—not for all your vaunted loveliness! Me—I just had a funny little mug.' She pulled a face, to illustrate. 'And that's why, now, you want to have your revenge. Turn me out. Lock me away. Bedlam.'

Her tone had turned to bitterness again. Memory of the present had come back to strike out triumphs of the past.

'Hell hath no fury like a woman scorned!'

She delivered this line, which had suddenly shaped itself out of her anguish, like the message of inspiration that it clearly was. And then she turned—swiftly and magnificently —to sweep back up the stairs. Yet even as she did so the magnificence acquired a quality of dizziness. She meant to thrust out her hands to slow down her accelerating world. (Where were her hands?) But her legs buckled under her, and she fell.

Part Six

47

'I don't want to die,' he said.

'I know, dear. I know.'

She took his hand and held it tightly and for sometime they just sat in silence.

'Your work!' she said. 'You've got to lose yourself in work. Work is the only thing that matters.'

'Work?' he repeated, bitterly.

'Yes!'

'No good. The poetry's all dried up.'

'What poppycock!'

'There's not a single thing I want to write about.'

'Write about Lourdes, of course.'

They'd only just come back.

'Oh, what's the use?' He pulled away his hand in disappointment and clenched his fists wildly, struggling to express himself. 'We're so alone,' he cried.

He looked—really he did look for just a minute—as though he might have been entered by the devil.

Yet then the feverish quality departed; the desperation and the drama; mere despondency remained.

'So alone,' he repeated.

Well, that was probably quite true. But it wasn't apropos, she thought, and it was better not to speak of it. Things somehow grew more real as soon as you tried to put them into words.

'It's the first line that's always the difficulty, isn't it?'

She took a sheet of paper from a pile she'd set beside his bed and sucked with much determination at a pencil.

Later she went out and bought him some more books, along with the groceries, hoping that stimulation might arrive through entertainment. She also bought him some more gramophone records. He liked Carroll Gibbons and Jack Payne.

She was broke; she didn't know where she would find the money. Somehow she always did. (But she categorically refused to go to his parents and ask for it.) For the time being she had given up her practice, both in Thayer Street and in the Harrow Road.

The following day she said to him: 'You were wrong, dear. You aren't alone. *I* shall be here. Always. Every moment. I do care. We all care. We none of us want you to die.'

Well, that was true enough, too, so far as it went. The world was founded on half-truths; while it ran terrified from whole ones.

But of course he did die. And she didn't know if he had ever quite believed her—even to cheap dance music. (During the last half hour, however, it had been entirely true; at least, she thought it had.) Later on, though, she'd remembered only her impatience—and she'd felt sad and worthless and ashamed.

'What will you do after I'm dead?' he had once asked her.

'Carry on as I did before,' she'd almost answered. But, thank goodness, her tact had stepped in. 'Oh, I don't know. Somehow, I suppose, I'll manage.'

'I only wish that I'd been able to provide.'

She merely smiled; and pursed her lips and shook her head.

'You've been a good wife, Daisy. You've been the best thing that happened to me. If anyone could ever have made anything out of me,' he said, 'that person would have been you.'

'You silly ass.' She busied herself, quite unnecessarily, with tucking in his blanket again—the blanket that Dan and Erica had given them.

'I hope that things go well for you.'

'Oh, perhaps I'll achieve something,' said Daisy. 'Of some sort. Despite myself!' She chuckled. 'And if you can achieve something *despite* yourself, that's quite a feather in your cap, Lord dild you!'

'Yes. It is. I really hope you will,' he repeated. '*Dild?*'

'Shame upon you! Don't you know your *Hamlet*? "Well, God dild you! They say the owl was a baker's daughter. Lord, we know what we are, but know not what we may be. God be at your table!" '

'Yes, and at yours, Daisy. May he be at it for ever!'

'Thank you, dear. I trust he will. I certainly sent him an invitation! But I forgot to put RSVP—so you can never be quite sure.'

'Oh, yes,' he said, 'I think you can.'

That was the Saturday before he died. He seemed to have found a certain strength during those latter days.

48

About one hour later Dr Ballad was at the door. By then Dan and Marsha had got Daisy into bed—she was only a small thing and even as a dead weight she was finally manageable for the two of them, although Dan was breathing very heavily, far more heavily than Marsha, and seemed to be looking to her for guidance as to every move. She didn't mind that. When Daisy was arranged neatly upon her bed, and the covers, too, pulled neatly across, right beneath her chin, Marsha led her brother down to the dining-room and sliced off the tops of his eggs for him, which mercifully had not grown hard—(she noted, with much gratitude, that had they eaten them as soon as she had got them out of the pan, they would surely have been watery; none of them enjoyed a watery egg). She cut his bread and butter into strips, so that he could dip them in the yolk. 'Soldiers,' she said, and smiled at him. 'I'll go and warm you some milk and put some sugar in it. I think you've had a shock.'

And, of course, they'd both had a shock—a dreadful shock. But she was stronger; she was younger; she could handle it. (All right, she *had* misjudged the timing of the eggs. Yet even that had turned out for the best.)

Daisy, too, must have received a shock. Poor thing. Even though, of course, she'd rather brought it on herself! One only hoped that it would be a lesson to her; a valuable and lasting lesson.

When she returned with the hot milk, Dan hadn't started on his meal; he was just sitting there at table, staring straight ahead of him. She didn't scold him. She dipped in the first of his bread-and-butter fingers, and held it out for him, and he obediently opened up his mouth, like a young bird.

'I wonder who first thought of calling them soldiers,' she said, while she watched him chew. 'And why.' She pursed her lips a second. 'I know that Daisy regards me as unintelligent, but I'm not so sure that that's true. I do wonder about things—I always have: things, maybe, that she just takes for granted, but doesn't really know the answer to.'

'Is the doctor coming?' asked Dan. He had asked her several times already.

'Now don't you worry your head about the doctor, darling. You just drink your milk and eat up those nice eggs. There's a jam swiss roll for afterwards. You know I phoned the doctor as soon as it happened, don't you?—though I'm not really sure I need have done so, now.'

'Why, is she dead?' He stopped his chewing and looked mildly interested.

'Good heavens, no, darling, she's not dead.' She handed him another strip of bread and he accepted it mechanically; she saw it now, not as a finger or a soldier, but as a fat, white, juicy worm, dripping with yellow goodness.

'Because I know I saw her breathing,' he said.

'Of course you saw her breathing. Of course you did. I only meant—one does so hate to trouble people without cause. Doctors are such busy folk, as well. It would be selfish if one brought them out for nothing.'

'I think I heard her moan a bit, too. I'm fairly sure I heard her moan.'

Marsha continued feeding him. 'Well, yes, of course. It would be only natural, after all.'

'She may have broken bones,' he persisted. 'In fact, probably she has. She looked quite *funny*, didn't she? All sort of twisted—before you straightened her and pushed her into place?'

242

'Dan, dear, I can see everything that's in your mouth. It isn't very nice. You must remember, too, that broken bones do knit. Everything heals with time. Well—nearly everything.'

Marsha scraped around the bottom of his first egg for him—got out every scrap of white, and then, with satisfaction, popped the spoon into his mouth. She always hated waste. Even the skin which had formed on the top of his milk she drew off with the same spoon and slipped carefully on to the congealing yolk of his second egg. The two other eggs —her own and Daisy's—she would boil up again tomorrow; she would use them either in sandwiches or a curry or a salad.

'Besides, Dan—what makes you speak of broken bones?' She shook her head at him with unchallengeable authority and gave him a broad and reassuring smile. 'Haven't you heard Daisy say—time and again—that people only need to know the proper way to fall? If there's one thing one can safely leave Daisy to get right, it's any problem which has to do with correct medical procedure—isn't that so?'

He nodded then, keeping perfect time with her own thoughtful nods. He seemed greatly comforted but—also —just a little bewildered. And, despite the care she'd taken when she put the cup to his lips and brought it down again, a particle of creamy skin dangled from one corner of his mouth. She ministered first to his physical needs and then to his mental.

'You see, Dan, all you need from now on is complete trust in my own judgement. Marsha knows what's best for the three of us. She'll look after you. She'll take care of things. You just have to relax—be totally at peace—rest easy in your mind. You haven't forgotten, have you, what happened here that day when you were out and there was a spider in the bath and *she*, silly thing'—Marsha jerked her head up at the ceiling—'was absolutely terrified? Well, who was the one who coped? Who was the one who brought tranquillity back into the house? And do you know how I did it? I put myself into that poor little spider's head and I thought, now what is the best way to set about this, not only from Daisy's point of view and from Marsha's point of view but from my own point

243

of view as well (said the spider!—oh what a clever old spider I am, I am! What a clever old spider I am).'

She laughed, wiped his mouth again on the crisply-laundered napkin (checked that it was well anchored in his collar and spread to its fullest extent across his front), then bent to kiss him gently on one cheek.

'She stoops to conquer!' she exclaimed merrily. 'And if you like, Dan, dear Dan, dear Desperate Dan, I'll tell you the whole long story later on. We'll call it "Spiders Under the Skin", shall we? I think that would be a good and thrilling title. But right now I've got to go and get ready for the doctor. So, darling, if I cut you an extra *large* slice of swiss roll, you'll promise me you won't leave any of it, there's a good boy? —not a single crumb, mind, not one sticky lick!'

Then she went upstairs and sat down at her dressing-table and looked at herself in the mirror. My goodness—what a fright! she thought. Oh, somehow I've got to do something about this!

And even fifteen minutes later, when the doctor came, she was barely ready for him—barely ready for him, although she had worked so hard and so fast, in the intervals between darting to the window to look out for his car.

In fact she actually had to keep him waiting for a few minutes but that didn't matter: she had always heard that it was best to keep a gentleman waiting a little, since that would serve to whet his appetite; and she knew, anyway, that Dan would never hear the bell. He never did, poor thing.

She took a final look in her full-length mirror before she left the room—swivelled and glanced across her shoulder, smoothing her hands down carefully, appraisingly, over her bottom. There! Would she pass mustard? She rather thought she would. She had quickly changed her dress—had chosen a little floral thing, simple but quite effective (sweet English roses for an English rose) which fitted snugly around the hips and really suited her quite nicely. She'd put on a spot of fresh make-up. (In fact, she'd put on a *lot* of fresh make-up—torn a leaf from *someone else's* book!) But she'd seen that she'd been looking a little pale and had needed to give herself a real lift. And with any luck the doctor wouldn't realize it was camouflage! With any luck he'd think it was the natural *her*! For Dr Ballad was young, you see, and very handsome. He made her think of Andrew.

She ran downstairs; or went as swiftly as she could; her chilblains were worse than ever these days and to add to that she had a corn.

But she reminded herself: not now; not any longer. No. All that was in the past.

She ran downstairs.

'Dr Ballad. How *could* I keep you waiting?'

'Oh, that's all right,' he said. He'd been standing in the road, looking up at the house, but now he came quickly forward. 'No doubt you had your hands full.'

'Yes.'

He stepped inside and Marsha closed the door. She found him looking at her in surprise. In admiration. Well, he'd never seen her so dressed up before.

She dimpled, shyly; looked down from under spiked, mascara-ed lashes.

'Do I really pass mustard?'

'Do you—? Oh, yes, certainly. Now, where shall I find Mrs Stormont?'

'In the lounge, Dr Ballad. Please step into the lounge.'

'This door?'

'No!' She said more gently: 'No, the other. Allow *me* to lead the way.'

He looked at her enquiringly when he saw an empty room. She closed the door behind them.

'Thank you so much, doctor, for turning out like this; I appreciate your promptness—although your wife told me you'd come as soon as you got back. That was your wife, I imagine? She had a sweet voice.'

He nodded.

'But I only hope I haven't brought you here upon a fool's errand.'

'I'm sorry—I don't understand. You said that Mrs Stormont had had a fall?'

'Yes.'

'Then, please, where is—?'

'I'm afraid it was very silly of me.' He was checked abruptly in mid-sentence.

'Silly?'

'You see, I know I did say Mrs Stormont. But I meant myself. I was rather shaken, doctor; I'd had a very nasty shock. It was the last in a long line of things, as well. Only this morning my older son and his family departed for Australia —'

'And?' Now it was his turn to interrupt. He did it gently, yet quite firmly.

'Well, foolishly—I don't know why it is—I often think of myself as Mrs Stormont, not as Mrs Poynton. But I'm sure you'll understand how that can happen. You grow up as *Miss* Stormont, you have a Mrs Stormont living under the same roof, you hear the name so often used . . . I imagine it could happen to anybody? I daresay it could happen even to you, doctor?'

'Er . . . yes . . . I'm certain that it could. But the main thing is, it's you, Mrs Poynton, who had the fall? Well, thank heaven, you don't appear to have hurt yourself too badly —not physically. But, as you say, it must have given you a very nasty jolt. Do, please, sit down. Have you taken anything to calm your nerves?'

'No, I haven't, doctor. But would you like to join me in a glass of sherry? I feel certain there's a little left.'

He was holding her wrist. She enjoyed that, and the sherry of course could wait.

'It happened on the stairs, my wife told me. Did you fall a long way?'

'No, no—hardly any distance. I'm afraid that on the telephone I may even have exaggerated.'

'Well, better safe than sorry; especially—I know you won't mind my saying this—if one's reached a certain age . . .' He added: 'Now, would you say that it was three stairs?—four?—more than that, or less, would you suppose?'

'But what has *age* got to do with it?' she laughed. 'It's the way you *feel* that counts.'

'Exactly, Mrs Poynton. I couldn't agree with you more.

246

Now if you'd like to lie on that settee for a moment I think I'd better give you a very quick once-over just to be on the safe side.' He helped her from her chair, then went down on his haunches to open up his large black bag.

'Shall I take my dress off?'

'No, I don't think that we need that.'

'But I wouldn't be embarrassed. Truly.'

Both the tone in which she said this and the smile that she gave him as she did so heightened his feelings of anxiety. Nor did her giggle when he used his stethoscope do anything to reassure him. He made the physical examination fairly short —after all, there were clearly no bones broken. Not even a ricked ankle. No obvious symptoms of internal bleeding. In fact, the whole thing was utterly amazing—in somebody of *her* age—if it really had been a serious sort of fall. And he wasn't happy about any of it—no, not in the slightest.

'Perhaps you would come and show me now precisely how far you did fall.'

'What a very lovely name it is—Ballad.'

'Thank you,' he said.

'Without a song,' she smiled, 'the day would never end. Did you know that? Without a song, the road would never bend. Without a song, a man would lose a friend. I was always extremely fond of singing,' she added.

He laughed politely; said nothing.

'People say I have a most delightful voice. I'm now going to tell you something. A pretty girl is like a melody.'

'I'm sure.'

But he wasn't certain what it was he was agreeing to. He was trying to remember how long ago he had last seen Mrs Poynton; he had only the haziest recollection of her and thought she must have been attended by one of his partners more often than by himself. Whenever he *had* last seen her, however, he was convinced that she hadn't behaved at all like this—or even looked at all like this. A rather nondescript sort of person, he would have said. If only he could remember, though, more clearly.

' "If you were the only boy in the world," ' sang Marsha, ' "and I were the only girl . . . nothing else would matter in this world today; we would go on loving in the same old way . . ."'

He put his hand out and touched her on the arm.

'I'm so sorry to have to stop you, Mrs Poynton—especially since I was enjoying it so much—you have a very charming voice—'

'As I said, people do always tell me that,' she interrupted him. 'I'm always in demand. "The life and soul of the party," they keep on saying; "a personality just as enchanting as her face!" Other songs they get me to sing are "Daisy, Daisy, give me your answer, do!" and "Pennies from Heaven" and—'

'But I'm afraid I do have other cases to attend to.'

'Oh, yes, of course. A doctor's life is such a busy one. I was just saying so, as a matter of fact, to my brother.'

'How is your brother?'

'Oh, just the same as usual. Infuriating. Placid. Kind.' A look of undeniable tenderness touched her face. 'Trusting. Very trusting.'

'I wonder if I could see him for a minute?'

'Oh, no, I'm afraid not.' She seemed to answer very quickly; even a little sharply.

'Not?'

'He's out.'

'Oh, I see. Will he be long?'

'Another hour or so. He went to the pictures.'

'Ah. And your sister-in-law? Is she at home?'

'No. No. That's why he went to the pictures. It was something which *she* wanted to see—some sort of sentimental rubbish. But we wouldn't have liked it if she'd gone alone.'

'No, naturally. How doubly fortunate then that you didn't hurt yourself when you fell. But would you like to come and show me where it was, now, please?'

On his way to the door, though, she called him back.

'In the hall, will you speak very softly,' she requested. 'You see, the neighbours are apt to complain.'

He said: 'Oh, surely one should be allowed to speak quite normally in one's own hallway.'

'But I'd much rather you didn't. I'd much rather you said anything you had to say, in here.'

He saw that she was getting perturbed. He decided not to press the issue.

'Well, there is just one more thing then, Mrs Poynton, before we do finish. I wonder if I could ask you to come and see me at the surgery—tomorrow morning, perhaps, before ten? The check-up I've just given you was necessarily brief. There could be ill effects we haven't bargained for. I'd like to see if I could maybe fix you up a day or two in hospital —purely for observation, you understand. It *would* be a safeguard. Would that be possible?'

'A day or two in hospital?'

He nodded.

'For observation?'

'Just in case there's something that I've overlooked.'

She smiled. 'You're right. A very sensible precaution. I'll call in at your surgery, then, at some time before ten.'

'Good. I'll warn Miss Clementson. I mean—I'll tell her.'

'Perfect. It will be so nice to renew our acquaintance so soon.'

She was smiling again, as she closed the front door. She was smiling because Dan hadn't come out of the dining-room; she'd been very frightened that he would. (And what would she have said then, oh Lord? The suspense had been quite gruelling!) She was smiling because Dr Ballad had forgotten to look at the staircase; she felt that she had rather caught him out there, after all the fuss that he had made about it! And she was smiling, as well, because in at least one further respect she felt that she'd outsmarted him. (For really Dr Ballad was *very* pleasant but he wasn't all that bright, was he?—which again, perhaps, was just like Andrew.) After all how could she *ever* think of leaving Daisy or of leaving Dan, even for a short time. They needed her; they both needed her! No. There'd be no appointment necessary, Miss Clementson, no need for any warning. Mrs Poynton would not be calling upon Dr Ballad. And Dr Ballad would find nobody at home, next time he called upon Mrs Poynton.

Nobody would. She would tell them so, quite clearly and unmistakably, through the letter box.

49

That night Marsha sat up with Daisy and every time Daisy moaned—as she did very frequently—Marsha applied a cold flannel to her forehead, and wiped the sides of her nose and her cheeks and her chin with it, too. And as she did so, the make-up came away. It was as though years and years of make-up came away, like layer after layer of heavy wallpaper, and the cold water in the pudding basin which Marsha had placed at the bedside soon became a stagnant khaki pool, with orange tints, leaving a thick sediment at the bottom when she emptied it. Marsha hadn't seen Daisy without make-up for nearly half a century, and the face just didn't look like Daisy—pallid, featureless, *embarrassingly* bare—although Marsha had little flashes of remembrance once or twice, in which she could suddenly imagine that all those years had rolled away and that she was once more looking at her sister-in-law as a young woman. At those moments she remembered two things more clearly than any other: Daisy posing statue-like in front of Andrew and threatening to remain fixed, and Dan saying, a little more recently (and yet, how strange—it didn't seem more recent—could she be getting slightly muddled?), 'Oh, at Shangri-La one *never* grows ancient!'

Many times, too, during that night Daisy did more than moan; she cried out. Then Marsha would start up from her doze and say, 'There, there, Daisy, *I*'m here, everything's all right; can I get you something, a nice cup of tea or a couple of aspirin?'—but she was always relieved to find that Daisy didn't answer, because she really wasn't up to the effort of making tea.

Having fetched the aspirin bottle, though, to have it close

at hand, Marsha was dismayed to find just one tablet left. She would have to send Dan out for a bottle in the morning. One bottle? No, why not two or even three? Why not ten? Then they wouldn't need to worry about aspirin again for ages —perhaps a year. Or, on the other hand, if he were to buy two hundred bottles, then they might last for ever. Twenty thousand aspirin. Didn't that sound peaceful? One thing that could be struck off her shopping list for all time; she didn't enjoy going shopping any more—except when she occasionally met people that she liked, and what was the point of that in any case?—she was fed up, worn out, with hoping. Besides, even running into people that she liked didn't, couldn't, take her mind off her worries, not for very long. She kept expecting things to happen—all sorts of things, horrible, shadowy things—she breathed a sigh of relief each time that she got home and closed the door. Safe. They can't reach me here, she said. Or, at any rate, not so easily. The handbag-snatchers, the rapists, the disease-carriers, the maniacs, the murderers in their motorcars. Not only them; they were just the fringe of it; all the others as well. She was so *thankful* to get home. But then she only had to screw up her courage all over again the next day and pray that, once more, she would run the gauntlet without mishap. They watched. They waited. She knew that they could pounce whenever they wanted. She wasn't nearly quick enough to avoid them.

'*Them*?' Daisy had once said. 'Who's *them*? No—don't tell me—so terrible that no word can ever describe *them*!'—and Marsha had laughed, with genuine amusement and genuine shame.

'The wolves and the bears,' she'd said.

'Yes, I know, dear. I think you must be loopy.'

'I shouldn't be at all surprised! But when I was a little girl I really believed that if I trod on the cracks in the pavement the wolves and the bears would make a rush for me and gobble me all up. I used to imagine what it would feel like to be gobbled up.'

'Uncomfortable.'

'I used to dream about the Christians being leapt on by the lions. I had a vivid imagination.'

251

'What happened to it?'

'What?'

'No—just my little joke, dear. They don't feed Christians to the lions any more—or so they tell me, anyway—not even here in Hendon.'

'It was horrible in some ways, being a child; horrible although of course it was lovely, too. I used to think that I'd be struck by lightning; even when I was inside the house; it would see me through the windows—flash straight through the glass at me. I can remember thinking, wouldn't it be nice if the windows were all boarded up—or at the very least, extremely dirty, so that I could lurk in the shadows and the thunderbolts would find it difficult to spot me. Also, the prowlers.'

'The prowlers as well, dear? You had a busy time.'

'Oh, yes. Even in a first-floor room or in a second-floor one, I sometimes used to think that if I looked up very quickly I would meet a pair of chilling eyes looking right back at me, through the window. So I hardly ever did—look up very quickly, I mean. I would try to give the intruder plenty of warning; I would only raise my eyes quite slowly.'

Marsha shrugged, and laughed again.

'And yet I think I was a happy child.'

'Well, just so long, dear, as you're not planning to recapture happiness and go through it all again! I can fight spiders, but I draw the line at wolves and bears and lions and thunderbolts and prowlers up on stilts!'

Yes, they had had a good little laugh about that; and of course it *was* ridiculous.

She didn't even like sending Dan out, either—in case something terrible might happen to *him*. So she wasn't only thinking of herself.

She fantasized, half sleeping, half wakeful, being jerked up automatically and stumbling to the bedside each time that Daisy moaned or cried out. Well, to begin with it was certainly each time—gradually, however, she got used to it.

She fantasized.

Supposing that Dan drew all his money out of the bank? —it wasn't very much, but it was a little over two thousand pounds. Supposing that he bought enough aspirin and den-tifrice and soap and tissues and toilet rolls to last them for a lifetime? She imagined the dining-room, stacked to the ceiling with toilet rolls. Supposing he bought enough tinned food—meat and fish and peas and macedoine and pears and milk and biscuits—there was nothing that you couldn't get in tins, even hams and chickens and steak-and-kidney pies—to last them for a lifetime? Supposing he bought enough jars of coffee and packets of tea and bags of sugar and huge contain-ers for the tea and for the sugar (sweet jars, maybe, from the confectioners?) to last them for a lifetime? Why not? Why not? It all seemed so perfectly possible. Of course it would need such very careful planning, and it would mean having to do without fresh fruit and vegetables, but you could get a balanced diet out of tins—more or less—surely? And, of course, it would mean that Dan was shopping regularly for weeks, and that she was stacking regularly for weeks—but Dan was strong, and she was tidy, and it would even be quite satisfying, *very* satisfying, stocking and ordering a fortress, independent, immune, impregnable. And after those few, frenzied, concentrated weeks, it would all be over, no more worry ever again—and how very peaceful *that* would be. Their own little island, their own little desert island, miles away from anywhere; their own little castle, surrounded by a moat.

And even during those few necessary weeks of shopping and stacking she could imagine that she'd be just too busy to worry about Dan and the dangers that might be besetting him outside the house. She'd have no time to stand there watching the clock, running to the front door to look out for him, wondering what on earth was taking him so long, trying to convince herself that all her fears were totally irrational.

She knew they were irrational, like a man wandering through a cemetery at dead of night might know that his were, too.

But their own little Shangri-La! What bliss! More, now, than just a name beside the door!

Even the thought of all that hard, hectic activity didn't make her feel bone-tired—no, on the contrary, it enlivened her. It would be creative; it would be exciting; it would be once-and-for-all . . . and not a bit like cleaning, for instance, which, almost as soon as you had finished, you knew would have to be done again. She was coming to hate cleaning. She *had* come to hate cleaning. But if they were going to have no visitors from now on—and that was all a part of it, of course, having no visitors—(not that, in fact, they'd ever had that many)—then it wouldn't really matter if things weren't always spotless. It wouldn't really matter if things weren't *ever* spotless! She laughed. Oh, what fun! What fun!

Yes, she was so tired of it all. She was so *tired* of having to pay the milkman, of having to wipe the milk bottles, of having to put out the dustbins, or having to remind Dan to put out the dustbins, of having to disinfect the dustbins, of having to tip the dustmen, of having to tip the milkman . . .

She was so *tired* of having to make the beds and air the blankets, of having to clean the washbasin and clean the bath and clean the lavatory, of having to plan the meals and prepare the meals and wash up after the meals . . .

She was so *tired* of having to dust and sweep and launder and scrub and iron and hoover and empty and polish and tidy . . .

The list was endless; it was endless; it was endless.

It was endless.

But in the new Shangri-La they would never need to worry about the little things like that (little things that grew to be bigger than you were). For what was the point? Life was too short. Although at Shangri-La, of course, didn't you get to be six hundred and still look like a young woman?

She smiled. Was she then, at last, about to come into her own; the state for which she had been truly destined? As a girl, she had always been known as such a bubbly little gadabout, such a pretty and fun-loving butterfly; until Andrew had put an end to all of that, for years and years and almost ever. (Andrew! Well, how glad she was that, earlier on this evening, she'd had the sense—the sense and the willpower—really to send him packing, that man! You didn't get taken in twice! Not by the same broad shoulders and the same fair hair. Thank heavens she had seen in time!) But now, she thought, the evil spell was lifting and everything was going to turn out happy-ever-after.

Because:

Apart from toilet rolls and food, they would buy lots and lots of books, for their fine citadel: lots and lots of records . . . and when she wasn't reading she would dance . . .

And they'd have to buy dozens of crates of champagne; and proper champagne glasses too—fifteen?—twenty?—to allow for breakages . . .

Daisy gave another cry. But Daisy's discomfort would only be a temporary thing—and, anyway, she *had* very much brought it on herself. Afterwards, when her poor broken body had mended, Daisy would be as happy as she'd ever been; they would all be as happy as they'd ever been— *happier*, because wiser.

Yes, it seemed so absolutely feasible. So tomorrow she would talk to Dan; tomorrow she would arrange it all; she knew that he would do anything—just anything—she asked. It was entirely true, as she had said to him a little earlier: Marsha knew best, Marsha would take marvellous care of all of them.

In fact, it suddenly occurred to her that it was so exciting —why wait until tomorrow? Why should they abide by rules of day and night any longer? They could make up their own rules as they went along. That was the best way.

50

Dan wasn't asleep—which was fortunate, since she certainly wouldn't have wished to wake him. 'I wondered if you'd like a cup of tea?' she asked, before she turned the light on. Her planning had revitalized her, to such an extent that she would have cooked him a full meal, if he'd wanted one.

'Who is it?'

She found the switch and a second later saw that he was

pushing back the bedclothes and on the point of getting up.

'No, no, Dan, you stay where you are. It isn't morning. I just felt like a chat. May I sit down?' She perched on the edge of the large bed.

'You're dressed,' he said.

'Am I? Oh, so I am.'

'Then has the doctor been again?'

'Do you like this dress?—you haven't told me. I rather think it suits me. Don't you?'

'What did he say?'

'Who?'

'The doctor.'

'Oh, the doctor? I told you, darling, what he said. Daisy is going to be fine. She'll be up and about in no time. Running around like nobody's business.'

'She'll be all right?'

'She's going to be fine,' repeated Marsha, with several energetic nods.

Then she said:

'We've got to be very careful, though.'

He looked at her enquiringly.

'Yes. You see, some people might get the idea that it was our fault—the fact she fell downstairs. I mean, some evil-minded old busybody, pushing his nose in where it wasn't wanted. They might say the accident was our fault. *Your* fault,' she added, loudly.

'My fault?'

'Yes; because you were the one who was on the telephone, weren't you? And—you remember, of course—you said that Daisy must have thought that you were speaking to the doctor. You'd told her that you were going to ring the doctor.'

'Was it the doctor who said that it was my fault?'

'Well, I'm afraid that it was, Dan. Yet that doesn't really matter. *I* know that it wasn't your fault. You mustn't feel at all guilty. But the only thing is—if the doctor comes back, you just mustn't let him in.' She told him this twice. 'Do you understand me?'

'Why? What would the doctor do?'

'Take you away, perhaps.'

'Take me away? I wouldn't want to go. I'd tell him that it wasn't my fault. It wasn't anybody's fault. I'd tell him that.'

'But he might not believe you. He might say that it's *always* somebody's fault when something like that happens.'

'Where would he want to take me, Marsha?'

'Oh. I don't know. Maybe to a kind of hospital.'

'To prison?'

'But you don't want to go anywhere, do you, Dan? You just want to stay here. At home. At Shangri-La. With Marsha. Don't you? And with Daisy.'

'I want to stay here.'

'Yes, darling. Of course you do. So just remember: don't open the door to the doctor!'

'But how will I know that it's the doctor?'

'Don't open the door to anyone! Not to anyone! Ever. That's the best way. Think of them—all—as being your enemies. They are all our enemies. They all want to find out our secrets. We don't want them to find out our secrets. They are all—uncaring—busybodies.'

'All?'

'Yes. That way you'll make no mistakes. That way we shan't fall into any traps.'

'But the doctor,' said Dan; 'the doctor might be bringing medicine for Daisy.'

'Medicine?'

'For Daisy.'

'Don't worry. Daisy's going to have her medicine.'

'What?'

'And, anyway, what Daisy really needs is aspirin. Lots and lots of aspirin.'

She told him then about her schemes for the future. It took her a long time. She told him in detail, and she wanted to be sure that he understood all the advantages.

'Do you remember that grocery shop you had when you were just a little boy? When I was two or three, I used to be your customer; they said that you were very kind to me. You must have been eleven by then, or twelve. Eventually you gave the grocery shop to *me* and you became *my* customer.

There must have been nearly fifty different things upon the shelves! Well, it will be just like playing grocery shops again—as though we were still at Ashford—you and me and Henry—and Mademoiselle.'

'I remember Mademoiselle!'

'Only instead of Henry, there'll be Daisy.'

'She was very pretty, wasn't she? I wonder what became of her.'

Marsha shrugged one shoulder, and smiled.

'I always said that I would marry her when I grew up. We'd have lots of children and live in a grand château and be very rich and very happy. She wanted to be a nurse. I hope she married someone very nice.'

'Yes. That's right. A nurse . . . She said that Andrew asked her to marry him, of course. That was a lie. That was a horrid lie.'

'She took me to the pictures once. We saw *Intolerance*.'

'However, I do believe this much. She absolutely ruined my life. If it hadn't been for her I'd still be married to him. Yes. We'd have been blissfully happy. It was a nearly perfect marriage—or it might have been.'

'Another time we saw a Charlie Chaplin film. There was a Pearl White serial, I remember.'

'I'm not so stupid as she thinks I am.'

'She was tied to the railway track . . .'

'And she's never once, you know, never once said she was sorry.'

They nodded at one another, companionably.

'Tomorrow—good and early—you must go to the bank,' she told him. 'Shall I come with you? We'll be safe—much safer—the two of us together.'

'Safe,' said Dan.

'Safe.'

Dan yawned.

'Oh, what a great big sleepy boy!' She stood up, smiling tenderly. 'Yes, I feel sleepy, too.'

'It *is* going to be all right, isn't it?'

'Of course it is. Like a storybook.'

'I wish Erica was here.'

'Yes. I know you do. But Marsha will take care of you, as well.'

'I did what Erica asked, though, didn't I? "Please be kind to Daisy," she said to me, the night before she died. "And may God forgive me, for not having tried to understand her better and to love her." "God *will* forgive you," I said; and I really knew that he would, too—especially if I invited Daisy to come and live here; if I offered her a home.'

Marsha had been told of this before. Well, it was easy enough for Erica, she had thought, the first time that she'd heard of it. After all, Erica had been upon her deathbed.

'But I really didn't mean that she should have this accident. I really didn't mean to try and send her away—not ever. I'm sure that nobody would think it was my fault.'

'They'd have no right to, dear, at any rate.'

She bent and kissed him on the forehead; then went to the door, and switched out the light. Dan settled down once more in bed.

On the landing, Marsha heard Daisy's groaning; it seemed to be getting louder; Marsha felt frightened, suddenly, of being alone.

She undressed herself in the darkness, letting her clothes lie exactly where they fell, all around her, near the staircase. She reopened the door that she'd just closed, walked back to the bed, got in upon Erica's side and put her arms around Dan's pyjama-ed chest.

'Erica?' said Dan, drowsily.

Marsha said: 'Happy dreams. Sweet repose. Half the bed and all the clothes.'

51

Perhaps the very nicest thing, Marsha found, about this period of her life was that Joan and Beryl got in touch with her again. Nobody else telephoned—which was surely just as well—but one or other of those two was always on the line, spending ever greater portions of each day gossiping about this and that and talking over old times—well, old times now were just like new times, of course—so that she often had to scold them, laughingly, for preventing her from getting on with the housework and for making her so lazy. 'Oh, it's all very well for the likes of you!' she'd say. '*You* may have nothing else to do! *You* may both be ladies of leisure . . . !' And, indeed, they probably were: Joan no longer worked in the film studios and had lost her second husband, tragically, through cancer, while Beryl, too, was now alone, having gone through all the miseries of a divorce, of being deserted for another woman. Well, Marsha could sympathize with her over that, of course; she could sympathize with them both and could bring them balm, maybe, as nobody else could. And she didn't mind that they'd neglected her for so long, either. The important thing was, they'd both returned when they had needed her; and not just good times, but really good times, were re-established. Paradise regained . . . she knew there'd been a book called that, although Daisy had always considered her quite badly read. And all those lovely long evenings in Paddington Street came back again—after a fashion—especially when Joan (or was it Beryl?) managed to contrive a three-way telephone system, and they could all talk to each other at the same time, which was glorious. (No wonder that she got so little of her work done! But then, of course—she had forgotten—it didn't need doing.) And oh —how they laughed again! How they talked about the things that really mattered! ('I shouldn't think,' said Malcolm, 'there are many ordinary homes where you get *three* such pretty women who spend so much time together!') How Beryl, still, was always popping out to Uncle with the brooch that Raymond never missed! How Joan, still, was always dashing out upon that frantic card-buying expedition! (Weren't there some discrepancies there?—were there?— never mind.) It was a lovely thing to happen to you when you had thought your life was ended and that there was nothing more to look forward to. Dan might complain that she was always on the telephone, but that was only jealousy, of course. Poor Dan. She had to be so kind to him; he had not been blessed with friends. How many people had? She was among the most fortunate of women.

52

As the months went by, Marsha spent more and more time sitting with Daisy—the emptied shell that was Daisy. Even at night she often felt reluctant to leave her.

'You just can't trust her an inch,' she'd say to Dan. 'You don't know what manner of mischief she'll be up to next, as soon as your back is turned. *I* had to find out the hard way, of course. Well, she doesn't get a second chance! Oh, no!'

'What sort of things does she get up to?' asked Dan, interested.

'Oh, you know that as well as I do. Flirting. Trying to steal other women's men. And not caring one scrap whom she may hurt in the process. Just doing it for the very hell of the thing; for the thrill of the chase.'

Marsha snorted.

She said to Daisy:

'After you get what you want—you don't want it. They should have called you Jezebel. You're nothing but a painted hussy!'

But she remembered that Bette Davis had played in *Jezebel*; and *she* hadn't been nearly wicked enough—oh, no, not nearly. All the time, you see, you'd wanted her to win back Henry Fonda in the end.

'That's the noise that Daisy used to make.'

'What?'

'That noise you made just now. I can't do it. I wish I could.'

Yet there were other reasons why she was reluctant to leave Daisy. Along with retribution, Marsha wanted forgiveness;

and she hoped all the time for moments of renewed intimacy that might be a sign of her getting it.

Also, during those long winter months, she wasn't always sure where day ended and where night began; and, even when she knew the difference, it was often something of an effort to get up from her chair and go through all the paraphernalia of getting ready for bed. It was easier to stay put. Dan didn't mind—he didn't even notice—whether she was there or not.

Sometimes he called her Erica.

One night he shouted up the stairs to her: 'Erica! Erica! Why is it so dark? Why don't the lights work? Is there a piece of cake or something anywhere?'

Marsha—sitting there with Daisy—heard his voice but not what he was saying. With a weary and impatient sigh she dragged herself out of her chair and picked up her candle. She went out on to the landing and spoke to him from there.

'What is it *now*, for heaven's sake?'

'What?'

'What do you *want*?'

He repeated his three questions, in precisely the same words and with precisely the same intonation.

'You know as well as I do why they don't work. You haven't paid any of the bills, have you?'

'That isn't my fault,' he said at last, sulkily, when he had grasped her meaning.

'Did I say that it was? I think you've got a very guilty conscience! And there may be some biscuits in the tin—you can feel for it in the dark. Whatever you do, don't take your candle, though. You know that you can't be trusted not to set the house on fire.'

He mumbled something which she didn't hear.

'And then go to bed, why don't you? It's getting very late. In fact—too late.'

'It's always too late.'

'And don't let the bugs bite!'

'I don't want to go to bed,' he answered; he spoke as petulantly as she did. 'And I feel cold as well!' This was delivered like some ultimatum.

'Then put on your cardigan.'

'It is on. I think.'

'Your overcoat, then. What's the *matter* with you? Do I have to supervise your every move?'

He turned this sharp interrogation aside, with an equally aggrieved one of his own.

'And why's there nothing on the wireless? Are they *still* on strike, then?'

'Yes, yes. I suppose so.' It was by far the easier.

He shambled back into the lounge, grumbling all the way. 'Nothing works. Nothing ever works. And you can never find a single thing you want. It's all rubbish—rubbish. *Rubbish!*' he said, defiantly, kicking some of it out of his path.

She didn't hear him. His voice simply trailed off into a meaningless jumble. She thought he must be asking for the biscuits again. He was always saying he was hungry.

'You're too *fat!*' she shouted after him. 'Fat, fat, fat!'

Hardly a day went by when she didn't tell him he was fat.

'I'm not!'

'Then, when,' she would ask, 'when did you last see yourself in a mirror? Of course, I can tell you when it *wasn't*. It *wasn't* while you were shaving.'

He had a six months' growth of beard; he always scratched it a great deal.

'The mirrors are all smeary,' he said, on one occasion.

'Well, you could wipe them then, I suppose? Or is that totally beyond you—something as difficult as that? In any case perhaps it's better not to. You'd see that you were fat.'

'And you'd see that your hair's all mucky-ucky,' he said. 'Hanging down with grease! And you'd see that your nose is dirty, too. You used to say that I was built for running. Like a whippet.'

'I never said that. Not once in my life!'

'Where did that slim one disappear to?'

'What?'

'The fat one. I don't like him. I don't like that fat one at all. When did he come in?'

'You're greedy—that's your trouble. You *eat* too much!'

263

'Where did the running one go?'

'I don't understand you, Dan. You're just not making sense.'

'*You*'re scratching now. You're always telling me that *I* scratch. You're always telling me that I say What? as well. You say it more than I do.'

'You're fat!'

'I want to get out,' he said.

He had said the same the following day. It was one of those phrases which seemed to have settled itself inside his brain and quickly worn a groove there.

'You can't get out,' said Marsha. 'So just do what I do. Pretend that it's a garden and that the sun is shining. All the time. Everyone is beautiful and everyone is happy.'

He chortled, gleefully. 'And no rats under the floor-boards?'

'Of course not.'

Then he remembered his imprisonment. 'Is this another story? Once upon a time?'

'No, no. This is the way that things are meant to be. *Were* meant to be. No fat men. No spiders. Just happiness. And sunshine. I'm wrong, of course: there's room in it for spiders. There's room in it for everything God made. There in the garden.'

'There's a spider dangling over Daisy. A big one. A fat one. Big and fat and black and hairy. On a long string.'

'I know there is. She doesn't mind. She hasn't said she minded.'

'Do you?'

'No. I quite enjoy watching it. I enjoy wondering just how far it will come. It's beautiful—when you look at it closely.'

'In the dark you can't see it. Does it go away?'

'Things change,' she said. 'Things change.'

'Yes. Did *you* tell me that story about a king who always wanted to be good—but then he got tired and he thought there was no point and because he was so tired he just gave up and after that he found it so much easier to be bad?'

'No, I didn't tell you that. I wouldn't like a story like that. It doesn't have a happy ending.'

Marsha's stories, indeed, were mainly stories about wicked stepsisters who finally got their come-uppance and had to learn repentance and turn over new leaves and live in the stables while the pretty heroines dined off golden plate and became much loved by the prince and by all his people. Marsha's stories were all the same story.

Sometimes Andrew was the name of the prince, and sometimes Andrew was the name of the magician.

And even when they first discovered that Daisy was dead, Marsha went on telling her this story.

'Are we just going to leave her here, then?' asked Dan, picking up one of Daisy's hands experimentally and watching it flop back on the sheet.

He did this several times.

'Yes. Why not? And please stop doing that, Dan—stop it! Why must you fidget? We don't want to let people inside the house; we said that from the start. And we can't just toss her from the window, can we, or push her through the letter box?'

'We could bury her in the back garden—in the middle of the night.'

'I want to keep her by me.'

'Why?'

'Because she never really learnt her lesson. She never said that she was sorry.'

'Well, she isn't going to learn it now.'

'We don't know that. We hope, indeed, she will.'

'She isn't going to say she's sorry. We do know that.' He added waggishly, and very much pleased with himself, 'We hope, indeed, she's not. Anyway, *I* do.'

'Perhaps her mouth will change,' said Marsha. 'If we watch it very closely; turn up at the corners; smile; show us in some small way that she wants to apologize.'

It occurred to her then to take out Daisy's dentures. They were pasted over with grey food. There was still slime inside the dead mouth.

Marsha, uncertain what to do with the dentures, was about to throw them in a corner, when apparently she changed her mind.

'Here.'

'*I* don't want them.'

'A keepsake.'

He didn't seem to understand.

'A souvenir!' she repeated. 'One for you and one for me.' Now she held only the top set out to him.

'Why do we need a souvenir?'

'Something to remember her by.'

'But I thought we were keeping *Daisy* here, to remember her by.'

Marsha had to admit that he was right. After a pause, she gave a slight shrug—and threw the dentures in the corner.

Something scuttled away in terror, as they landed.

Without her teeth, Daisy's face looked smaller.

'She stinks—doesn't she?'

'No! Of course not! Darling, you don't say things like that. Not about the dead. And even if she does—a very little —well, just remember, so do you.'

'No, I don't. Not half so much as you.'

'Yes, you do.'

'No, I don't.'

'Yes. Yes, yes.' She nodded categorically. 'Much worse.'

'Prove it!'

These days their moods changed as quickly as their topics of conversation; or as quickly as their variations upon a single topic. Marsha said, soon afterwards:

'Perhaps she's gone to that place which she once told me of, where things were as they might have been. As they might have been at their very best. I wonder. I do hope so. What do you think, Dan? Do you think that's where she's gone?'

He considered the question carefully; and then gave a series of wise nods. 'There's life in the old dog yet,' he said.

They both laughed—affectionate laughter; and they both grieved a little too.

'In any case she looks so peaceful, Dan.'

'Does she?'

'Yes. It would be a pity to disturb her. Even if we dared.'

'It's up to you, old girl. Why don't you sing a hymn? Like in a funeral service? Ashes to ashes and dust to dust.'

'I don't know any hymns.'

'Oh. Sing "Daisy, Daisy", then. To cheer her on her way. Also, it would tell God who was coming—just in case he might have missed her in this gloom.'

So Marsha did so; Dan stood to attention.

Marsha sang it more sweetly than her sister-in-law had ever sung it, but her own rendering lacked the vitality of Daisy's. It somehow lacked the oomph.

'It won't be a stylish marriage—
I can't afford a carriage—
But you'll look sweet
Upon the seat
Of a bicycle made for two.'

'That's all either of us ever wanted, Daisy, isn't it—deep down? A bicycle made for two. And we each had one for such a very little time. Even your children in the end, the very best of them, grow up and desert you and don't care a tittle whether you're on your own or not.'

'I wonder if she's run into Mother,' said Dan. He grinned at his sister, impishly.

'I wonder if she's met her own, yet,' smiled Marsha, suddenly just as impish. There were traces, briefly, of the children they'd once been.

In any case, they felt it was a good send-off she'd been given.

Except, of course, that they had only *half* sent her off; they fully realized that. They watched out for alteration over the succeeding months—Dan with every bit as much interest, finally, as Marsha. It was a fascinating game. And although in their main objective they were somewhat disappointed, alteration they certainly did see.

Gradually, like a figurehead being gnawed at from within, the flesh began to fall away from Daisy's coloured, leathery old face (Marsha had reapplied her make-up; she could no longer bear the nakedness), until the very whiteness of the bone at last gleamed through. Beneath the blankets and the striped pyjamas, too, a change was taking place. They didn't look to examine the extent of it, but both hands still lay upon the sheet like conflicting pointers to a buried treasure, far beyond the tea-stains; and the weight of the hearing-aid in the breast pocket, its cord still stretching tautly to a vanished ear, emphasized the contour of the caved-in chest, especially on the left, above that off-white tideline, sprinkled with her fallen fingernails.

And Daisy *did* stink; it was no good pretending that she didn't. Every day Marsha would spray the room with a sweet and heady air freshener intended for the lavatory—luckily, they'd bought a dozen cans of that—yet as time went by (it's still the same old story; a fight for love and glory; a fight to do or die) their nostrils not only grew acclimatized to it but even came to welcome it. It turned almost to the smell of safety.

When Marsha reapplied the make-up Dan had watched her.

'Oh, this takes me back to 1935!' she said.

'Do you wish it really did?'

She didn't answer. But her hand shook as she put on the lipstick; and tears trembled on her lids and blurred her vision. Neither of them spoke again until the work was done. Then she turned to him and shook her head forlornly. Her nose ran and she wiped it on her sleeve.

'I haven't done much reading,' she said. 'You know, it hasn't been the way I pictured it. I haven't done much dancing, either. No. Hardly any at all.'

'Never mind.' For a moment, he lay his hand, with its very long-nailed fingers, tenderly on hers. He could see that she needed reassurance for something—even if he didn't quite understand for what.

'I've dozed and dreamed, and dozed and dreamed, and wished my time away. It isn't very much; there's not a lot to show. The trouble is—I feel so tired.'

'Is it nearly March?'

'Why?'

'It's my birthday, of course, in March.' The sudden excitement of his smile then quickly faded. 'Oh. Have we had Christmas?'

'What?'

'Christmas!'

'Christmas?' she said, vaguely. 'Is it? Is it really? Then

268

happy Christmas, darling.' But she added instantly: 'I don't want Christmas. No. I haven't got anything prepared.'

'Never mind. It was fun last year. It was nice having Daisy with us. We had jelly and tinned pineapple and we played cards. There were some chocolates, too. We sat round the bed, and it was light.'

She caught his air of wistfulness; for his sake, she really made an effort. 'Would you like . . . ?'

'Yes?'

'Would you like . . . a humming competition? Do you remember . . . when we were very small, and staying on that farm in Lincolnshire . . . you gave me half-a-crown?'

He smiled. 'Oh yes; I thought it was a shilling.'

'My voice has probably got rusty, though—I warn you! Croak, croak, croak! And *you* could never hum in tune, anyway. But I'm game if you are. My turn first? A penny for each song you recognize?'

'I haven't any pennies. And nor have you.'

She considered carefully and then hummed the tune of 'We'll gather lilacs in the spring again'. He tried very hard; adopted a tremendous air of concentration. But he didn't know it.

She couldn't remember what it was, either.

'Your turn,' she said.

He thought and thought; made two or three false starts. 'No. I can't think of anything. You have another go.'

She tried 'Putting on the Ritz' and 'I'll be your sweetheart'. 'Oh, this is no good,' she said, crossly. 'If you don't know this one I'm not going on!'

But he did; mercifully he did.

'Sing louder,' he said. 'I've almost got it.'

'Yes?'

'Something in Paris . . . April?'

'Yes!'

He was enormously pleased with himself. '*And* I've never been to Paris!'

'Nor me.'

'I don't suppose I ever shall—now.'

'No.'

'Everybody speaks of Paris, and we shall never see it. Never! Oh, dear. But is it nearly March?'

'*I* don't know!'

'March the twenty-something?' He stopped, puzzled. 'The twenty-sixth? Or twenty-seventh? Oh, Erica.' His face twisted, in anguish. 'Which day is it—my birthday?'

'March the twenty-third,' she said.

'Are you sure?'

'March the twenty-third.' He needed to know, and what on earth did it matter—a day or two earlier, a day or two later? That day could even be the right day.

But on March the twenty-third there appeared in the *Guardian* the following report:

'An inquest is to be held on the two elderly women whose bodies were found on Monday in the dilapidated North London house they shared with a man who was the brother of one of them and the brother-in-law of the other. Post-mortem examinations yesterday revealed that they had both died from natural causes—but that the older woman had been dead for up to a year . . .'